Three In The Key

by KC Avalon

KC Avalon

KC Avalon

Cover Design by KC Avalon

ISBN 9781076762160

This book is dedicated to the three men in my life. I love you with all of my heart. My youngest son inspired me with the idea of a basketball romance story and wrote the game content. My oldest son helped me realize you are never too old to follow your dreams. My loving husband never doubted my ability to write a book.

Contents

Title Page

Copyright   3

Dedication   4

Chapter 1 - A Fortunate Encounter   12

Chapter 2 - More Than A Casual Connection   29

Chapter 3 - Will I Ever See You Again?   57

Chapter 4 - Cowboy Take Me Away   78

Chapter 5 - Romantic Roommates   104

Chapter 6 - No Time for a Young Filly   120

Chapter 7 - Out of Sight But In The Picture   149

Chapter 8 Two Steppin Good Ol' Boy   165

Chapter 9 - Undying Love   187

Chapter 10 - Game Changer   216

Epilogue   232

About the Author   242

Prologue

"With the first pick in the 2016 draft, the Philadelphia 76ers select Jaxon Jones from Elgin, Texas and the University of Texas as their power forward." It took a second or two for Jax's brain to process what he heard. Did they just say my name, or am I imagining it? It is every little boy's dream to grow up and become a professional athlete, and to have his family watch him on television and play in front of an arena of fans. An entire lifetime of dreams was coming true in a couple seconds time. The anxiety of possibly not getting drafted tonight quickly turned into the greatest excitement I ever felt.

The adrenaline rushing through my body at this moment was off the charts. The feeling was more powerful than any energy drink on the market. As luck would have it, all of my wishes were being granted at once. A small town Texas farm boy was picked first in the NBA draft. Did I fall asleep waiting for the draft to start? Was I going to wake up all of a sudden and realize I was dreaming? I sure hope not! I wanted to take in the moment and savor it, but the moment felt like an out of body experience. It was moving too fast!

Earlier in the day, my parents gave me a custom navy blue pinstripe suit for the occasion with brown oxford dress shoes. I wore a crisp white shirt and a dark blue tie with white and red diagonal stripes and a brown leather belt with a gold belt buckle adorned with a Texas longhorn. They took care of every detail. I insisted I was fine buying a store bought suit, but my parents insisted on having a suit made for such an important occasion. They felt I should look my best for my big day so I could represent Texas properly. The suit fit like a glove and not only was it sharp, but it was high quality material paired with fine craftsmanship. It was considerably different from my everyday attire which consisted of jeans, tee shirt, and Timberland boots or my white and orange basketball uniform at the University of Texas. I felt a little out of my comfort zone, but I had to admit the suit gave me swag. When I wore it, I walked with confidence and stood out from the crowd, like Al Pacino in Scarface. Okay, maybe the comparison is a little far fetched, but damn I never looked so good. Mom helped me with my tie and smiled up at me with such a loving look in her eyes. She always had my back and loved me no matter what the circumstance. Even if I failed at something, I could count on her to say at least I tried my best and to her, I was the best. It was nice to have the one person in your corner who was your number one fan, a friend, partner in crime, and shoulder to cry on, all in one. His mother's voice interrupted his thoughts.

"Jaxon, you look so handsome. Dad and I are so proud of your accomplishments. It is truly amazing you made it here today. For most people, this is just something in a dream which never becomes a reality. Don't fool yourself though, because you worked so hard to be here today and deserve to be among the best draft picks. You have a brighter future ahead of you in basketball than the family farming business. As much as you enjoyed the work, money pays the bills. We wanted you to have a choice in your career instead of the pressure of carrying on the family business. Dad and I do not want to watch you struggle in a business where it is hard to earn money. You have such drive and determination to succeed. This is your time to shine and get paid for something you love to do. There are really no words to express how happy you have made us both. We are proud of the man standing in front of us. You cannot forget where you came from though. Stay humble and kind, and make sure fame does not spoil you. or else you will have to deal with me. Remember, you deserve this. I love you so much!!"

She was crying and laughing at the same time and hugging me. She kissed my cheek and then wiped off the lipstick. My mom was so sentimental and proud of her only child. I could never do any wrong in her eyes. She alway saw the positive side of life, and I would always be her baby no matter how old I became.

"Okay mom, watch the threads," I said laughing. "I love you too, and thank you for everything. None of this would be possible without the support of you and dad. It means the world to me." I started choking up, and dad came to the rescue.

He pulled me in for a hug and slapped me on the back. He said, "Son, we love you and are damn proud of you. I agree with everything your mother said. This is a damn big deal today. I am sure you are overwhelmed, but take a second to enjoy the moment and take it all in. You will get picked by a team today. I have no doubt in my mind whatsoever. Try your best, but most of all, love what you do. It is not worth it if you do not have a passion for it. This is a huge accomplishment and a day you will never forget. Hell, I feel like I am walking around in a dream. Not many people get the opportunity to play in the NBA. Keep it real, and I better not see you on television acting like you are entitled just because you are making the big bucks. If you let the fame go to your head, it will all come tumbling down, and then I would have no choice but to whoop your ass." He had to get all tough guy with me so his emotions would not get the best of him.

I said, "Thank you both. Today is as much your day as it is mine. You were both great role models and gave me the love and support I needed. You stuck with me through good times and bad. I can always count on you to be there for me in any circumstance. I love you both."

   My parents had given up so much for me to be here. For years they made a living farming. Their hard work made it possible for me to go to college. They did the best they could and saved as much money as possible. It was a tough business, and every year it was harder to earn a decent living. Hard work and actual blood, sweat, and tears went into farming. After much thought, they sold the farm recently to a developer who bought the six acres of land to build townhouses. For now, my parents were looking to rent a condominium in Austin until they found a new home to start the next chapter of their lives together. They had until September 1st to move. They wanted to take their time exploring different areas in order to find the perfect place to live. I hoped to return the favor one day by doing something for them to show my appreciation.

Chapter 1 - A Fortunate Encounter

Sydney Fox was excited to accept her diploma at Stockton University. She had her Bachelor of Arts degree in special education. People always said time flew, and she agreed it was really true.

It seemed like not so long ago I graduated from high school. I remember being nervous about meeting new people and going to a new school after having so many friends at my old school. Thankfully, I made friends easily. On orientation day, I met my best friend Nina.

I actually met her in the women's bathroom. I was wearing these cute white capris I bought off the clearance rack. The material was kind of strange, and I did not give it much thought until the seam ripped at my ass. I was horrified and ran to the bathroom as quick as possible. Nina saw what happened and followed me. She just so happened to have a pair of shorts, because she was going to work out after orientation and insisted I take them.

Then she started laughing saying she was glad to give me **ass**istance and she was looking forward to **ass**ociating with me. We both started laughing hysterically. The unfortunate event was our first introduction. Needless to say, our bond was instant. We took a lot of classes together, since we had the same major. Everything worked out better than I could have imagined.

College was so much different than high school. Professors did not harass you to go to class. They could have cared less. After all, it was your money to waste. I felt like I was treated as an adult in college. Professors had more respect for the students than in high school. Instead of a dictatorship, college was more like an adult talking to a peer whom he/she respected. I enjoyed college so much more than high school. Another great advantage was how the students were friendlier than high school, and there was no pressure to act a certain way in order to be accepted as a friend. It was a great experience, and here I was four years later accepting my degree. My graduation cap was designed as a colorful puzzle piece to honor autistic children. Most of the young women graduating, custom designed their caps to show the crowd their personal message. There was a variety: song lyrics, blingy designs, names, shout outs to parents, how much money was spent, future career, etc. I also bought a sash with the Australian flag. It was perfect since my name was Sydney. The weather was 75 degrees and sunny with no clouds in the clear blue sky.

It was showtime! The band started playing, and the crowd eagerly stood on their feet and applauded as each major walked out in a procession to their seats. They each had their own section. As soon as the music started, I became choked up and overcome with such emotion. I felt like a VIP and I could not stop smiling. I was extremely proud of my accomplishments which brought me to this happy day. I worked so hard to be here with my classmates today. The University issued a honorary degree to a graduate from 1964. He was the special guest and spoke to the graduates about his ventures in life. He failed at his first business miserably but learned from his mistakes and ended up making millions of dollars. We all learned some valuable life lessons from his speech. The first piece of advice was to take responsibility for our actions and not blame everyone else, or we would make the same mistakes again. He also said the people we worked with would be our most valuable assets. The last piece of advice was to keep our reputation, because this is what would determine our success. Then he gave us a standing ovation as a gift. The man was the best speaker I ever heard at a graduation ceremony and kept me captivated the entire time.

Next, the President of the University brought a fellow student onto the stage. She was also an education major like Sydney. He took the time to honor the people in the military who were unable to be at graduation today and asked everyone to give them a round of applause. Everyone showed their appreciation with a standing ovation. He went on to tell the crowd how Rosanna's sister was serving in the Middle East for the last three years, and how it was a huge sacrifice she gave in order for us to enjoy our freedom. As the crowd broke into applause again, Rosanna's sister came out from behind the curtain with a bouquet of flowers for her sister. Rosanna stood there with her hands up to her face in astonishment. They were both crying along with every person in the audience. Rosanna had no idea the University made plans to fly her sister in for her graduation. I had tears running down my face. What a wonderful gesture it was to unite the two sisters on such a happy occasion.

As if the crowd was not emotional enough, the President asked us to stand and move our tassels from the right side to the left side because it was time to receive our diplomas. I was sitting in the front row, so we were asked to stand first. I was hoping and praying I would not fall flat on my face while walking across the stage. It felt exhilarating and satisfying to hear my name called. I could hear my family and friends yelling out. It actually gave me the poise I needed to walk across the stage and shake the President's hand to accept my diploma. It was nice to go first, but now I had a long wait, about 45 minutes to be exact, until the rest of the names were called. I was clapping for my classmates and talking to Nina the entire time.

When the ceremony was over, they played our alma mater

and I tossed my cap in the air with the rest of the graduating class. This small tradition brought such excitement and happiness to me. I was truly a grown up with my entire life in front of me. It was one of the happiest days of my life to graduate college.

It was also a little overwhelming to think I was officially an adult with the responsibility to go to work and earn money instead of mom and dad taking care of me all the time. I really liked mommy and daddy taking care of me. It made me feel secure. Maybe they would let me ease into being an adult. After all, college took four years. She could not be expected to transform overnight. Wow, all this adult thinking was making my head spin. At least I would be able to enjoy the summer if I could find a job. I passed my elementary school Praxis tests for New Jersey in reading and language, math, science and social studies. This was required before I was able to complete student teaching in my last semester of college. Sydney loved working with kids and helping others. She wanted to have a fulfilling and meaningful career. Four years of college was gone with the toss of a cap, but now she would have to pay off the student loans. She could worry about being a responsible adult on another day. She was going to enjoy the night.

Sydney searched through the crowd for her parents. She ran through people until her eyes locked on them. Mom had tears in her eyes and dad was holding a colorful arrangement of daisies. They were Sydney's "happy" flower and her favorite.

She said, "Thank you mom and dad! I cannot believe I did it! It was far from easy, but I stuck with it and worked hard so you would be proud of me. There were times where I thought I wanted to give up, but you both helped me through it."

Mom said, "We are very proud of you. You made it, and all of your hard work will pay off with a job you will love." She kissed me on the cheek.

Dad gathered me in his arms for a big hug and kissed the top of my head. "Honey, it means the world to me to see you so happy and I am so proud. I wish mom and I did not have to leave so quickly, but we have to get to your aunt's surprise party in Virginia Beach. We will be back Sunday afternoon and can have dinner to celebrate your graduation. You are not allowed to drink and drive, so before we go, let me drop you off at Boogie Nights Club in Atlantic City, and you can order an Uber home after you are done partying. Go have some fun with your friends. I will feel much better knowing you are safe. Although I know you will be dancing more than drinking. It is impossible for you to sit still when you hear music. Enjoy yourself sweetheart, and call us if you need anything."

When we arrived at the club, I kissed mom and dad goodbye and wished them a safe trip. I told them there was no need to feel guilty leaving since I would be partying even if they were home. I was so excited for the night ahead. I always listened to seventies music with my parents and loved disco. I loved music from the time I was a little kid. On Saturday nights we would sit around and sing and dance and pretend to play instruments. I could not dry dishes without singing into any utensil remotely resembling a microphone.

The club was amazing. It instantly brought you back to the seventies with the biggest lit up disco ball I had ever seen. It was so blingy and mesmerizing. The light reflected off each mirrored piece.

I saw my friend at a table with zebra patterned chairs and a lava lamp on the table. Nina had to yell over the music to be heard. We reached for each other and exchanged air kisses so we did not mess up our makeup. "Hey Sydney, congrats on your graduation and to us. Girlfriend, we did it!

"Yes WE did Nina. It was so crowded at graduation I missed a chance to get any pictures with you after the ceremony. Once I started looking for my parents, I lost you and was unable to find you again. They were short on time since they had a six hour drive ahead of them."

"No worries. It is okay. I was in such a rush to party, so I rushed my family out of there. I would have been happy skipping it and having my diploma mailed to me, but my parents would have freaked."

"You know deep down those are not your true feelings. No one wants to sit for a long time, yet it is so nice to see everyone and celebrate together as a group. It is a tradition."

"Sydney, I swear to God you better stop with the blah blah blah. Now let's do some serious partying. I ordered you a drink. It should be here any minute." Arriving on cue, Roller Girl skates up to us in her little, tight cutoff tee shirt which ended just before the bottom of her perfect melon shaped breasts. She also had shiny, white hot pant shorts and tube socks and a serving tray with two shots and two Rum Punches. KC and the Sunshine Band was playing "*Get Down Tonight*". I grabbed Nina's hand and ran to the dance floor. We just kept dancing as the DJ spun the tunes: *Hot Stuff, Funky Town, Knock on Wood, Dancing Queen*, and now *It's Raining Men*. We were singing to the music and throwing our hands in the air. Nina and I were laughing and dancing. I was having a blast when someone grabbed my hand. I just pulled it away and continued dancing. I thought someone grabbed it by mistake since we were all crowded on the dance floor. Whoever it was, grabbed my hand more forcefully this time. I turned around and met the eye of a shit faced blonde thirty something guy who obviously thought he was a Greek God I should be falling all over. I was totally unimpressed.

"What's up babe," he slurred as he was trying to grind up on me. "Come over here so I can show you a good time."

"Sorry, but I am here with my friend tonight. I am already having a good time. Get lost!"

Mr. Dick Head pulled me in close enough to smell his stale beer breath and said, "You are going home with me tonight."

Some guys just refuse to get a hint. I tried to pull away, but his grip grew even tighter. He tried to take my hand and rub it on his pathetic little penis which felt more like a door knob than an ankle slapper. Enough is enough. It was necessary to introduce his penis to my kneecap and his rib cage met my elbow. I felt a little sorry for him since I threw a mean elbow, and he took a big hit. As he lay there breathless and bent in half on the floor, I said, "Now this is what I call a good time. What? Did you say something? Sorry for breaking your balls dude. I am not attracted to assholes." I turned my drink upside down on him and said, "You look like you could use some ice."

Nina was laughing hysterical. "Oh my God Syd! What a fucking jerk. He totally got what he deserved!! Where did you learn all those kung fu moves?"

I said, "I have no idea what he was thinking. I was not even paying attention to him or looking his way to even give him the wrong idea."

They almost forgot about the guy on the floor. After he was done groaning, he tried to get up and lunged at Sydney while saying, "I will show you bitch!" Fortunately he never had the chance. Security ran out and escorted him out the door before he could even lay one finger on Sydney.

I was a little shaken from the incident but refused to let one jackass ruin my entire night. I turned to Nina and said, "I am going to the bathroom before we do another dance floor marathon. The asshole definitely had it coming and got what he deserved."

When I came out of the bathroom, Nina was slow dancing with a sharp dressed muscular Italian guy. He was about 6'3" and had dark hair and dark eyes and a nice tan. One look at her and I can tell she is hooked. She wasted no time while I was gone. It could not be helped. My best friend was quite the looker. Men just waited to make their move. She excused herself and ran over. "Syd, I am soooo sorry! I know we are doing a girls night, but this guy is so hot I need to take him home. I swear I had no plans of looking for a man. It just happened. And God! He is making me so horny, and I deserve a good graduation gift!"

We laughed and hugged. "Stop apologizing. You cannot help being gorgeous. It is completely my fault for leaving you all alone. Please there is no need to worry about me. I am a big girl. Go get your man. He is hot as hell, and I doubt you will be disappointed. He looks like the kind of gift that keeps giving."

Jax was in Atlantic City for the NBA combine May 10 -13th, 2016. The combine consisted of four days of workouts to showcase players' skills with roughly seventy other draft candidates. We performed drills similar to those we used to do in basketball camps growing up, along with fitness and agility tests. NBA general managers, coaches and scouts observed the talent.

ESPN had my name positioned on the winners side. They commented, "Jaxon the Jaguar Jones was one of the ten fastest power forwards at the 2016 combine. He was 85% in free throws and 50% in three pointers. At one point Jax was looking like King James with his layup abilities. He made it look effortless as he dribbled around his back and through his own legs and his teammates legs to get to the rim and make a perfect layup. Fans think layups are easy and expect players to make them. The layup is actually the hardest shot to make even though it is the shot taken the most often in a game.

Jax averaged thirty minutes per game in his college days. He has a smaller frame than other players in his position but plays with such confidence. He can compensate for his size by remaining in his lane against bigger guys. If he can do this, it will help him succeed. Jones measured 6'7" barefoot and 6'9" in shoes and weighs 240 pounds. Jax seems to possess a mental sharpness and seems to have the capability to think and react quickly to changing game situations. I believe Jaxon Jones will be a household name in basketball for a long time. It is really way too soon to say, however, he seems to have the superstar quality."

Yes!! My discipline and hard work paid off on this great night, yet it was only the beginning of a difficult journey. Part of me worried my performance was too good, and maybe it would be hard to live up to consistently. Maybe I should have set the bar a little lower. Unfortunately, I was incapable of holding back. I was always in competition with myself and it was ingrained in my DNA to reach for the stars.

Right now was a time for celebration. I could worry about the battle ahead of me later. I like the nickname ESPN gave me "Jags (short for Jaguar)". Very catchy! Maybe the nickname was in anticipation of me being picked by the Sixers. They already had a JJ on the team. I had no control over which team I would be joining, so it would be senseless to overthink it. The only thing I knew for sure was how I finally finished an exhausting four days of combine workouts. It felt great to get positive feedback and praise. I could only hope the positive press would continue.

Even though I was dog-tired and could easily fall fast asleep in my hotel's comfortable king size bed, I decided to venture out to the Tropicana Boogie Nights Club for a few drinks. It would be a shame not to celebrate.

I listened to all types of music but mostly country. Disco and seventies music gave me the energy I needed to stay awake tonight, and I desperately needed to do something other than basketball. Well, Boogie Nights was definitely different in a good way. The crowd was mixed in age. The DJ was named Mr. Boogie and kept the party atmosphere alive, and professional dancers lined the side of the dance floor. This club had an amazing party vibe and everyone seemed to be having a lot of fun. I grabbed a seat overlooking the dance floor. The lit dance floor looked like the one from Saturday Night Fever starring John Travolta. It belonged in the movies or on a television show, since it had a celebrity feel to it. It had multi colored lights underneath. I could imagine John Travolta in his white suit and black shirt doing the dance floor some justice. I surely did not feel worthy of dancing on such a fine dance floor.

I was people watching and enjoying the music when I saw her. WOW! She was 5'10" with brown eyes, curly long dark brown hair with caramel highlights, curvy with an incredible ass, and a smile which could light up a room. She was laughing and having fun, and it was easy to see she enjoyed life. Her laugh was infectious and hearty. Talk about hearts. Mine was beating quick, and my horny friend was trying to pop up to get a look at her too. "Whoa there buddy. Down boy!" It was an involuntary reaction to an incredibly beautiful woman. It was not my intention to come here and take someone home for the night. I was not a player who went to bars for one night stands. I LOVED sex like any other hot blooded man but preferred it to be meaningful. I had my share of friends with benefits in college. Back then, I had no time for anything more than a one night stand. The time part was still the same, if not worse, but I needed a relationship at this stage of my life.

I felt like a little boy who just realized he likes girls in a "more than friends" kind of way. I mean I REALLY liked her, and I was drawn to her like a moth is drawn to a flame. There were half dressed girls on the floor shaking their tits and ass to snag a man for the night. This one was different. She was sexier than any of

Three in the Key

them, wearing distressed, comfortable looking black jeans with a two tone gray silk spaghetti strap top with little crystals and a scoop neck showing the shape of her perfect breasts, without them plunging out in my face. I know guys say the bigger tits the better but I was an ass man. Her shirt was strappy in the back, and when she danced with her hands in the air, you could see a hint of the shape of her breast on the side. She had a light, creamy complexion. Her lips were sexy with a mauve lip gloss. They shined like they were begging me to kiss them. When she talked to her friend, she smiled with her teeth showing and her top teeth were biting her bottom lip playfully as she was listening intently. This woman had no idea how sexy she was or the things I was thinking of doing to her right then and there. Her shoes were black, gladiator four inch high heels.

I felt like my brain shut down just looking at her. My other head kicked into high alert. It was straining against my jeans trying to get out. Her clothing left something to the imagination, although I mentally undressed her in seconds. Then some jerk started bothering her and put hands on her. I was about to get up and teach him some respect, but this woman needed no rescuing. It seemed like a reflex when she gave him a knee kick to the dick and an elbow right under his ribs. Well God Damn!! A woman with spunk. She possessed so many qualities I wanted. The jerk thought he was gonna get a piece of ass, and he got an ass kicking instead. He was curled up like a baby with his ego all over the dance floor. Two bouncers picked him up and showed him the way out. I laughed out loud and slapped my knee. She had physical beauty and personality, and I had to meet her as soon as possible.

∞∞∞

Sydney went back to her table and ordered another rum punch. She sipped her drink to relax as her body moved in the chair to the rhythm of the music. Her alone time was suddenly interrupted to her dismay. Why did people feel the need to bother her when she was minding her own business?

A voice at the table next to mine said in an awe shucks, down home Texas drawl, "Darlin I am not fixin to mess with you anytime soon. You gave the poor some beach a beatin!" I turned to give him some attitude, and my heart skipped more than a few beats.

First of all, his voice sounded intelligent and was sexy as hell. It was the type of voice that could convince you to do anything. My eyes did not disappoint me either. He was very tall with an athletic, muscular build, wavy dark brown hair which curled so sexy on the nape of his neck, brown eyes appearing kind and appreciative, and a smile which could easily make my panties fall to the floor. His hair was tousled and looked sexy as hell. I wanted to run my fingers through it. His smile widened as if he knew the effect he was having on me.

I laughed and answered, "I was trying to celebrate my college graduation, but the dumb ass had other ideas. I am in no mood for men who want to grind up on me, and I hope to God you are not trying to sleep with me too."

"Well I need to mention how any hot blooded male would be a fool not to wanna take you home to warm up his bed, but no, I am not tired enough to sleep with you yet."

I let out a loud, appreciative laugh I was unable to hold back, smiled and replied, "My name is Sydney, and it is a pleasure to make your acquaintance. I took my drink over to his table and shook his hand. He took my hand in his, slowly bringing it to his lips while maintaining eye contact and kissed it. Electricity ran through my entire body and the kiss felt like super slow motion. I sensed my mouth dropping open on the floor. He was so God Damn sexy. I was staring at his lips wanting them all over my body. Boy, I could only hope he was unable to read my mind right now. He smiled at me again and let my hand go and motioned for me to sit down and join him. "My girlfriend Nina is here with me, however she ditched me for a hot Italian guy she is taking home."

His beautiful smile revealed perfect white teeth. He said, "Much obliged Sydney. My name is Jax. Congratulations on your graduation. I am happy to celebrate with you." This cowboy talked smooth and enunciated his words slowly like Matthew McConaughey, who also made me weak in the knees. Jax had on jeans accentuating a nice ass, a belt with a gold Texas longhorn buckle, worn brown cowboy boots, and a deep blue tee shirt with a vee neck and short sleeves. His shirt was fitted and showed off cut arms, muscular biceps, and olive skin. His chiseled biceps gave me the butterflies, and I blushed because it made me imagine him on top of me while flexing those biceps. I was glad to see his ring finger was bare and very relieved he was unable to read my mind. On the other hand, maybe he could. I did not care. He was so gorgeous. We made small talk for a few minutes.

"So Jax. Lucky for you, I hope you can dance, because I am looking to raise the roof in this place tonight."

He grinned at me devilishly and said, "Indeed, well then I better not disappoint you." He gave me his hand and led me out to the dance floor. His touch immediately sent tingles up and down my body. My body felt as if it had a fever. I felt like fireworks were going to light up the sky.

We danced to *You Sexy Thing, Don't Stop Til You Get Enough, Bad Girls, Shake Your Groove Thing*, and *Ring My Bell*. Then a slow song began to play, and he pulled me in closer. He smelled so good. I recognized the Giorgio Armani Acqua Di Gio cologne. His hands were on the small of my back and moved lower until they rested on my ass. I looked at him and after giving me a wicked grin, he moved them up a little. He knew he could take me right on the dance floor if he desired.

We continued dancing to *More Than A Woman* and then *Let's Get It On*. Without heels, my head would probably be even with his chest, but I was wearing high heeled sandals and he was bending down. My lips were now even with his neck. I had to hold myself back from trailing kisses up and down his neck. Our chemistry was explosive. If Jax pulled me like the dumbass earlier tonight, I would have followed him like a puppy dog with no questions asked. I tried to catch myself. I was completely misbehaving. What was I thinking? I needed to get control of myself! Thank God the music ended before I had sex with him right on the dance floor. Oh my God! Here I go again. I was insatiable when it came to wanting this man who I just met. I never had this feeling with anyone. I felt like I had to argue with myself to keep my hands off of him.

His voice brought me back to reality. "Sydney, are you okay? The music stopped about thirty seconds ago."

"Yes, I am fine. Sorry, I must have zoned out from all of the dancing."

Jax smiled at me. He saw right through my little white lie. He was so confident, but not in a cocky way. His slow talking put me at ease. I would have left with him right there and then, but he took my hand and walked me back to his table. We sat down and ordered a drink and tried to get to know each other a little better. It was a slow torture for my body. Jax said he enjoyed growing up on a farm in Elgin, Texas. The town was five square miles with a population of approximately 8,000 people. He was an only child and helped his parents with farm chores. The main crop was corn and they also had chicken eggs, milk from the cows, and they raised pigs. Everything they produced was sold at the market. They spent money as well. There was upkeep to the farm such as painting barns and outside buildings, repairing and painting fences, greasing farm machinery, sharpening hoes, shovels, and post hole diggers.

Sydney said, "So what did you do for fun out in the country?"

"Well when the day's work is done, I can listen to country music in the bed of my pickup truck, drink sweet tea, or some moonshine, and look up at the stars. You can see the constellations on a clear night, and the sky is beautiful with hundreds of stars. There was no cable television, so you made your own fun. We had horses, so I could take a horse and go riding and explore nature. It is so quiet outside. I can walk around naked on the farm if I wanted.

Oh how I would love to see him naked I thought to myself, but instead blurted out, "Not the best idea with a horse. He might think it is a carrot." Sydney laughed out loud at her own joke.

Jax loved how she had a sense of humor. "Good one! I love your wit. I did not really walk around naked. I am just saying I could if I chose to do so, because the nearest neighbor was a mile away. You made your own fun on the farm. Some nights I would get a gun from the collection and shoot beer cans off the wall or fence. Mostly the guns are for protecting the animals from coyotes, but there is no harm in having some fun now and again. I never had to worry about going to a gym. You work muscles you never knew existed. I spent a lot of time with my family. Enough about me. Tell me about yourself Sydney."

She was almost at a loss for words. When he looked at her, she felt like the only woman in the room. Jax gave her his undivided attention, and he was not just making small talk to get into my pants. He was truly interested in learning more about me. I was unused to someone caring about what I had to say, plus I was mesmerized by his seductive good looks.

He smiled and said "C'mon you cannot hold back on me."

I cleared my throat and said, "Oh, sorry. It is not often someone asks about me. The house I live in with my parents in Sea Isle used to be my grandparents. They owned a bakery. They left the house to us in the will and we moved in when I was twelve years old. My father is a carpenter. He used to work in Philadelphia on commercial buildings and renovations. Once we moved to Sea Isle, he opened up his own business and does residential remodeling work for residents and landlords. He can have as much work as he is able to handle. Everyone likes him, because he is friendly and is good at what he does. Plus he charges a reasonable price not trying to rip people off. He comes from a long line of carpenters. I am an only child as well. My mother stayed home to take care of me. When my grandparents were alive, she helped them with the business. She could have taken over the bakery but it would have been too much of a commitment. She preferred to spend quality time with her family. It is pretty quiet here from Labor Day to Memorial Day. Weekends are the busiest during the in season. During the off season you have to travel twenty minutes to get to the nearest open grocery store. Then during the season, I am surrounded by crowds of people. It is a tourist area, so I get to meet different people all the time. Most people rent the houses for a one week vacation. They try to fit as many people as they can onto one island. I get the best of both worlds since I it is quiet during the off season. The majority of people do not live here year round."

Jax listened intently the entire time and leaned into to show his interest. "See, it was not so difficult to tell me about yourself. Opening up is a great feeling. Sounds like a great place to live. You will definitely have to tell me more." The crowd in the club was thinning out. Jax said, "Do you have a ride home?"

Sydney shook her head. "Nina and I were going to order an Uber, however she is long gone."

Jax quickly offered, "I have a rental car, so I would be more than happy to give you a ride home. It is no problem at all. No strings attached. I promise. I am loving our time spent together and do not want the night to end yet."

"I live thirty minutes away."

He exaggerated his southern accent in response. "Well I reckon it it is a good thing I did not bring my horse Cracker." Jax chuckled and so did I. "I have GPS but you can easily show me the way."

"Well if you insist. And Cracker, really? You came up with a funny name on the fly. Cracker Jax. Good one!" I know I just met him, but he made me feel safe and comfortable. He could easily be a serial killer or a rapist yet I was pretty sure he was neither. Although if he was a rapist, I would not give him much of a fight. It sounded ridiculous, nevertheless if I did not know any better, I would say I just met my soulmate.

I reached for his hand and said, "Follow me. I will show you where I live."

Chapter 2 - More Than A Casual Connection

They arrived on 57th Street in Sea Isle City a short twenty minutes later. There were hardly any cars on the road at 2 a.m. and Jax was a cowboy with a heavy foot. Sydney's parents were away until Sunday afternoon, so no one was home. She was very thankful they were six hours away. They pulled up to a gray cedar shake siding three story house. Her parents owned the east unit. Sydney gave Jax the grand tour. They entered the house through the garage. There were two guest bedrooms on the lower floor with a bathroom and a laundry area. This floor was your typical shore home.

The next floor was an open concept masterpiece including an enormous family room with a vaulted ceiling, featuring wood beams and a fabulous fireplace. There was shiplap on the wall surrounding the fireplace, floor to ceiling. Shiplap is milled so the planks fit together and overlap similar to siding, whereas tongue and groove joins and interlocks. The wood was white and light gray multicolor with a beech wood beam mantle. Two built in bookcases flanked each side of the fireplace. The outer wall was entirely glass, consisting of sliding door window panes with the two center doors gliding away from you as you exit outdoors onto a Trex deck. I loved the unobstructed deck view with cedar railings and see thru glass panels.

Back inside, the dining room contained an oversized re-claimed pine, naturally finished wood table with two chairs at each end and two huge benches on either side. An orbital chandelier hung from the ceiling. The kitchen was designed with white cabinets and black granite countertops and stain-less steel appliances. The kitchen island had a radius edge coun-tertop with a breakfast bar. A master bedroom and bathroom decorated with a nautical theme were beyond the kitchen.

The top floor consisted of a fourth bedroom and ensuite bath-room. This was Sydney's room. The bed was queen size with posts and a frame going around the top. There were white sheers draped around the bed. Very romantic and seductive. Jax loved the house, and was glad no one was home. He was alone with the woman of his dreams.

Sydney ran back downstairs with him and handed him a glass of Merlot and turned on some country music. I said, "So just be-cause I am a cowboy, you turn on the country music?"

She laughed. "No, not at all. Believe it or not, I like listening to country music. I am not stereotyping you at all. In fact, feel free to change it if you would rather listen to something else."

"No, I am only kiddin with ya girl. I love country. Turn it up!"

Sydney thought it was so cute how he exaggerated his accent when he was making a joke. "Make yourself at home. I will be right back."

"You promise? Or is there an outdoor stairway for you to escape?"

"Jax, even if there was, I have no plans of running away from you. You could not keep me away if you tried." She smiled at him as she walked away.

Jax kicked off his shoes and relaxed on the beige leather family room couch while Sydney changed. He felt very at home here. The house was warm and inviting. Even though it was Friday the thirteenth, he felt like his luck could not get any better. Hot damn, he possessed no self control when this woman was in his presence. He was a hot blooded male, but his desire for her was unlike any he ever experienced. They had chemistry, and it was off the charts. He enjoyed her company as well. Conversation was intimate and easy. Wow, to think he was so close to returning to his hotel room and passing out instead of going out for a drink. He would have been a damn fool.

Five minutes passed and then Sydney opened the door to her room. I gazed up at her from my seat on the couch. I had to catch my breath. Good Lord, she was even beautiful dressed down. She wore baby blue yoga pants with a matching hoodie showing a hint of cleavage, and her dark curly thick hair was pulled back into a ponytail. Dang she was sexy. A couple tendrils of hair escaped the rubber band and framed her face. Her contacts were replaced with stylish black frames. If it was possible, she was more adorable and even better looking in casual clothes, glasses and those curls. The best part about it was how Sydney had no clue the effect she was having on me.

"WOW girl. You are quite the looker."

"Well howdy yourself cowboy." As she came down the steps Luke Bryan was singing M-O-V-E. She was dancing to the beat as Luke sang,

"Right about then, you lock eyes on me
You got me where you want me, where I wanna be
All up in the middle of your left and right
Just side to side, yeah, you're right on time when you
M-O-V-E"

Luke had the right idea. I wanted to be all up in the middle of her left and right and then explore every inch of her body.

Almost as if she read my mind, Sydney bit her bottom lip and smiled at me shyly and the feller in my pants was at full attention. Thank God for the strategically placed pillow blocking her view. As she moved closer to the couch, I stood up and she threw her arms around me to give me a hug and giggled. Sweet Jesus, she smelled good enough to devour. I caressed the side of her cheek with the side of my hand. I backed her up against the wall, leaned down and kissed her on her lips. Her lip gloss tasted like cherries. I took my tongue and parted her lips, and her tongue met mine. Their tongues did a little tango, and we kissed some more. Her tongue was so gentle and she was going slow and teasing me. Then she ran her fingers through my hair and arched her body into mine. A little moan escaped her lips. Oh my God, this vixen was going to make me explode in my pants if she kept kissing me and moaning. She backed me up and pushed me down so we were on the couch, and she stopped long enough to remove her hoodie.

"It is getting so hot in here." She straddled me on the couch and we kissed some more. I could kiss her for hours even though her tongue was tantalizing me.

I stopped her for a second and said, "Wait Sydney, I am going to be a gentleman and say if you keep going, I am not going to be able to stop."

She answered me by taking her shirt off and replied, "I sure hope not." A low growl escaped my throat. Her breasts were perky and looked very eager to please. I kissed her nipples and teased them with my tongue. She grabbed the back of my head and pulled it toward her so her breast was in my mouth. Well it would not be fair if I said hello to one and ignored the other one, so I gave her other breast some love too and suckled it until it hardened. Our eyes locked and the sexual tension between us was mounting, and we both were incapable of stopping until we were satisfied. She unzipped my pants and grabbed my friend who was more than happy to finally get some attention. Sydney kissed it and I thought I was going to lose it. She was holding it and kissing it and teasing it some more. I pulled her up and we kissed again only this time with so much passion and urgency. Clothes flew off in all directions, and then we fell onto the floor.

We were laughing and kissing and I regained my balance. I was on top of her and hesitated a second to make sure she did not have a change of heart. She smiled at me and grabbed my cock and guided it, making it easy to enter her. Sydney was so hot, wet, and ready and her body wrapped around me as if it were made for mine. It felt like I was home, and I never wanted to leave. It felt so good. I kissed her and she lightly bit my bottom lip. Her hand cupped the cheek of my ass and pulled me in deeper. I moved in a steady rhythm until I felt the spasms of her climax and then moved faster and harder. She put her legs up in the air and arched her back. It was all I could take. The volcano could not be held back any longer. I came so hard, and it felt spectacular. It was better than I ever could have imagined. She knew how to satisfy me like no other, and she thoroughly enjoyed herself.

Sydney kissed me and laughed while saying, "Thank you Jax for making my graduation day so special. This is a night I will always remember."

I chuckled and said, "Anytime. I was more than happy to oblige. By the way, the night is far from over. I will give you a lot more to remember if you so desire. I am so glad I decided to go to the club instead of going back to my room all alone. So are you ready for round two?"

We both laughed as I carried Sydney upstairs to her bed, I devoured her again, only much slower this time so I could explore every inch of her body. I needed to memorize every curve, since she was someone I never wanted to forget. It was satisfying to leisurely give attention to every part of her and to see what excited her the most. It enhanced my pleasure to see her squeal in delight as she responded to me. Sydney wanted the same thing.

She pushed me down on the bed and took advantage of kissing and touching my body all over. She did not stop until I was spent. When we were finished, we fell asleep intertwined and naked in her bed. It was a long day, and we were both exhausted, happy, and completely satisfied.

∞∞∞

Sydney woke up Saturday morning and the sun was shining through the window. The weather was reflected her mood, bright, happy, and full of sunshine. She rolled over to smile at Jax, but her hand found the other side of the bed empty. The only thing she grabbed were rumpled sheets and air. Sydney's heart felt heavy with disappointment. It seemed like more than a one night stand to her. Jax did things to her and made her feel like no one else did. The sex was absolutely unbelievable. She swore they shared an intimate connection which she never experienced before. The night was so extraordinary, fireworks should have lit up the sky. It was an epic night she would remember forever.

Guess she was all alone in those feelings. How could she be so stupid and careless? Sydney was so angry she rolled over onto her stomach, buried her face in the pillow, and started kicking her feet and punching the mattress while yelling "You stupid ass!! God dammit!! What were you thinking?"

As she was carrying on, Jax had strolled into the room with two coffees. To his amusement, he witnessed Sydney beating the shit out of her bed and talking to herself. He started laughing and said, "Hey be nice. You really should not call me a stupid ass. I rushed as fast as I could to get your coffee. I better not interrupt you. Should I go?" He placed the coffee on the dresser and said, "I was not familiar with my surroundings, so I was pretty lucky to find my way back to you."

Sydney rolled over slowly and looked at him timidly. Her cheeks were flushed with embarrassment, and she looked adorable. When her eyes met his, her face broke out into a big smile and she started giggling. She hesitated a second, stood up on her bed, and then jumped off into his arms.

It was unexpected, however Jax had no problem catching her. "Well, good morning to you gorgeous! I enjoyed the show."

"I totally apologize. I really thought you snuck out while I was sleeping and were never coming back."

"I should give you a good spanking for thinking I would sneak out on you. You might enjoy it too much, so I promise not to spank you. Darlin, you are too special to be anyone's one night stand. I wanted you to get some sleep, so I ventured out to find coffee. It was so peaceful and nice outside. It gave me time to think about last night. I want you to know I had no intention of meeting anyone at the bar. I needed a break, so I simply went out for a few drinks after a hard week. It turned out to be one of the smartest decisions of my life." Jax looked at her with a devilish grin.

Sydney kissed him and said, "I am glad you decided to go out and came home with me. I thoroughly enjoyed last night too. I have never brought anyone home and had sex on the first night. I thought I was having a girls night out, and meeting you was a nice surprise. I feel like I have known you for years. You are so easy to talk to, and my body responds to yours automatically. I honestly have to say I have never felt this way before. It is a little scary."

I kissed her on her cute nose. "I agree completely. There is an underlying current between us. I am insatiable when it comes to you. We should go sit on the deck and drink our coffee, before I keep you locked up in this bedroom all day. As much as I would love nothing more, the weather is so beautiful. It would be a shame to stay inside and waste such a beautiful day.

When they were comfortably sitting outside on the deck, Sydney said, "I forgot to ask you what you are doing in New Jersey. I noticed from your accent, you are not from around here."

"I am here for the NBA draft. Well, actually the draft is next month. The combine workouts were from Tuesday to Friday, and I just finished up yesterday. I have to fly back to Austin, Texas tomorrow morning."

"So you are a basketball player? The workouts sound exhausting."

"The workouts were brutal. Hopefully you are looking at a future NBA player. The draft is coming up shortly, and I will find out if I am picked by a team."

Sydney's smile disappeared. "So I was right. I was a one night stand. Athletes are notorious for being players on and off the field. You have no idea where you will be playing. You will have no time for a relationship or me."

"I need and want to see you again," Jax said. "I wish we met earlier and were at least from the same state, but neither one of us has control over fate. The draft is June 23rd. I had zero spring breaks in my four years at the University of Texas. I was so inundated with basketball. Listen, if you can pick me up at the Atlantic City airport on June 13th, we can spend June 13th to the 22nd together. We can figure out the rest later after the draft."

"Deal."

Jax was enjoying Sydney's company. She asked him if he wanted to take a walk on the beach, and she seemed shocked when he informed her it would be his first time. The only place he had seen a beach was on television, in pictures, or in the movies. They held hands with interlaced fingers and walked in comfortable silence. Jax was taking in his surroundings, and

Sydney was thinking about how lucky she was to have met Jax. She felt like she needed to pinch herself to prove it was real. They walked up a couple wooden steps to the promenade. The promenade was a wooden boardwalk with concrete sections spanning 27th Street to 57th Street. People walked, jogged, and rode bicycles on the promenade. There were not any stores on this part of the boardwalk, just houses. The stores were in the center of town.

They crossed the boardwalk and went onto the sand path leading to the ocean. The path went up a small hill. Once they cleared the hill, the spectacular sight of the ocean lay before them.

Jax was utterly amazed. It was like nothing he ever experienced before. The path opened up to what looked like a big sand field going on for miles. It was cool and silky against my feet, and it slid between my toes. The sun reflected off the water in a perfect light. It was high tide, so the ocean was in further covering up some of the sand. Sydney explained how during low tide, the waves were calm and the sand field was larger. Right now, the waves were approximately three feet high. I could hear the waves crashing down as they came in, and the water flowing in after the wave hit. The waves were white around the edges with salt, looking like snow. I could smell the salt air and hear the seagulls fighting over little crabs in shells. If I looked out into the ocean, I could not tell where the water ended and the sky began. The ocean faded into the horizon. The wind gently blew our hair. It was very calming and breathtakingly beautiful.

Sydney grabbed my hand excitedly and pulled me toward the water. "Come on Jax! Hurry and put your feet in the water." We ran the rest of the way to the water and laughed.

The water hit my shins and was refreshingly cool. It was only 70 degrees out but it was May 14, so not exactly summer weather yet. "Oh my God girl. This is a little cold, but I love it."

Something hit my foot. I bent down to get it and it was a fan shell. It was gray and white.

Sydney said, "Let's walk in the sand along the water, and we can look for more shells. Next time you visit, the water will be warmer to swim in. It is a little nippy right now."

While we were walking, I asked her, "What will you do now, since you graduated college?"

"I have to take my certification test for New Jersey. The results will automatically be recorded in a database, so I can apply for a teaching job in special education."

"I think it is great you want a career working with children. Which age group are you most interested in teaching?"

"I completed my student teaching at an elementary school in Galloway, five minutes away from college. The students were great, and I really enjoyed the younger kids."

"What sparked your interest in special education?"

"I know it will sound like a cliche, but I feel like I can make a difference teaching the children. I can relate to what they experience socially. Kids can be so cruel to other children. Then you take a child with a learning disability, emotional issues, or even autism and it is so much worse and compounds problems. The child is sometimes singled out and ridiculed or laughed at or treated as if he or she has some sort of catchy disease. It is so unfair, and I want to be of service by making the child's life easier if I possibly can."

I looked at her appreciatively. "God you are an amazing and caring woman Sydney. You have such a big heart. How can you relate to what the children are going through? You are so beautiful, I simply cannot imagine anyone ever making fun of you or bullying you."

"You really are too sweet Jax. Anyone can be affected by this type of behavior. In fact, you would be surprised how many kids have to deal with being treated unfairly sometime during their school years. When I was in elementary school, glasses were far from popular. Kids made fun of me like something was wrong with me, because I was unable to see like everyone else. In middle school, I was skinny with no shape so kids called me Olive Oyl from the Popeye cartoon. It hurt my feelings, because I only wanted to have friends like everyone else. The other kids also want to be accepted, so they joined in the name calling. They all thought it was a big joke. I thought it was mean and unfair. At first my reaction was to be defensive, but this only made them say it more. Then I figured if I let them get it out of their system, they would move on and stop calling me those names. I concentrated on school instead, resulting in straight A's. This only complicated the problem by giving them something else to make fun of and destroyed my self esteem for a long time.

As a result, I am always sensitive to other people's feelings and tend to befriend the underdog. I am not a follower and do what I feel is right, regardless of what others think. I empathize with children going through a similar situation and want to be there for them. I want to help them deal with mean people by not retaliating or being defensive. Let the mean person look bad with their behavior. You should be yourself and act nice to everyone no matter how you are treated. Listen to me going on and on. I apologize for boring you."

"Nonsense Sydney. I am so sorry you had to go through those bad experiences. No one deserves to be treated like an outcast. What a bunch of assholes. You are a good person for dealing with the situation the way you did and overcoming it. You have a lot of strength and courage."

"Jax, thank you so much. They probably had no idea how bad they made me feel, nonetheless everything worked out eventually. It was not my intention to have you pity me. I simply want to use my teaching skills to make a positive difference in the lives of the children I teach. I am not selecting a career for the amount of money it pays. I am choosing a job which I will love on most days."

"The more I talk to you, the more admirable qualities I uncover. I am confident you are making a great choice and will make a huge difference in children's lives.

"Thank you for believing in me. Your words mean so much. Again, sorry for going on about myself. Sometimes I have such a passion for something, I cannot help myself."

"Sydney, I asked you to tell me about yourself. I am intrigued and far from bored." We stopped walking long enough for me to kiss her. Her lips tasted like salt air and coffee. "Sydney, I am starving. Is there any place good to eat which is open this time of year?"

"Most places are not open yet since it is the off season. You are in luck though. I know a coffee shop open on weekends."

We walked into the small but cozy coffee shop. Sydney knew the college student working the grill and ran over to give him a big hug. "Hey Mike! I did not realize you would be working already. Long time no see! How are you?"

"I am doing great Sydney. I just finished my semester and am here until the end of summer. I just returned from Australia. I spent a semester abroad and completed an internship while I was there. It was a lot of fun and a once in a lifetime opportunity. I was able to do some sight seeing in my free time and visited New Zealand on my spring break."

"How exciting! Where did you study abroad in Australia?"

"Sydney."

"What?"

Mike cracked up. "I went to Sydney, Australia. It was the best decision. I will show you some pictures soon."

"Of course. I know you are busy working. Can we have two of your famous egg sandwiches with bacon and extra cheese?" She turned to me and said, "Mike's sandwiches are the best, but he is stingy with the cheese!"

Mike turned to me and said, "She has an addiction to cheese. She puts it on everything."

Sydney was about to introduce Jax to Mike, however no introductions were necessary. He shook Jax's hand and said, "Great to meet you Jax. I picked the right day to come back to work! It is so nice to meet you. Everyone is saying great things about your play. Good luck with the draft. I hope you will be a Sixer soon."

Jax shook Mike's hand and said, "You too man." He looked at Sydney and smiled, "Yes, I would love to be a Sixer, and the location is perfect."

Sydney turned to Mike, "Well I will let you get back to work, but do you have time to take a selfie with us real quick?"

Mike gladly obliged then went back to the grill to work on the sandwiches.

Sydney asked, "Mike, how did you know who Jax was?"

"Oh my God. Seriously? He is only on the front page of every sports section and all over the internet lately. Tell me you had no idea who he was?" Mike slapped himself in the forehead in disbelief.

Sydney held her hands up. "Hey in my defense, I do not really follow basketball, so no I had no clue."

Mike shook his head, laughed, and handed Sydney her sandwiches in a small bag. "You are so unbelievable. Have a wonderful day, and I will be seeing you around this summer!"

∞∞∞

Jax still could not believe how captivated he was by the ocean. The beauty of the ocean and sound of the waves made him feel at peace. It was hypnotic, and he felt happy in its presence. Combine the beach with the vivaciousness of Sydney and he had everything he could possibly want. His mind was telling him, "Whoa, hit the brakes, you just met her last night." His heart was telling him, "You better not dare let this girl out of your sight. Ever. She is everything you are looking for in a partner."

Sydney interrupted his little argument with himself by asking, "Jax, everything okay? You look like you are deep in thought."

I smiled at her and said, "I was just thinking how great of a time I am having with you, and I wish I could slow it down."

She smiled back at me and said, "Well since that is impossible, we should just make the most of our time together. If you are feeling up to it, I would love to take you crabbing at one of my secret spots."

"Just when I think you cannot impress me anymore, you do it again. I would love to go anywhere with you."

Every inch of Syd was all woman, and she was no priss. She was up for just about anything and was so carefree. After we took the top off, we went for a short ride in her Jeep. She turned the music up and the wind was blowing through her hair while she sung along to the song on the radio. I seemed to have a smile permanently plastered to my face, but it could not be helped. Sydney's love for life was contagious. She did not take anything for granted and had the best time no matter what she was doing.

After approximately fifteen minutes, she pulled off the rode onto a dirt trail. I have no idea how she even found it. She went back a distance and parked at a marshy area. Sydney pulled out some string attached to a triangle and handed me a net. She undid the bottom of the triangle and attached something sausage shaped to it.

She caught me staring at her.

"Okay you are looking at me very strangely. This is chicken neck I attached as bait to my hand line. You want to cast this into the water and when you feel something on the other end, you pull in the line real slow so the crab does not feel you on the other end. When I say now, you put the net in the water and scoop up the crab and put it in the plastic bucket. You will be able to see it by the time I tell you to scoop it. I put a little bit of cold water in the bottom of the bucket so they stay alive. When we are done crabbing, we can check the crabs to see if they are keepers."

"Are you seriously going to catch crabs with this hand line?"

"I sure am. Watch and learn baby!"

She must have felt something on the line, since she started pulling the string in super slow motion. Less than thirty seconds later, she said, "NOW" and I saw the crab and scooped it up. It was an exciting moment, especially since I was not expecting her to catch anything. Not because I doubted her skill. The equipment just seemed to be lacking. I figured I would humor her a bit and go along with it. Boy was I wrong.

After I put the crab in the bucket, the son of a bitch was pissed. It was trying to get out, and you could hear the claws clicking. I am glad it was in the bucket. The crab would have loved to get his claws on me.

She caught half a dozen and then switched and told me it was my turn. Sydney talked me through it like a champ. I was like a little kid when I felt the crab on the other end of my line. I wanted to pull it up as quickly as I could, but Sydney told me to resist yanking the crab. I was to do it very slowly, or the crab would let go. It seemed like it took an eternity to bring the crab up close enough to grab with the net, but I felt very accomplished!

After we were finished catching the crabs, Sydney took out a plastic ruler with a cutout. She explained how the crabs needed to be so big to keep them, unless it was a male. You could keep any size male. The pregnant females had to be thrown back in the water. They had orange sponges attached to the underneath of their shell. The males had something which looked like a penis on the apron of the shell, and the females shell was rounded.

"Syd, I am impressed as hell at your crabbing abilities. Here I thought we were going to throw a cage in the water and sit around and wait."

"Crabbing is very relaxing to me, and I get more pleasure from catching them this way. It is very rewarding to know I can catch my own dinner with a string and a net. Since we are going out to dinner, I am going to put them all back. Otherwise, I would take them home and put them in the sink and pour ice over them until they were nice and numb. I wear rubber gloves so the claws cannot hurt me. The ice paralyzes them, so I can break their back. Then I pull up the apron and clean the dirt out. It is a lot of work, but I thoroughly enjoy it."

"Sweetheart, watching you catch crabs turned me on. You are one remarkable woman. I wish it was possible for me to spend the entire summer here with you."

"Anytime Jax. I would love nothing more. Being near the water is so relaxing and enjoyable. This place makes me so happy and satisfied."

"Hey!" Jax protested, "You are supposed to describe me with those words."

She walked up to me and reached up on her tippy toes to give me a long deep kiss. After lingering for a few minutes, we separated and she replied, "Well, you should already know I feel happy and satisfied without me having to say it." She threw me the keys and got in on the passenger's side.

They drove back to the house and Jax asked Sydney if he could take his shower first so he could take a nap before dinner. She motioned for him to come here with her pointer finger, kissed him on the lips, and told him to go for it. Then she gave him a big slap on the ass as he walked away. While Jax was taking a shower, Sydney called Nina.

Nina picked up and answered on the first ring, "I am so sorry about last night. I felt horrible for leaving you. I promise you, it was unplanned. Please try not to hate me."

"You are being ridiculous Nina. There is absolutely no need to be sorry. Everything worked out for both of us. I met someone after you left. A smooth talking cowboy who I took home last night. He let me ride his horse."

"Oh my God Syd. You are so corny, you little slut. How was it? Spill the details. It is so out of character for you to take a stranger home."

"Nina, it was the best sex I ever had in my life. Unfortunately for me, he is flying back to Texas tomorrow morning. He promised to come back in a month, before the NBA draft."

"Oh my God, seriously!! Of all the people you could possibly meet, you meet a player. I swear to God he better not break your fucking heart, or I will kick his ass! And it is a promise." Nina knew Sydney dated very little and did not open up her heart to many guys. Syd's attraction to this guy was very obvious to

Nina, especially after having sex on the first date. She normally dated guys for at least a month before giving it up.

"Down Girl! Thanks for looking out for me, but I believe he will keep his word. Nina, he has a southern drawl like Matthew McConaughey. It is so DAMN sexy! I will try my best not to get my hopes up, but it may be too late. He seems like he is being honest with me. How was your date with the hot Italian?"

"His name is Vincenzo Bellini. Chenzo for short. And no, he is not a mobster. He very well may be a keeper. I never let him go home."

Sydney was happy for Nina. She dated guys who only seemed to be looking for casual sex and not worthy of a relationship. Nina was a good person and deserved a good guy. She seemed to attract jerks, and her luck was due to change. "My tall, dark, and handsome guy's name is Jax, and I love everything about him. Except for where he lives. I want to see him all the time."

Nina paused for a second and then yelled into the phone, "Wait, what? Holy shit, Syd, are you dating Jaxon Jones, the frigging number one draft pick from Texas?!"

"The one and only. Why does everyone seem to know who he is besides me? Mike at the bagel shop said his name before I had the chance to introduce the two. I slept with him and had no idea who he was. Well he did mention he played basketball. You know basketball is not my thing. I love sports, but I only seem to watch hockey and football."

"You are something else! Turn on a television once in a while. Or look on the internet. The next hottest NBA star everyone is talking about is Jaxon Jones, who is staying at your house and you have no idea who the hell he is! You must be living under a rock. I do not know if you deserve him. Get a clue." They both burst out laughing.

Jax came out of the bathroom with a towel wrapped around

his waist looking sexy as hell. "Umm Nina, I have to go. Jax just came out from the shower. His towel just dropped and umm ...well....I think he needs me. I have to go." Sydney hung up the phone and left Nina screaming in excitement on the other end.

"What was all the commotion about?" Jax knowingly smiled.

"Well you sure know how to get a girl's attention and make her stutter like an idiot. I just talked to my best friend Nina who I was out with last night. I told her about my incredible night with you and not just the sex. I definitely loved the sex, but I also enjoyed talking to you and getting to know you. She was making fun of me because I slept with an up and coming basketball star and had no idea who you were. She was screaming on the other end of the phone. I tried to explain to her how I really do not follow basketball too much."

"Well, I would say now is a good time to start."

Jax insisted on taking Sydney to a nice restaurant. She suggested they go to the Lobster House in Cape May. When she came out of her room, she was stunning. The girl had me head over heels in twenty four hours. She was wearing a dark denim sleeveless dress with a zipper ending right at her cleavage. The zipper was begging me to pull it down. Her shoes were tan sparkly wedges and her earrings were gold crystal hoops. Her hair was pulled back in a ponytail with wisps of curly hair sneaking out on the side. "Good God Sydney, I have no idea if I can make it through dinner. The only thing I am hungry for is you."

"We have to keep up your strength Jax. After all we just finished," Sydney laughed. "You are insatiable. Save me for dessert."

"Okay we better go before I change my mind and skip dinner and go straight to dessert."

Our table was on the outside deck overlooking the water. The ambiance was perfect. The sun was setting, and the view was spectacular. We ordered shrimp cocktail for our appetizer and lobster bisque soup. Sydney asked, "So did you play basketball on the farm?"

"Yes, one of the best Christmas gifts I ever received was when I was eight years old. There was very little spare time after helping my parents do chores on the farm. Any free time I had was spent playing basketball. My dad saw my growing interest in the game and found an old basketball hoop and attached it to a backboard made out of pallets. He hung it on the side of the barn and poured a cement court. I watched Allen Iverson and the 76er's when the games were televised. Cable was unavailable where we lived. On special occasions my mom and dad took me to The Tavern in Austin, TX where families gathered to eat and watch the game. I remember the 76ers were in the NBA finals in 2001 for the first time in over twenty years against the Lakers who were the defending champs. The Sixers won the first game in overtime but lost the remaining games, to my disappointment. I believe Iverson was twenty five years old at the time and scored forty eight points in the game they won. He pretty much single handedly carried the team to the finals. In my opinion, the Sixers played better basketball than the Lakers in the finals, but the Lakers still won. Iverson sadly never made it back to the Finals again. The Lakers had Shaquille O'Neal and Kobe Bryant. For a thin, short guard in a league where others were taller and heavier than him, Allen Iverson matched the big guys and was never intimidated. He was very competitive and crossed up more players with his deadly crossover move. It tripped other players up due to the fact he hesitated before executing the move. It looked like a fake. AI was very skilled at stealing the ball. Besides those skills, he was quick, so it gave other defenses a lot of trouble. I watched the Sixers due to Iverson. It was so exciting to watch him play."

Sydney was smiling and nodding, and she gave me her full attention when I was telling her about one of my childhood idols who happened to be someone other than Michael Jordan. It seemed as if everyone loved Michael Jordan. He was a legend and undeniably one of the greatest basketball players of all time. Today, many feel LeBron James fits the modern day definition of a GOAT. I personally believe Kevin Durant would have fit the definition if he was not playing for the Warriors. There are multiple good players on the team, so Durant does not get the opportunity to score as many points as he is capable of scoring if he were still with OKC. However, Durant beat James twice in the Finals.

Sydney commented, "I am so excited listening to you talk about the sport you love so passionately. I do know who Allen Iverson is, and it seems like people either love or hate him for his attitude. I remember my dad saying his crossover move was exciting to watch, because he was so good at it and fast. I must confess, I usually watch basketball games during playoffs. Well not the entire game, but at least for the last two minutes anyway." She laughed. "I hate to admit I am such a disgrace, and apologize for being one of those bandwagon fans. At least now I have a reason to watch."

"Are you saying I need to visit all the women who currently do not follow basketball and sleep with them so they start watching?" Jax smirked.

"No smartass, and you better not if you know what is good for you. So tell me, when did you realize you wanted to play basketball?"

"You are good for me, and I have no interest in anyone else. To answer your question, I am not really sure I ever realized I wanted to do this as a career. I played because I loved to play.

I always assumed there would be no choice to play due to the family farming business. I naturally assumed farming would be my career. I practiced dribbling and shooting baskets and spent hours working on drills. I took advantage of every minute. Basketball became my favorite past time, and with a lot of practice, I became really skilled at shooting and ball handling. I was homeschooled in elementary and middle school. I went to the public high school in Elgin and played point guard on the Elgin Wildcats team. In my senior year, I caught the attention of a scout who happened to be at one of our playoff games to see his nephew play. A week later, I was offered a full scholarship to play basketball at the University of Texas with the Longhorns."

"Were your parents upset or disappointed about you not taking over the family business?"

"Not at all, and quite the opposite. They are so supportive and actually made the decision for me. They told me how they did not want me to have an unstable future. Successful farming was determined by weather, government funding, and petroleum cost. So much more is involved in farming than just planting a crop and harvesting it, or gathering eggs in a basket. It is not so simple. There are a lot of outside elements which can make farming challenging as a living. My parents sold the farm to a developer and are waiting to find a house so they can begin their retirement."

"Jax, it is so wonderful to have parents who believe in making your dreams a reality. You are very fortunate to be so loved and supported. They obviously must be so proud of you. And it is extremely important to choose an occupation doing something you love. I would enjoy seeing you play sometime."

"Nothing would make me happier than to see you in the crowd."

Sydney and I were never at a loss for conversation. We were both trying to find out as much as we could about the other since time was not on our side. I was enjoying her company. The waitress arrived with our dinner. I had a succulent, melt in your mouth filet mignon, broiled lobster, and the creamiest, most delicious mashed potatoes. Everything was seasoned and cooked to perfection. Sydney had lobster, scallops and shrimp over linguini in a blush sauce. The seafood was very tender and delicious. We were so full after such a massive dinner. Sydney drove us back to Sea Isle and took me to Townsends Inlet to work off some of the food we ate. She took a blanket out of the trunk of her car and handed it to me, and we walked up a hill along a sandy path and kicked off our shoes. When we reached the top of the hill and started going down the other side, the view was extraordinary. This was where the bay and ocean met, and we were below the bridge which took you to Avalon and Stone Harbor. We could hear the cars above us. There were boats in the bay and people fishing along the shore. Kids were playing with dogs on the sand and other couples like us were strolling along the water.

Sydney did not want their time together to end. Her parents were coming back tomorrow to take her out for her graduation dinner. Right now I had Jax with me for the rest of the night. I refused to let the looming time constraint put a damper on our fun.

I looked over at Jax. He was so damn hot. He was wearing a black pocket tee with white lips on the pocket, light gray khakis, and black Sperry loafers trimmed in gray. We held hands as we walked. It was hard to believe how comfortable we were with each other in such a short period of time. "Jax, I still cannot believe you have never been to an ocean before this weekend. What was your first impression?"

"I felt like a little kid seeing it for the first time this morning. If I did not know any better, I would think the sand was a large plain extending as far as the eye can see." His eyes were dancing with excitement, and he instantly transformed into a six year old while he was talking. The more he talked, the more excited he became.

Jax continued, "It is an amazing part of nature like the Grand Canyon. The waves in the ocean look so powerful and demand respect, and yet the water is so calming to look at and makes me so happy. I felt mesmerized and could not stop looking at it. It is captivating just like you Sydney." He quickly closed the distance between them, pulled her into him, and gave her a long, passionate kiss.

Sydney slowly licked her lips and said, "I live here every day and I never get tired of looking at the ocean. I come to Townsends Inlet when I want to look for shells and take a long walk and think about life. The ocean is so big and makes me and my problems feel so small. I feel every grain of sand pull my feet in. I love walking in the water and feeling the ocean as it comes in and touches my feet and then goes back out. It feels like the breeze wraps around and hugs you. This is where I belong and where I feel the most at home. It is like heaven on earth to witness God's creation and to be lucky enough to be able to appreciate the beauty. Oh geez, there I go getting all philosophical. Hey do you want to race?"

Sydney took off before she even finished the sentence and was giggling so hard, I am surprised she did not fall over. She kept running. I counted to three to myself and then took off. I had to make her think she had half a chance. When she heard me coming she was laughing uncontrollably. "You sound like a herd of buffalo."

I scooped her up in my arms and dropped the blanket. It was so big it wrapped around us. She was still laughing and snorting.

"You okay Syd or are you planning on dying on me?"

I finally caught my breath and then pulled him on top of me. We kissed so long my lips were numb. "Thanks for the CPR Jax. You are definitely a lifesaver"

He unzipped my dress to reveal my dark navy bra and kissed the top of my breasts. "Mmm. I want some dessert."

"Oh my God Jax. What are you doing? Not here. There are people walking around." He met my eyes and smiled to acknowledge he heard what I was saying. Then he quickly disappeared under the blanket. I tapped him on the head because I was mortified someone would see us. Jax responded by going lower. He was trailing kisses from my chest to my navel. He lifted my denim dress up to my waist and his finger hooked on the elastic of my bikini panties. He pulled them down to my knees and then his tongue softly tickled my clit. I almost stopped breathing. It felt sensational. He kept a steady pace then moved two fingers inside me. Oh my God!! I started to arch my back in response to my arousal, and he laughed because he knew I was completely surrendering myself to him. He had me right where he wanted me and he damn well knew it. The thrill of possibly getting caught made me climax pretty quickly. It felt so intoxicating, I wanted the feeling to last forever.

Now it was my turn to return the favor. I disappeared under the blanket. Jax had no complaints. He felt as if he died and went to heaven when Sydney unzipped his pants. She wasted no time pulling his penis out of his pants with her soft, warm hands and then wrapping her hot, soft, wet lips around his shaft. The warmth of her mouth gave him the most intense spine tingling sensation. Adrenaline rushed through his body, and he was in pure ecstasy. She lifted his penis up and kissed and licked the underside, which was so sensitive to her touch. Syd was so tender and loving. He lifted the blanket up for a second to catch a peek and her eyes looked up at him. She laughed in response, and the result was a wonderful humming sensation. He practically jumped off the blanket between the vibration and the sensation shooting through his body. It was like jolts of electricity and euphoria. She put me back in her mouth and gently sucked in a steady rhythm as she caressed my balls and squeezed lightly. I could feel the back of her throat and shuddered again. I was surrounded by an intense warmness and suppleness of her mouth and her lips. To say I was in ecstasy would be an understatement. I could not hold back any longer, although I honestly was never in control. I tapped Sydney on the shoulder to let her know I was ready to cum and she continued anyway. "Oh my God, yesssss." In this moment, I experienced the most powerful sensational feeling, and my brain shut off to hold onto the moment for as long as possible. If I died right there and then, I would have died a very happy man. She smiled at me and we lay there cuddling for a while in the blanket. After some time, we felt chilly and walked back to the Jeep. It took less than five minutes to get back to the house.

We shared a bottle of wine and watched *Ghosts of Girlfriends Past*. What a coincidence to see Matthew in a movie. I smiled at Jax and told him they could pass as brothers. Jax enjoyed romantic comedies as much as I did. After the movie, I took Jax upstairs one last time. He had to leave early in the morning to catch a flight home. We made love with such passion and hunger, and I was so fearful I would never see him again.

Jax woke me up early in the morning to offer me a tender goodbye kiss. "Baby, I really hate to wake you up. You look like an angel sleeping. The last thing I want is for you to wake up in an empty bed. It really pains me to leave you. Thank you for sharing the best weekend of my life with me. It is a weekend I shall never forget."

I wrapped my arms around him as if my very life depended on it. More than anything, I wish he could change his mind and stay with me. I knew I was acting unreasonable and childish, but it could not be helped. He slowly carried me downstairs. It was not hard to tell how it killed him just as much to leave me. I kissed him and spoke with a big lump stuck in my throat, "Jax, I enjoyed every single second with you and absolutely have no regrets. The more time I spend with you, the more I realize we are made for each other. It sounds ridiculous in such a short period of time, but I just know. If I could do anything for you to stay, I would. I am not ready for this." The dam broke as my tears started to flow, and Jax gently wiped them away.

"You are not being ridiculous if I feel the same way. Who cares what anyone else thinks. Our chemistry is insane. We hugged and kissed passionately for a considerable amount of time, and then he involuntary pulled himself away. Jax said he had to go before he missed his flight and promised to return before the draft.

As he reached for the door knob I started sobbing uncontrollably with my back against the living room wall. He turned to look at me as tears ran down my face. His face was full of concern, but his eyes were full of compassion and love. He took three big strides and pinned me to the wall with a kiss saying more than words could at this moment. "Baby, please I beg you not to cry. I do not know what to say to make you believe me, but just have some faith. I have not given you any reason not to trust me yet. You will see me again. Go get some sleep. If I do not leave right now, chances are I never will. I unfortunately have a plane to catch."

I gave him one last quick kiss and leaned against the door after he left to listen as his car pulled away. I went back to my bed and crawled under the warm sheets. His scent and indentation were still there. I wrapped the sheets around me and hugged his pillow. Then I cried myself back to sleep. Maybe I would spend time with him in my dreams until I could see him again.

Chapter 3 - Will I Ever See You Again?

Sydney celebrated her graduation at the Tuckahoe Inn with her parents. The restaurant overlooked the bay and offered excellent seafood. She told her parents about meeting Jax at the club and spending the weekend together. Her mom and dad looked at each other quizzically. Mom wore a disapproving look on her face. Dad seemed disappointed. She was immediately bombarded with questions.

"Who is he? Where is he from? How come he did not come to dinner? Is it because he is a player? He stayed in our house? You let a stranger into our home? Did you sleep in separate bedrooms? Oh my God Sydney, have some self respect. Who has sex with someone the minute they meet? I hope you stayed away from our bed. I am sure you gave him the wrong idea. He better not break your heart or else!"

"Mom and dad! Slow down and relax. Give me a chance to respond." I laughed. My parents obviously were not finding the situation funny in the least bit.

"Okay to answer your questions, his name is Jax Jones and he is from Texas. I met him at Boogie Nights in Atlantic City. We really hit it off and wanted to spend more time together. I showed him around Sea Isle. Yes dad, he is a player but not in the way you may think. He plays basketball. I have plenty of self respect, however I am old enough to make my own decisions."

My dad interrupted, "Wait. What? Hold on, you mean The Jax Jones who is in the NBA draft? Are you kidding me? The sports analysts have been talking about him for weeks now. What are the chances?"

"Geez dad. Thanks for the vote of confidence. I am not good enough to snag a prospective NBA basketball player?"

"There you go twisting my words around. You know what I mean. I meant, what are the chances of you both being at the same place at the same time and meeting? And then spending the weekend together?"

"Actually he initiated a conversation with me. I had no idea who he was until he told me. His name was not familiar to me at all."

"Are you kidding me? How did you meet someone who is the best player in the NBA draft and the Sixers best chance of winning a lot of games, and you had no idea?"

"Hon, my mom chimed in. Stop acting like a prosecutor and let Syd talk. I am sure he is a nice guy."

"Oh c'mon Jen. Be realistic. How nice is a prospective NBA star who has his pick from thousands of women? What are the chances he will stay faithful to our daughter?"

"Rob! You are making me mad! On second thought, make it furious! You have not even met him, and it is not your job to pass judgment. The words coming out of your mouth right now are ludicrous. Sydney has a good head on her shoulders, and I trust her."

"Thanks mom, I said. At least someone does." I gave my dad a dirty look.

Rob rolled his eyes. "Sydney, I am just looking out for my little girl."

"Yeah dad, I know, but I am grown now. Leave the relationships to me."

"Well, judging by your last choice, you sure know how to pick them and can use all the help you can get," he replied.

"Really, dad! What a low blow. I would not expect such a hurtful comment from you of all people."

My mom shot him the death glare, and he shut his mouth real quick. My ex boyfriend, Paul was off limits for conversation. Dad knew better than to bring it up.

I met Paul at college. He was good looking with dirty blonde hair, blue eyes, an athletic build, and a beautiful smile. He reminded me of Paul Walker from *The Fast and The Furious.* Needless to say, I was more than willing when he asked me out. Paul was the All American male who all moms and dads could not help but adore. He had one hell of a life planned for himself. His career plan was to become a state trooper. He successfully completed his basic training and was finishing up his degree in criminal justice while he interned at the State Police Station in Atlantic City. If things worked out, we would have a great life ahead of us. Sounded like a perfect little dream come true.

Until we became a couple, and it all started to unravel. After I became his girlfriend, everything changed dramatically. The dream became a nightmare. He seemed caring but was really jealous and controlling. I had no identity of my own. When I went out with friends, he texted me so much it was not worth going out anymore. He criticized and berated me on every little subject, from how I dressed to how I cooked and how I spoke. Nothing I did made him happy, but yet he refused to let me go. He let me know he was better than me through his words and actions.

He cheated on me but always came crawling back. Somehow,

he believed I was his property. I became afraid of him and was too embarrassed to tell my parents or Nina. They all thought Paul was so perfect, and I would look like a failure if they found out otherwise. They would not believe me if I told them. After much despair, I finally confided in Nina, and she told me to leave him. When I finally gained the courage to leave him, it did not go well. He kept calling and texting me nonstop and slashed my tires when I ignored him. Nina helped me get a restraining order against him. He was a ladies man, and it did not take him long to find his next victim. Hopefully she would come to her senses quicker than I did.

My dad cleared his throat to get my attention and brought me out of my bad memories and back to reality. "I am so sorry honey. Forgive me. It was unfair of me to say, especially since he fooled everyone. I am only trying to protect you. Hey, do you think I can get some tickets to Jax's games?"

They all burst out laughing. It was typical of dad to cash in on Jax's fame. The cheerful mood returned, and the waitress arrived with dinner. Our meal was marvelous, and we laughed and enjoyed each other's company despite the earlier awkwardness. Nothing more was mentioned about Jax or Paul. I knew Jax was a good guy. We had pleasant conversations, and I felt as if I knew him my entire life. We shared a mutual respect for each other that I never had with Paul. Paul was a selfish egomaniac and only cared about himself and his needs. Sex with Paul was unspectacular and robotic. There was very little pleasure involved. I had no idea at the time, since I had no comparison. Paul was my first love, or so I thought. Jax was different and better than Paul on every level. When I stood up from the table, I realized my fingers were crossed.

∞∞∞

Jax was overcome with emotion when it was time to leave

Sydney. Before he woke her, he was watching her sleep. She looked like a peaceful angel sleeping, with her curly dark hair laying against her white pillow and a smile on her face. Sydney seemed to be cheerful all the time and was always laughing or smiling. She enjoyed life and even smiled in her sleep. Jax secretly hoped she was dreaming of him. Her joyfulness was contagious. It was difficult not to be happy while spending time with her.

He was totally unlucky with relationships back home in Texas. Basketball took up the majority of his time, and the few women he did date wanted more attention than he was able to offer. And to be honest, he was not interested enough to put in the work to save the relationship. The girls were drop dead gorgeous yet very high maintenance and whiny. It started out fun until they tried to change him and monopolize the little time he had to himself. He avoided head games and drama.

Jax was too busy with the farm and his chores to date in his teens and had no opportunity to date until college. At first he enjoyed the occasional one night stand because of the sex. There were no strings attached which meant no relationship worries. The girl would go home, and he would play basketball. It should have been the perfect arrangement, yet now he yearned for a relationship. His parents were married for twenty five years and despite some hard times, were still very much in love.

Jax grew up in a very loving environment, and they managed to have fun when the work was finished. Both parents were there for him every day and supported all of his dreams, and would do anything to make those dreams become a reality. Jax wanted a loving relationship like his parents, so his children could be part of a happy family. He wanted someone to love who would love and cherish him in return. His soulmate was somewhere waiting for him, and he longed to share the rest of his life with her as equal partners. So far he struggled to find her, until he met Sydney. She probably doubted his sincerity to see her before the draft, but Jax knew he was going to keep his promise.

In the month following the combine, Jax found little free time. He was on a mission to find an agent as soon as he returned to Texas. The clock was ticking with only ten days left to find one. I was getting plenty of calls and had a big decision to make. I needed an agent who had experience with the league and also had strong family values. I planned on staying in the business as long as possible and wanted my career to grow with my agent. The average life of an NBA player lasted 4.5 years, unless he was a star. It was a necessity for my agent to care about my needs as well as my future family, in addition to fulfilling his own agenda. I had met with several agents during my college basketball season. They attended my games and each one was bursting at the seams to tell me how they were worthier than the other agents. It seemed like one big pissing contest to get my attention.

The big agencies tried to entice you with their high profile player list and promised to focus their time and energy equally. Sorry, if I refused to buy into the bullshit. If a high profile player demanded the agent's time, I am sure the agent would drop everything to do so, because the athlete was their livelihood and essentially paid their salary. I would be brushed aside like a gnat. The small companies were out to prove they could accomplish the same as the bigger companies, even if they did not have the clientele or the money to back it up.

The NBA was a big multi billion dollar monopoly with labor contracts, bargaining agreements, salary caps, luxury taxes, and many more rules. Players needed agents to manage their professional life. Agents understand market value, collective bargaining agreements, and the negotiation process. They also take care of phone calls, interviews, public appearances, endorsements, and prevent the player from going bankrupt trying to manage their own money.

Agents are always searching for potential sponsors and business deals, and I had no interest in the business practices of basketball. Even if I was savvy enough to handle the business, it should be managed by a professional who possessed the right qualifications and experience. My calling was to play basketball. The meetings were a hassle, although they were crucial to protect my future. Essentially, it was a business marriage, and I needed a suitable partner. Time was running out.

With hardly no time to spare, I decided to sign with an agent who met with me and my parents informally and unannounced on a family outing at Barton Springs pool in Austin. First and foremost, this guy was motivated to track me down at this location. If you have never been there, it is quite the experience. The pool is three acres long, and the water is supplied by underground natural springs. It is open year round, and the water temperature remains at a nippy seventy degrees. The view of the pool was breathtaking and unlike any pool you have ever laid eyes on in your lifetime. I am not talking about your everyday swim club with a diving board or two and a half asleep lifeguard who may or may not be able to save someone. This was literally water which extended three football fields and was surrounded by beautiful parks. I thought this was the coolest place I had ever been to until I saw the ocean for the first time recently.

Anyway, after a nice swim, the family was picnicking on the grass when this guy in designer frames and swim trunks adorned with palm trees strolls up to us with an IPad. He definitely looked out of place. Surprisingly he strolls right up to us and knew our names even though we never laid eyes on him previously. He apologized for the intrusion and introduced himself to us as Joe Fortunato. Joe explained he was an agent and wanted to speak to all of us, however he felt it would be more suitable to spend family time with us before discussing business. His concept was to observe me outside of basketball to see what was important to me off the court.

Although the guy obviously stalked me to find out where I would be today, he really did his homework and took a unique approach in order to meet with me. His actions demonstrated perseverance, dedication, and motivation without even giving a formal presentation. My family and I were intrigued and invited him to join us for the day.

It was a very enjoyable day. We swam, ate, and conversed with Joe as if he was part of the family. As a matter of fact, he was not in any particular rush at all and was enjoying himself. He was very animated and friendly and included everyone in the conversation. There was absolutely zero awkwardness all day long.

Eventually, we had to remind Joe how he traveled here today for a specific purpose. After convincing him we were very interested to hear what he had to say, Joe apologized again for interrupting our family gathering. None of us minded and were glad to meet him. He knew all about my basketball career and followed my games. Without bad mouthing his competition, he explained what he had to offer as my agent and clarified how my success and happiness were his main priority. It was in his best interest to balance my professional life, my endorsements, and appearances so I still had time enough to spend with my family. The goal was to make money without taking advantage of me in the process.

His goal was to represent a well rounded athlete with strong family ties. Joe expressed why the deal needed to be mutually beneficial. It was vital for me to make enough money to have a comfortable career and retirement, and Joe wanted to take the journey with me. Despite owning a small company which he founded, Joe Fortunato was a good fit for my career. He felt it was of the utmost importance to have a balance and not burn myself out. It was not necessary to make every last dollar available to me. There needed to be boundaries.

His commitment was to take care of the business end of basketball and look out for my best interests in the process while advising me on a regular basis. Any final decision was mine to make. My assignment was to play basketball and pick an endorsement to benefit my life. It was important not to sell out to any brand for the sake of a few dollars. Choosing a specific endorsement should have special meaning to me. Joe would find endorsement deals for me, and I would decide which to choose. I trusted him and my family trusted him. He was a very likable man with good values. It was unconventional to sign a deal while sitting in swim trunks at a lake, but it was exactly how it went down. I was very fortunate Joe found me.

Sydney's heart ached after Jax went home, and she felt an emptiness she could not explain. One thing was for certain. There was a lot to accomplish before Jax returned,, and little time to be bored. She was thankful to be busy. Maybe the days would fly by, so the time would be closer to seeing Jax again. Sydney was a teacher's aide in a fourth grade special education class, so her days were full. She was assigned to an autistic little boy named Max.

I learned a lot from my experience with Max to benefit me in my future career. He had an individualized education program (IEP) which was customized to meet his learning needs. It logged Max's learning and objectives to help educate him more effectively. He required a routine, so I gave him a piece of paper listing activities in order without specific times. There was a question mark before lunch and before the end of the day to help introduce the unknown items of the day. The teacher listed the activity with a picture beside it so Max knew his plans for the day.

This type of daily schedule made learning easier for Max instead of adding unnecessary stress. It allowed him to look forward to new activities without any surprises. I learned autistic children have trouble in social situations. Each child is different with regard to behavior. Max's parents thought Max was just a shy child, since he showed no interest interacting with other children. He experienced difficulty with conversations and making eye contact. As time passed, I noticed his extreme interest with buttons. His mother informed us he had a collection at home of different colors, shapes and sizes. Max had to be reminded not to touch or follow strangers for their buttons.

His parents were concerned about his fixation. We explained how obsessions with items are different for each autistic child. Max found comfort playing with them. I spent my time with him during my student teaching showing him different activities using buttons and turned his obsession into a hobby he could use in his everyday life in a productive way. I bought a bunch of different buttons from the craft store and put them in a container for Max. We made different crafts, and Max looked forward to each project. We made button magnets, clips, pictures, bracelets, and decorative bowls. Then we decorated his shoes with them. When we played games, we used the buttons as the "men". We even made bicycles out of paper clips and buttons. I showed Max how to make gifts and greeting cards out of them. I was able to teach him how to tell time from a round clock using buttons as the hours of the day. The buttons were convenient and assisted in teaching. We were able to sort, count, and make letters with them.

Another concern for Max's parents was how Max rocked his body back and forth in stressful situations. His parents wanted it to stop, but we explained how it was a coping mechanism which soothed him like a pacifier comforts a baby. We tried to determine when the rocking occurred to identify the trigger, in order to reduce or eliminate the problem . I also learned Max was not showing defiance when he did not do what was asked of him. He simply did not understand what was expected of him. Sometimes it was easier if he had a picture showing him how to do something.

Furthermore, Max needed guidance and coaching in order to interact with other children. It was difficult for him to comprehend a long discussion. I learned to get to the point using fewer words. Max was a great kid and was very intelligent. The special education teacher I was working with expressed how I worked well with Max and should definitely pursue a career teaching autistic children. Max's parents were very pleased with the way I worked with him and communicated his progress to them. My teacher's feedback revealed I was compassionate, creative, understanding, patient, and intuitive to Max's educational requirements. His parents commented how I possessed a calmness which in turn helped reduce Max's stress level.

My work day was far from perfect and demanded tremendous patience and kindness. I was tired and aggravated at times like anyone else. I enjoyed a challenge, and it was very rewarding to see the results of my hard work. It helped to be young and approachable, and I loved children. The school provided a good support system. It was essential for everyone to work together as professionals to fulfill each child's needs, and to communicate progress with the parents in order for them to support the child at home. Individualized Education Plans were quite a lengthy process. The IEP's were only as successful as the follow up and tweaking of the plan. It was important to realize situations changed constantly, and nothing was written in stone.

My personal feeling was the process ran smoothly if the parents had an open mind and kept us informed of changes at home and followed our suggestions. It was constantly a work in progress. Everyone needed to work together. There was an abundance of information given at the meeting, and the goal was to meet each child's academic needs. Objectives needed to be realistic and not too general if they were to be achieved. I found it helpful working with the same child every day. I found it helped me become more aware of his needs. I was able to find ways to guide Max in effectively communicating. If it became obvious a goal was not going to be reached, I suggested a more feasible backup plan. Communicating with the parents on a regular basis was key to the child, parent, teacher relationship. Max was the ultimate reason I wanted to pursue a profession mentoring autistic students through education.

∞∞∞

I completed applications online for special education, specifically autism. In the meantime, I studied for my Praxis exams which were necessary to pass, in order to become certified. Not long after Jax left, I received a call from Bancroft School in Haddonfield, New Jersey. It was a part time teaching position, but had the potential to become full time after one year. The open position was for an assistant teacher. A full time position with their organization required a minimum of one year prior teaching experience in the field.

My initial interview went well and was very informative. Bancroft was one of the first private schools in the United States for developmental disabilities and learning difficulties. The company upheld high standards and strived to meet the needs of every child. My student teacher supervisor had a lengthy discussion with the Bancroft teacher who was hiring an assistant teacher to support her with the class. My reviews were excellent, and I was encouraged to pursue the position. My student teaching would count toward previous teaching experience in addition to one school year as an assistant teacher, in the event I decided to apply for a full time teaching job the following school year. The administration was pleased with the progress I made with Max, and felt my skills would be a good fit with their school. Max's parents gave the school wonderful feedback, and said I was an asset to the school and highly recommended me for the position.

I was invited to create and teach a sample lesson in the elementary classroom in two weeks. It seemed like a really great opportunity, so I agreed to return. I took the Praxis test the week after my interview.

As promised, two weeks later I arrived at Bancroft to teach a small group of elementary students a lesson. First, I showed them a blue plastic bag and then a yellow plastic bag. Then I pulled out items from each bag, and together we recited the names and colors of each item. Once the students were familiar with all of the items, I held up one item at a time and took turns asking each student to put the item into the bag where the item belonged. If the item was placed into the wrong bag, I waited until after the lesson to tell the child privately and explained why the item belonged in a certain group. The kids seemed to have fun, and the lesson was successful. I made sure the activity was fun and without pressure. No one was forced to participate. I met with the director following the lesson, and he said the job was mine. I was encouraged to go home and think it over, and let him know my decision in a week or two.

The position required five hours a day assisting the teacher. I would work one on one with each student based on the student's individualized plan, and I would offer input for the teacher with regard to the ongoing plan. After one year, I would be considered for a full time teaching job if there was an opening, or continue as an assistant teacher. Each class utilized three assistant teachers, since spending sufficient time with each student was a priority.

I was so exhilarated and over the moon after my triumphant meeting. I was dancing and singing on my way out to the car and I was smiling from ear to ear. My career was off to a good start, and I was astonished and proud I was able to get a job so quickly after graduation. I decided not to wait a minute longer and sent Jax a quick text sharing my new job offer. When I hit send, I started to doubt myself. Maybe I should have waited to send a message. Would he remember who I was? God I seemed so desperate. Why am I so impulsive!! He obviously does not want to hear from you or else he would have texted you.

As I was busy arguing with myself, three bubbles popped up on the screen. He was replying! What was it going to say? Well

I did not have to wait long. A text came through from "My cowboy". This was the nickname I gave him in my contact list. "Wow you were able to get a job so quickly. You sure did not waste any time." It continued, "Good job! Those kids are lucky to have you as their teacher. I promise, we will celebrate soon." The text ended with a winky emoji and a heart.

"Sorry, I hope you were not in the middle of something. I should not have bothered you. I sent the message before deciding if it was a good idea. I tend to be a bit impulsive at times."

"Sydney, I am so glad you texted. Impulsive is good in this instance. I am on my way to a meeting now, but I will text you before your pretty little head hits the pillow tonight. Text me ANY TIME. If I am busy, I will wait until I have some free time. There is no need for any apologies."

I texted back, "Looking forward to it. I anxiously await to hear from you. I miss you in my bed. Have a nice day." I inserted a kiss emoji and decided to go have some lunch. I was starving!

Hearing from Jax awakened the longing inside of me, and I suddenly could not wait to see him again. My heart ached for him ever since he left, and he was always on my mind. We were only together for one weekend, but our connection was so strong. I realized in two short days, Jax was my soulmate. He was so easy to talk to, and I felt like we knew each other for years. My heart felt full when he was by my side. I would do anything to make a relationship work with Jax, especially since we were so compatible. It was unfair he lived so far away. Of course I meet the perfect guy and man of my dreams, while my fate was hanging by a thread.

The little voice in my head advised me to proceed with caution, but I told it to shut the hell up. Was it possible to love someone so soon? Was I confusing love and lust? Our sexual chemistry was intense and undeniable. He made my body react and respond in ways it never had before. On the other hand, I believe we had love too. Jax was my best friend whom I cared about considerably, and we shared our deepest thoughts and feelings in conversations which continued for hours. I truly cared about him, and dreaming of a future together, made me realize my strong desire to take the journey.

I was on my way back to my car when my phone rang, as if he knew I was thinking of him. I blushed. It was preposterous to think he read my private thoughts. My heart skipped a few beats as I answered.

"Jax, I thought you were waiting until tonight to text me?"

"Hey Syd, sorry I could not call any sooner. After you texted me, I had to talk to you and hear your voice. I needed more than a text. Especially after you said you missed me in your bed. Life has been crazy since I left you, but you are never far from my thoughts. I need you to know how I feel."

"There is no need to explain. I completely understand how crazy your life must be right now. I figured I was the furthest thing from your mind. Apparently, we both have been thinking about each other a lot. You have no idea how happy you have made me."

"You should never question it. I have not stopped thinking of you since I left your house to catch my flight. It was sheer torture returning to Texas when I longed to be with you. It was an impossible situation. I felt better after reminding myself we would see each other in a month. I had a lot deadlines to meet before the draft. Jax went on to tell me about the deadline imposed for obtaining an agent. He described his first meeting with the agent he chose, Joe Fortunato. Jax highlighted the reasons behind his decision to sign with Joe. I was laughing. "He seems like a genuine man and really dedicated to go above and beyond what is required to get you to sign."

"This is the interesting part Syd. He seemed as if he forgot the purpose of his visit, and thoroughly enjoyed spending time with me and my family. The agenda was put aside, and there was no rush to get back to it. The entire experience made me appreciate Joe as a person and trust him to look out for my best interest. He actually took the time to give a damn."

"I am so happy for you. It seems like you made the right choice. The process has to be difficult when you are choosing someone you never met to handle your career, which is your life. At least you know he will have your back."

Jax paused for a second or two as if he was unsure about his next sentence.

The hesitation scared the hell out of Sydney. She was thinking, *"Oh God, here it comes. He wants to end it."*

He cleared his throat and continued, "I know I promised to visit you before the draft...."

Sydney's heart sank. *"Dammit. I should have known better. Here comes the big blow off. Why did I open up my heart to him?"*

"....but I was thinking, you should fly to Texas so you can meet my parents, and I can show you off and around a little? So what do you think?"

Sydney was so excited. What a complete 360 to the scenario she was dreaming up! She was so relieved and began jumping up and down and screaming in the parking lot like she won a new car. She was laughing and crying at the same time. Sydney told Jax customers from the hamburger store were staring out the window watching her behave like a maniac. Here she thought Jax was politely giving her the boot, but instead was inviting her to Texas before the draft to meet his mom and dad. It took her a second to find her voice. She was flooded with emotions and almost started to cry again. Syd choked up. "Oh my God Jax, really?

"Yes but, I might have to reconsider after you broke my eardrum screaming. Now I lost my hearing. Did you just say something?"

"Smart ass! I would love to but I can only make it down for a few days if it is okay?"

"Any time with you will be alright baby. I will book your flight and text you the flight information later today."

They spoke again for an hour before bedtime to catch up on their lives since they had last been together. There were no uncomfortable silences. They were both excited to hear about the other and what had happened in the time they were apart. Sydney found it hard to believe how much went on behind the scenes in the NBA.

"Wow, babe your mind must be spinning. Your whole world is changing at once with a lot of unknowns. I feel overwhelmed just accomplishing what I need to in order to get a job. Here you are trying to get into the NBA, and it is not an everyday occurrence like a teaching job. You are experiencing a whole new world, and I want you to know I am here for you every step of the way, and anytime you need to talk."

"I appreciate the support and would love nothing more than to talk to you. Everything is new to me, so I will learn as I go. I will enjoy sharing my day with you and taking this journey together. Enough about me. You can read it on the internet later. Tell me all about your job search and interview experience."

Sydney was more than happy to discuss what she accomplished since Jax left. Jax was excited to hear about Sydney's job search and learned more about teaching requirements and the process of obtaining a job in the education field. He was extremely happy for her, and her success was just as important to him as his own. Their conversation was so easy, and they both had so much to say to each other. It was obvious by their excitement and fast talking how they truly missed each other. As a result, they both promised to at least text each other before bed every night, if it was not possible to call. It was so important to keep in touch, and they both were determined to make this relationship work.

Sydney thought about him every minute she was not occupied. She should have texted him sooner but was afraid of being disappointed or even worse, rejected if he changed his mind about her. Luckily she was mistaken, however she managed to get in her own head by overthinking and second guessing his feelings.

Likewise, Jax thought about Sydney constantly. It would have been truly difficult to forget someone as incredible as her. In his case, he was hard pressed for time and so consumed with deadlines needing to be met before draft day, and time simply got away from him. Sydney was never far from his thoughts. He found himself always wanting to tell her about his day and the good things happening in his life. She was one of them, and it was unthinkable to get her out of his mind even if he tried, and he did not want to either.

Jax reluctantly informed Sydney it was time to hang up.

"Nooooo. I cannot bear to hang up. I finally get to talk to you, and I never want to let you go."

"C'mon Syd, the sooner you hang up the sooner we see each other in person. We both need to get these days done, so I can hold you in my arms again."

"Jax, it would be so rude for me to hang up on you. You do it."

After playfully bantering about who was going to hang up first, Jax suggested they both hang up at the same time. "On three. 1, 2, see you in Texas soon baby, 3." The line went dead.

Sydney felt incredible. Since Jax was not there to hug, she fell backwards onto her bed and hugged her pillow. She was so thrilled! She was going to Texas to see Jax! She needed to tell someone quick before she burst at the seams. So, Sydney called Nina.

Nina barely had a chance to say hello before Syd was talking a mile a minute in her ear.

"Nina, you will never believe this, but Jax just called and he is flying me to Texas to meet his parents and to show me where he grew up. The way he was talking, I was preparing for a big disappointment. If you remember, he was supposed to come to Sea Isle. I jumped to conclusions like I always do thinking he was cancelling his trip. Well he did, but he is bringing me to Texas! It is so exciting. I cannot wait to go. I have no idea what I am going to wear. Maybe we should go shopping together. You are going to have to help me pack. Nina?"

"Holy shit, Syd! You are talking so fast, my head is spinning. Did you drink a pot of espresso? Nina responded, "Take a deep breath. You still have plenty of time, and of course I will help you shop and pack. That is wonderful news, however please be careful. I desperately want to be a supportive friend, but make sure this is really what you want. I need to be your voice of reason. You do realize, he will be drafted to an NBA team. It could be anywhere in the United States. You need to think long and hard about this. You are just beginning your career, so you are in no position to relocate for him. Do you want to maintain a long distance relationship? And more importantly, do you want to be with a man who has women throwing themselves at him every night? You need to think about how your life is going to change, and if you are up for the challenge. You just met Jax and really do not know him very well to make an informed decision. Think about yourself for once instead of putting the other person first. Last time you put HIM first, and look how it ended. I just want to help protect your heart."

Sydney was at a loss for words for a few seconds then angrily replied, "Nina, you really know how to bring me down real quick and focus on the negative. You are a real buzz kill. I call you to share my excitement with you, and you shoot everything down and turn it into something bad. I was looking for your support, not your approval. Thank you for being a friend, but I deserve Jax and want to enjoy myself. How can you judge him before spending any time with him? He is a decent and caring man. I am a big girl and will be fine. I realize this entire situation seems crazy, but I feel like I love him already. Jax may be the ONE, and I will not pass up the chance to find out in order to save myself from hurting in the end. It is a chance I need to take, with or without your support. I do not dare tell my parents after my disaster with Paul, or they will think I totally lost it."

"Okay, okay, I am so sorry. You do not understand how I blame myself for failing you by not seeing the warning signs in your last relationship. I know how you suffered as a result of Paul and want you to have the perfect relationship. From what you have shared with me so far, Jax seems like a dream come true, and I hope he continues to treat you well. Pay attention to any red flags. Maybe slow down a tiny bit. There is no rush."

"I am well aware how valuable your friendship is to me, and I know you always have my back. I promise to be careful. Paul had everyone under his spell. I blame myself for not getting out after seeing the warning signs. I never knew you felt responsible for my failed relationship. It was completely out of your control and no fault of yours. He fooled everyone and was one smooth character, with an evil side behind closed doors. There is no way in hell I will let history repeat itself. I learned to respect myself and to speak up. After Paul, I cannot disapprove if you appear skeptical or overprotective. You need to give Jax a fair chance and remember, he is not Paul. I refuse to let Paul ruin my future relationships."

"You are absolutely right. I promise not to hold Jax responsible for Paul being such an asshole. I love you Sydney, and value our friendship. I expect you to enjoy yourself and give me plenty of details when you get back!"

"I love you too, and you will be the first person I call."

∞∞∞

Sydney informed her parents of the good news next. They were protective, of course, and advised her to take things slow, especially since she had no idea which city Jax would call home. Their biggest concern was I would fall head over heels in love, only to get my heart crushed in the end.

I assured my parents I was up for the challenge of a long distance relationship. I needed to take my chances, for the simple reason Jax was worth taking the risk. Mom and Dad were resigned to the fact my mind was already made up and could only hope for the best.

The remaining days flew by, and I kept myself very busy. I continued to try my wardrobe on at night to see what I wanted to pack for Texas. I went shopping for new outfits and bikinis. A girl needed to have options. Half the time, my closet was on the floor. I just could not decide what to bring and tried on everything. In the end, Nina came to the rescue. Not only did she tell me which clothes I should bring, but also packed my suitcase for me. I honestly would not know what to do without her. She was a complete life saver.

Chapter 4 - Cowboy Take Me Away

J ax was at the Austin-Bergstrom airport looking for Syd. He checked on her flight, and it had landed fifteen minutes ago. I was nervous with the anticipation of seeing her again. I kept scanning the crowd, and then I saw her.

Sydney was a vision wearing sexy cutoff shorts, brown cowboy boots with a chunky heel, and a beige spaghetti string midriff top with crocheted sections which hung down from the midriff into points with fringe. She finished off the look with a beige cowboy hat. Drop dead gorgeous. God help me, she was the hottest cowgirl I ever saw, and she was all mine.

When our eyes met, she paused and smiled at me, and her smile lit up the entire room. She started walking faster until she was running, then jumped into my arms and wrapped her legs around me. I caught her and spun her around. Our lips met for a quick kiss until I pulled her in for a deeper kiss.

"Let me take a look at you. WOW! You look amazing and sexy as hell! I love the cowgirl hat, and especially the boots. What a nice touch. These people probably think you are a supermodel who jumped right out of the pages of a fashion magazine."

She giggled and could not stop smiling at me. Her white teeth were beautiful and those lips…. my God. Syd did a little curtsy and said, "Thanks so much! You are much too kind. I bought them for you. I could not resist, especially since I was coming to Texas. I have to say, you are looking damn hot yourself."

Jax was wearing tan khaki shorts with a tight black tee,

showing off his biceps. He wore tan and black Sperry shoes to match. Jax was wearing a light tan straw cowboy hat with a black braided band. We walked a few feet until Syd pulled me back, stretched up on her tippy toes, wrapped her arms around my neck, and pulled me down for a longer sensual kiss. Her lips tasted fruity, and she smelled so good. People were rushing around us to get to their destinations, and as far as we were concerned, we were the only two people in the room. Our tongues explored each other's mouths. Kissing her made me realize how much I really missed and longed for her.

Unfortunately the kiss ended, and I took her hand after telling her I was taking her home with me. Our fingers were intertwined as we walked out to the parking lot. I opened up the trunk to my white Jeep and loaded her bags. Sydney was so excited the Jeep was mine. The top was off since the weather was expected to be beautiful during Sydney's stay.

"I love your ride. You have excellent taste."

"How funny is it that we both own Jeeps? Coincidence?"

"We both have so much in common. I think it was fate, and we were brought together for a reason. I look forward to finding out. How far is your family's farm from here?"

"Thirty to forty five minutes depending on traffic."

"Perfect. I would be totally disappointed to take a short ride in a Jeep."

Sydney was far from a prissy girl and completely down to earth. Before we pulled away, she removed her cowgirl hat and grabbed a clip from her bag and quickly pulled her hair back. Not once did she complain about her hair getting messed up in the wind. She turned the music up and was singing and dancing and throwing her hands up in the air. She was laughing and truly enjoying herself.

Her happiness was contagious. I could not stop smiling at her. Nothing gave me more satisfaction than to see her comfortable in front of me and be herself. Sydney was completely genuine, and did not pretend to be someone she was not. I admired her generosity and kindness toward others. I think I was falling for her...HARD.

∞∞∞

Laying eyes on Jax at the airport for the first time since Sea Isle gave me the butterflies. I felt like a big part of me was missing when we were apart. Running into his arms made me feel safe and loved. The feeling was hard to explain, but it just felt right and fabulous. I belonged in his arms. Kissing Jax was like watching fireworks. It was thrilling and satisfying and left me wanting more. I could have kissed him forever, but it was time to go and meet Jax's parents. He opened the trunk to a nice white Jeep. The top was down and I was so excited. I loved Jeeps!! I turned the music up and danced in my seat. When we turned off of the highway and took back country roads, it was easier to talk.

"Jax, I love your Jeep! I love the freedom and the wind whipping through my hair. I love the outdoors."

"He laughed. I feel the same way and love taking it out for a ride. Are you nervous to meet my parents?"

"I am not scared about meeting them. I am nervous about them liking me."

"Nonsense, you have nothing to worry about. How can they not love you? Just be yourself. You are so genuine and cheerful. Honestly, they will think you are perfect for me."

"Thanks for the vote of confidence. You are very impressive yourself Jax! When you meet my parents, they will see how you are a true gentleman."

Jax pulled up to a white farmhouse with a long winding driveway. It had a huge, wrap around porch and plenty of trees. One of the trees had a tire swing attached to it and two other trees had a hammock tied to the two tree trunks. It looked so inviting and relaxing. Jax parked and grabbed Sydney's hand and squeezed it gently with encouragement. The fields with crops were in back of the house along with a big red barn and a hen house. "I will show you around later. I want you to meet my parents first."

There were four white rocking chairs on the porch and a little table with a glass pitcher of cold, sweet tea. My death grip on Jax's hand tightened. He gave me a reassuring squeeze and rubbed the outside of my hand with his thumb. I loosened my grip. I was unaware of how hard I was squeezing his hand. Jax continued caressing my hand in hopes of soothing my nerves.

The worn wooden screen door flew open as we climbed the steps. His parents had big smiles on their faces. They hugged and kissed Jax and were hugging and kissing me before Jax had the chance to introduce me. I was instantly put at ease. They loved me before they even knew me.

"You must be Sydney!! I am so delighted to finally meet you. Please call me Mary. Every time Jaxon mentions your name, he gets a big goofy smile on his face."

Jax said, "MOM!!"

"Oh stop being dramatic Jax. I am sure knowing this will make Sydney happy."

I laughed and offered my hand and Mary grabbed it and pulled me in for a big hug and kiss. "We do not shake hands around here Sydney. I am a big hug and kiss person. Oh and this is my husband Frank."

"Frank grabbed my hand and kissed it and gave me a big hug too. Welcome to our home. We are excited to have you spend time with us. Please make yourself at home while you are here."

They were so friendly and welcoming and it surely did not feel like a first meeting. Frank and Mary made me feel at home instantly. I could easily see where Jax's kindness came from. His parents were two very special people, and I was very thankful. I felt foolish for worrying so much. I gave myself pains in the stomach with the anxiety of seeking their approval.

"Sydney," Mary said, "Come sit down beside me on the porch and enjoy a nice, cold glass of sweet tea." She patted the chair next to her. "Sweetheart, I know you had a long trip. It is such a nice day, I thought we could relax and enjoy the outdoors a little bit."

Frank returned with mason jars for the tea and a plate of cut up sandwiches. He poured everyone some sweet tea and then put the plate of chopped beef brisket sandwiches with barbecue sauce on the table. "I cut these in quarters so they are less messy. Sydney, I chose this meal so you were able to get a taste of Texas."

I said, "Thank you so much. You are very thoughtful. I really appreciate you going out of your way to make me feel at home."

"It is no trouble at all," Mary said. "Anyone who is special to my son is like family to me. There will only be a problem if you are one of those girls who eat like an anorexic bird. I know you are only here for four days, so we want to make your stay memorable and relaxing."

Jax almost choked from laughing, "Sydney, an anorexic bird? Oh my God! This girl can house some food! She should be 300 pounds."

Syd elbowed Jax and laughed. "Hey leave me alone Jax. So what, I love food! And I have to say, I am completely famished. The food on the plane looked very unappetizing so I politely declined. I will take Jax's portion too."

Everyone laughed. Frank and Mary had no idea what to expect when Jax told them about Sydney's visit. They wanted a girl for Jax who would make him happy, and to their relief, it was obvious Sydney was that girl. The foursome made small talk while they ate and enjoyed each other's company. Sydney never ate brisket before and absolutely loved it. "The sandwiches hit the spot. Thanks again, Frank and Mary," Sydney said.

"You are very welcome dear, and you better stop thanking me so much since I plan on spoiling you. Get used to it. You are so sweet. Jax told us about your interest in teaching special education. How is your progress with your job search?"

"Actually, I was recently offered a job an hour and a half from home. It will be too far to commute every day, so if I accept, I need to relocate and find an apartment. They gave me another week to think about their offer and make my decision, but it really seems like a great opportunity."

Frank said, "Congratulations young lady. If this is something you really want to do, then everything else will fall into place. It looks like we need to help you celebrate your success while you are visiting in Texas. We have plenty to celebrate. Jax has just about made it to the NBA with the draft quickly approaching, and you have a promising career ahead of you. Sydney, you should also be proud of yourself accomplishing so much so soon after graduation."

"Dad," Jax said "Please try not to get your hopes up too much. I am not definitely guaranteed a place in the NBA. I am lucky enough to be part of the draft. I feel as if it will be difficult to breathe until it is all over. There is so much pressure."

"Son, you underestimate your talent. You have worked extremely hard and never had anything handed to you. It is easy for your mother and I to see how these teams will be fighting over you. In our mind, it is not a matter of making it. It is a matter of which team will get you. There should be no pressure since we are happy for you no matter what happens."

Jax replied, "Thanks for your confidence in my abilities mom and dad. It honestly means the world to me."

I stood up to carry the empty plates into the house, however Mary stopped me dead in my tracks. "Jax, go show Sydney around. I will clean up. Sydney I appreciate you trying to help, but you are our guest, and I will not have you cleaning up after us. It was very thoughtful of you to offer."

Jax smiled at me and grabbed my hand. "Let's go Syd. We can explore outside first. I can show you inside later."

∞∞∞

Jax was so happy his parents loved Sydney. He did not even have to ask what they thought of her. Their actions told him everything he needed to know. They were the type of parents who only wanted happiness for him. Whatever made him happy was what they wanted for him. And it was obvious to everyone, Sydney made him very happy. They were holding hands and walking. There was a big tree with a tire swing attached. "Get on. I will push you." Syd kicked her shoes off, slid her legs through the tire, and held onto the rope as Jax pushed her. She was kicking her feet back and forth with her head back laughing like a little kid. Ah, her laugh was so infectious and delightful, like music to his ears. When the swing came to a stop, he knelt down to kiss her. At the exact same time, Syd started to get up and they bumped heads. They both cracked up laughing and fell to the ground. Both of them were on their backs. Jax rolled over and cradled her head in his arms so she would not move again. He bent down and rubbed her nose with his in a cute eskimo kiss. Then he kissed her on her beautiful, succulent, moist lips. They were perfectly rounded bow shaped lips. A feeling of electricity jolted through his body. He gently parted her lips with his tongue and their tongues began to circle like hungry sharks. She tasted like sweet tea. Yummy. Dammit, he had to stop now. "We better get up before it becomes impossible for me to move. You already make it very difficult for me to walk. I am pitching a tent here."

Syd gave me a huge devilish grin and grabbed my hand to pull me to my feet. What a little vixen! I took her to the hen house to collect eggs from the chickens. I gave her a basket and said, "Let's go gather some eggs." She was like a little kid bubbling with enthusiasm and giggling. The nests were all clean. "How do you know when to collect the eggs?" "We collect them twice a day in the morning and at night. You want to dispose of the broken eggs so the chickens cannot eat them. If they sit for hours they will get bacteria. You will hear them start to cluck louder when they are laying eggs."

"Awe they are so cute!!" Sydney put her hand in very cautiously for the first one and put the egg in the basket. "I love animals. I really think I would love life on a farm."

"Unfortunately the work outweighs the fun. Believe me, the novelty wears off quick. It would be more fun if you did not rely on farming as your only source of income."

"Why is it so hard to make a living?"

"There is an extreme amount of pressure to produce crops while dealing with weather problems, equipment problems, government mandates, market price, as well as supply and demand fluctuations. To compound problems, you have large companies taking over the farming industry. Farming is a high stress occupation. It is very frustrating and disheartening, since it is the one job where working harder does not necessarily equate to more money or success. Oh Sydney, please accept my apology. It definitely was not my intention to be negative and destroy your good time by discussing family business. It frustrates me to see my parents struggle year after year."

"Jax, honestly, there is really no need to apologize. I guess I never put much thought into how much was involved in farming. Most of us take it for granted assuming the crops are planted, the crops grow, and then you pick the crops and take them to market and get paid. You opened my eyes by sharing insight as to what really happens. I understand where you are coming from and agree completely. Given those facts, farming would undoubtedly be more fun as a hobby to alleviate the pressures of earning a living. I can only imagine the anxiety caused by the unexpected situations which arise and are out of anyone's control. Supporting a family is no easy task in today's world."

"Farming can be the best job there ever was when the crops are plentiful and everything works out as planned, but there are so many unknown factors, and Mother Nature is the most fickle of them all. The pressure became too much for my parents after many years of farming, and they have arrived at the stage of their life where they deserve to enjoy themselves. They sold the farm to a local developer and have to move in September. After the NBA draft, they will begin looking for a new home. I told them all about enjoying my time in Sea Isle and seeing the ocean for the first time. It was fascinating and mesmerizing at the same time. I explained how it stretches the horizon as far as the eye can see just like wheat fields, and how it is different shades of blue depending on the way the sun shines. The moment you see it, you are reminded how three quarters of the earth is water. The waves crash in and roll back out as if there is a machine somewhere out there making it happen. Seagulls are squawking, and you can smell coconut sunscreen, the salt in the air, and sometimes even a fish aroma. The ocean is wondrous to look at and makes me feel happy and peaceful."

"Wow, Jax! The ocean made quite an impression on you. You really described it perfectly, and it seems like you may appreciate living by the ocean someday. It is not like we saw too much of the outdoors during your last visit." She winked and smiled at me like a sexy temptress.

"Careful baby girl. It will not take much for me to rip your clothes off and devour your perfect body. My desire for you is more tempestuous than any stormy ocean." I smiled at her and smacked her ass before taking the basket from her. "Let me be a gentleman and finish showing you around."

∞∞∞

Mary rang a bell to let them know dinner was ready. It was perfect timing since Jax just finished giving Sydney the grand tour of the farm. They took a lot of breaks in between each stop to soak in some sun. The weather was beautiful. Dinner was served in the house on the back porch which was screened in. They enjoyed another scrumptious home cooked meal. Mary was a great cook. She served chicken fried steak with gravy, homemade biscuits with melted butter, and mashed potatoes. The salad was delicious. It had spinach leaves, apples, cinnamon and warm pecans coated in brown sugar. The dressing was apple cider vinegar and oil. Sydney could not stop complimenting Mary. "Mary this is absolutely delicious. I would literally gain fifty pounds if I ate here every day. Everything is cooked to perfection, and I love it! Thank you so much!"

"Thank you so much Sydney. I love to cook, so there is no need to thank me. I am more than happy to feed you. I am delighted you are savoring some Southern specialties. Hopefully you are ready for dessert. You are in for a treat."

"Oh I am so full," Sydney started to say as Mary served her a dessert looking so mouth watering, there was no way she could possible refuse it. "Um, I mean thank you."

"I thought you would change your mind," Mary winked.

"What is this? It looks too good to eat."

"It is called Sopapilla cheesecake. Believe me, you might want seconds."

"Mmm," Sydney moaned between each bite. "Absolutely delectable." Cheesecake surrounded by cinnamon roll pastry. "Oh my God, I think I died and went to heaven."

Sydney and Mary cleaned the dishes and Frank and Jax sat out on the front porch.

Frank told his son, "Jax you picked out a good girl, especially since you were not even looking to find someone."

"Thanks dad. It is too soon to tell, but so far I feel like we were made for each other. The more time I spend with her, the more I never want to leave her side. We are so compatible and get along very well."

"Hold onto her, son. I know the circumstances are not ideal with the NBA draft. If she makes you happy, you will find a way to make it work."

Mary and Sydney came outside to challenge the boys to some Texas hold 'em. Frank and Jax gladly accepted.

Sydney slept well and felt revived in the morning. Today was going to be a wonderful day no matter what the plans. Jax informed her last night that the family had a surprise outing planned for her. Sydney was told to wear a bathing suit and bring a towel. No more details were given, however there was obviously swimming involved and Jax's parents were going too. She chose her fire engine red bikini with a cute white long sleeve cover up. It had open strips of lattice material across the midriff and on the forearm. It was a beautiful day. Sydney smelled coffee and breakfast the minute she opened her door. It smelled absolutely delicious. The food was so good, she devoured biscuits in sausage gravy, sunny side up eggs, and fruit salad with a hot cup of coffee. An empty plate was all the thanks Frank and Mary needed. The smiles on their faces showed their satisfaction.

An hour later, they all jumped into the Jeep with a picnic basket full of goodies. The weather was sunny with a light breeze. Their destination was a place called Barton Springs. Now it was

Sydney's turn to be amazed. She was not sure what to expect, yet it was the most incredible place she had ever seen. Here she was in the middle of Austin, Texas with natural springs stretching for blocks. Instead of paved city asphalt, the streets were replaced with beautiful aqua water. It was a sensational oasis with a beautiful skyline. She felt like she was a little kid again and could not fight the anticipation of wanting to get in the water before it disappeared. She never saw or experienced anything like this, and it was amazing. Syd grabbed an intertube and told Jax he was it as she tapped him and started to run as fast as her legs would take her. His parents burst out laughing, and they seemed content to see us enjoying ourselves.

I thought I had a good head start since I cheated, but then I heard Jax catching up. It was hard to keep my composure since his feet sounded like a herd of buffalo closing in. We landed in the water together gasping for air from laughing so hard. Jax and I wrapped our arms around each other and kissed in the water. It was very frigid at first, yet refreshing. The water temperature caught Sydney by surprise, even though she was used to the changing water temperature in the ocean. At first she felt like every muscle in her body was paralyzed, but as she swam around, she became more accustomed to it. Since it was a hot summer day, she was expecting the water to feel like a bath. She was hugging Jax when she felt something on her leg.

She let out a little squeal. "Oh my God!! What the hell is that? Was it you?"

"Was what me?" Jax smirked.

"C'mon Jax, quit playing around. I am freaking out here. I just felt something on my leg! If it is not you what is it?"

"Oh, you must be talking about the fish. There are fish in the water."

Sure enough I looked closer and there were fish. "I still cannot get over this place. You get to swim with fish. It is similar to what I would imagine Neverland to be like in Peter Pan. Once you go through the gates of Barton Springs, it is as if you are transported to a different time. It seems like a magical setting where everyone of all ages has fun. I will always remember this place with the gigantic trees, the gentle slopes leading down to the aqua water, and the beautiful park surrounding it. The grounds are so pristine."

Jax said, "I am delighted you are enjoying yourself. I will always remember the big smile on your face, how you look so beautiful in your fire engine red hot bikini, and how your body is torturing me. It hugs every curve and looks great with your dark hair and beautiful curls. And I must say you did a beautiful job with the landscaping."

I laughed out loud, then I gave Jax a kiss. "Thank you for the compliment! You know how to make a girl feel special."

"And you know how to tease me. Now I will be forced to stay in the water all day to hide my one eyed trouser snake."

"Or I could just play rings with the inner tubes." I laughed and almost took in a mouth of water. Jax grabbed me and dunked me.

"Oh so you think you are funny, do you? You are a comedian. Let's float so maybe I can take in some scenery and get my mind off of how bad I want you."

We held hands to keep our tubes together and floated on the long sea of water. Now I knew how Jax felt when he saw the ocean for the first time. It makes such an impression and fills you with such wonderment and awe, you want to share the experience with others. I always assumed people were missing out if they never saw the ocean, but there are other gems just as amazing. I felt closer to Jax sharing a place he loved to visit. As we slowly floated, we took in the Austin skyline. I looked over to the bank of the spring and saw a pair of ducks. I was taken off guard and nearly fell off my tube. I was so excited, I started hitting Jax.

"Babe, look over there. Oh my God! There are ducks in the water!"

"Yes there are. I am so used to seeing them, so I forgot to tell you. It is something you never get to see in the ocean. You get to experience nature when you swim in this water."

"This is great, and I love the ducks! My eyes find it hard to believe what they are seeing. Look at the male! He is so beautiful. His glossy emerald green head is majestic."

"I love ducks too. Did you ever notice, they travel in pairs? The male has the green head, and the other one is the female. They always stay together, since they mate for life."

I leaned over and kissed him. "That is the most romantic thing I ever heard. It explains why I love them." I opened my eyes as we finished our kiss and started laughing so hard, I did fall off the tube.

Jax was confused by my laughter and followed my gaze to see turtles sunbathing. He thought she found his kiss funny, because there was not anything funny about the turtles. He looked a little further, and immediately understood what happened. "Oh, I forgot to tell you a small detail. Clothing is optional in some areas. Are you going to be okay?"

He was laughing too. I grabbed onto him and tried to whisper in his ear but was laughing too hard. I finally whispered, "Her nipples look like sunny side up eggs. Oh my God! Take a quick look but for God's sake, do not make it obvious. You cannot make eye contact, or she will know."

Jax spun me around, so he could catch a glimpse. When he did, he started laughing uncontrollably too. We managed to get back on the tubes and floated back down to where we started.

Our blankets and chairs were set up under big shade trees. There were plenty of trees around. We ate a fried chicken and hush puppy packed lunch along with sweet tea, of course. I learned a hush puppy was corn bread, and it was delicious with melted butter. I was enjoying Texan food. The weather was perfect. It was hot, yet there was a nice, gentle breeze. Frank and Mary were so nice and down to earth, and the conversation flowed easily. We swam, played rings and bocce ball, and relaxed while appreciating each other's company. It was as if time slowed down in order for us to bond and thoroughly enjoy our day together.

Later the same night, Jax drove me around the farm in an old pickup truck. We parked in a field. When I got out of the truck, I saw the barn with the basketball rim and net Jax told me about. It was exactly as he described, and I could see him as a little boy practicing his shots and celebrating the baskets he made.

"So this is where it all started and where you became a basketball star?!"

"Yep, this is where I spent most of my time growing up. I practiced until there was no more sunlight. It relaxed me and gave me something to look forward to at the end of each day."

After he put blankets in the bed of the truck, Jax turned the radio on and we lay there holding hands and looking up at the stars. He said, "Look to your left. There is the Big Dipper. Do you see the three stars in the handle and the four stars in the bowl?"

"Yes! I do. It kind of looks like a kite. I can connect the dots. How cool!"

"Do you know how to find the North star?"

"I pointed randomly and said, this one?"

"Jax laughed. Good try. See the last two stars in the bottom of the bowl or ladle? Draw an imaginary line through them and it takes you to the North star!"

Sydney cuddled up next to Jax and said, "I am impressed, you even know astronomy."

"I learned about it in school and then spent a lot of time outdoors, which helped me find them. This is a perfectly clear night for you to see the Little Dipper too. The North star starts the beginning of the handle of the Little Dipper. They both have seven stars."

"Wow Jackson, you never cease to amaze me. You are so smart! Thank you so much for the astronomy lesson!"

"Now it is time for your anatomy lesson."

We both laughed so hard until we cried. When we finally finished laughing, he pulled me into him, and we kissed. It was a seductive kiss, sending a whirlwind of sparks throughout my body. Jax nibbled on my ear and played with my soft ear lobe as he smiled at me. The man had a look in his eyes as if he wanted to devour me. He moved to my neck and sucked it, but not hard enough to leave a mark. I could smell his cologne. It smelled light and clean and turned me on. Our lips met again. Longing cascaded all through my body. Jax was driving me completely insane. He slowly lifted up my dress and let out a deep groan when his hand found skin instead of underwear. His finger slipped inside of me and he kept a slow, steady pace going until I climaxed. Then he unzipped his pants and pulled me on top of him. He wanted me to orgasm again, and I never wanted it to end.

We both lay in the bed of the truck content with smiles on our faces. We cuddled and talked late into the night. "So tell me about your last serious relationship."

"I dated a girl in college named Ginger. She hung out with some of the other girls in my circle of friends. We were the only two not dating anyone, so we gave it a try. We had fun and kept it casual but nothing serious. It was strictly hanging out and hooking up. Neither one of us cared about getting to know each other better or spending quality time together. It worked out perfectly for both of us. How about you? Anyone special?"

"Well I dated a guy named Paul. He was perfect in the beginning of our relationship. My parents were crazy about him. He was the type of guy who was good at everything he attempted to do and very popular with parents and peers. Paul knew all the right things to say and do, and was quite the charmer. After we started dating, he became increasingly possessive and jealous, and matters progressively became worse. He berated me and picked on every little thing I said or did. I started to think I was the problem and lost confidence and self worth in myself. Everyone loved this guy, so it had to be me. How could I speak up without being blamed for everything happening. I felt as if everyone would be disappointed in me. During one argument, Paul shoved me so hard, I fell down the stairs. At this point, I decided I needed to leave and take a chance confiding in my parents and Nina. I had enough of his condescending behavior, and was afraid his violence would grow. I decided to file a restraining order against him. I was scared, but my parents and Nina convinced me it was what needed to be done to get away from him once and for all."

Jax grabbed her and pulled her in for a hug while kissing the top of her head. "Oh Sydney, I am so sorry for your experience, and I had no idea. As hard as your decision may have been, it was the right one. No one should be laying hands on you and treating you any other way than how a lady should be treated. You will never have to worry about that type of behavior again. I know how to treat a woman. I would never hurt you or any other woman for that matter. So did Paul leave you alone after the restraining order?"

"Yes and no. I had no idea of the repercussions of filing a restraining order. Paul finished the police academy successfully and was fulfilling his requirements to become a part of the state police. In fact, he was in the middle of his internship when his boss regretfully informed him he would not be able to hold a state, local, or any government position due to the restraining order. When the police department told me, I tried to take back my statement, but it was too late. The damage was already done. I know he believes I destroyed his life, and I was afraid he would take some sort of revenge, but thankfully he found a new girlfriend. Hopefully he will forget I exist.

"Sydney, I hope you realize you were not the reason Paul lost his job. He ruined his own life due to the fact he has no idea how to treat a woman.

She smiled at him and took his hand and gave it a squeeze. "I am so glad and thankful we met. The more time I spend with you, the more I never want to leave you. We are so compatible, and our relationship seems so easy. How come it takes me all these years to meet the right guy, and he lives over a thousand miles away? Sometimes love does not play fair!"

"I feel the same way about you. We have fun together and share similar interests and values. I promise you I am willing to put in the effort to make this work, as long as you can handle a long distance relationship."

"Nothing would make me happier, and I would love to give it a try."

We slowly made our way back to the house. My dreams were all happy dreams about life with Jax. He was everything I ever wanted and needed for a happily ever after.

∞∞∞

Jax was sitting at the table with his parents when Sydney joined them for breakfast the next morning. "It feels like the middle of the night. Are you sure it is morning?"

Jax and his parents laughed. Sydney wanted to help with some farm chores, so she was given a wakeup time of 5 a.m. It was obvious she was not an early riser. She looked like a pirate with one eye open and one eye closed and half asleep. "Grab some breakfast tacos before we start working, and of course some coffee. Well maybe you should drink the whole pot!"

"Very funny Jackson. It takes a couple hours for me to wake up completely."

"You will be waking up quicker, since there are many chores to be done."

Breakfast was delicious, and she was trying her hardest to be alert. Who gets up at this time anyway, other than chickens? Sydney never heard of tacos for breakfast, but these were warm tortillas with eggs, cheddar, bacon, and hash browns. She could get used to these down home meals. After a huge cup of coffee, she was ready to start working.

First, Jax took Sydney to the horses. I showed her how to check them from nose to tail for injury, swelling, or ticks. Next, we brushed the horses. Sydney jumped right in to help. I told her the horses enjoyed being brushed. Since the weather was warm, we applied anti fly treatment and then cleaned the stalls.

"Well this was fun!" Sydney said. "Except for the smell of horse poop. I could do without the smell first thing in the morning. It turns my stomach."

"I am sure you will find it hard to believe, but after a while, you get used to the smell. Not so fast, we have more work to do with the horses. Clean the bucket and put some fresh water in there. It is important to keep the water free of bacteria."

"Duh, I forgot they had to eat. What are we feeding them?"

"Horse tacos."

Sydney gave me a look of disbelief.

"Only kidding, but the look on your face was priceless. We are going to put hay in the hay trough so the horses can feed throughout the day whenever they feel hungry. Now put a scoop of oats and feed treatment in the feed bucket. The hard part is finished. We just need to check the stall for any wasp nests or anything to spook the horses."

"Is it time to take them for a run?"

"We can come back later after dad finishes tacking up the horses so they are ready to ride. You having fun so far?"

"Syd gave me a quick kiss and said you betcha!"

"Now it is time to go visit the chickens. We are going to let them out of their runs and clean up the poop. There are dropping boards in the coops, so we just have to rake the waste into buckets and then use it in compost. Then we have to fill up the chicken feed, scrub the waterers and fill the waterers. Eggs are collected later in the day to give them time to lay."

"Alright I am ready to help you. Just guide me along as we go. I will watch what you do first and then do the same."

Sydney would do just fine on a farm. She was not afraid to get dirty and had no problem doing chores. Her love for the animals was very apparent. I think she enjoyed the experience besides having to get up at the ass crack of dawn.

"We can go shoot some hoops now," Jax said.

"What about the rest of our chores?"

"You did not come all this way to work. The fields need to be fertilized, and then we weed and seed. When hay is ready, we cut, rake and bale the hay. There are a lot of maintenance items and animal health issues to handle. Since you wanted to help, I gave you a couple chores to see what life on a farm is like. I have to say you would be a gorgeous farmer's daughter, especially with those cute curly pigtails. No work would get done, since you would be too much of a distraction for the workers to get anything done."

"Well Jax, you would be the only worker I would be interested in." Sydney gave him a kiss.

Jax smiled, grabbed Syd's hand, and walked with her to the barn she saw when they arrived on her first day. He gave her a basketball and told her to shoot. She threw the ball so hard, it almost clobbered him in the head.

Jax laughed and yelled. "Oh my God, it was not a baseball I gave you to throw. Take it easy now, or I will be unconscious for draft day."

Sydney was doubled over laughing. "I am so sorry. I swear I did not do it on purpose. I thought I had to throw hard enough in order for the ball to go in the basket. I guess I did not realize my own strength."

"You threw hard enough for the ball to go into the chicken coops. Here, step aside so I can show you how to do it. You want to start small and end tall."

"Jax, what in the world did you just say? Do I need to lay on the ground?"

Jax shook his head no and chuckled. "Oh girl, you are not being serious right now, are you? Let me explain the concept. You want to explode into your shot by pushing your hips back and to accomplish this, you need to bend your knees. End your shot by extending your body until you are standing tall. Hopefully this makes better sense. Here, give it a try."

Sydney talked herself through it, and the ball went up and almost went into the net. She jumped up and down happily and clapped her hands. "Jax, it almost worked. It makes complete sense."

"Good job. You did much better. Now make sure you extend your follow through by snapping the elbow. Okay, not literally. You are looking at me like I have two heads right now. To do this, you extend your arm which automatically snaps the wrist. You will get a nice arch on the ball."

She gave it another attempt, and the result was a beautiful basket where the ball only touched net. You might have thought she won a million dollars. Sydney was jumping up and down again and cheering while doing a celebration dance. She threw her arms around him and gave him a kiss.

"Now I hope you realize this type of behavior is not permitted in a game. No kissing and hugging the coach or the players."

Sydney laughed. "Well how am I supposed to have any fun with all of these rules. Let me see you shoot hot shot."

Jax practiced his shooting and Sydney watched him proudly with the biggest smile on her face. It took very little to make her happy. She could watch him play all day.

They played until Mary called everyone in for lunch.

Jax treated everyone to dinner at a restaurant called Truluck's. They served mouthwatering, perfectly seasoned steak and the freshest and finest seafood. Each main course was carefully paired with the perfect wine selection. The dinner was very delicious and satisfying. I was quickly learning Texans were very serious about their food.

After dinner Jax's parents decided to go home and let us explore Rainey Street on our own. Jax noted how it was packed on weekends, and weekdays were the best time to go to be able to truly appreciate the mood. The street was lined with adorable little old houses converted into bars of all different colors. Most of the houses were bungalows. Many people socialized outside on the patios which were adorned with string lighting overhead. There were food trucks, hammocks, games, entertainment and plenty of patios and decks. This was a playland for adults with some of the best craft beers in Texas. It was truly a unique experience and was something you needed to see with your own eyes, since describing it did not do it justice. Jax said most tourists went to drink on 6th Street. Rainey Street reminded me of upscale college parties for adults. I especially liked the ambiance, since it was very cozy and casual.

We enjoyed a couple drinks at the Bungalow. It was a Craftsman house looking very inviting on the outside. The inside featured glass walls, making it easier to people watch. A DJ was playing music, and the rhythm enticed you into having nothing less than a good time.

Afterwards, we hung out at Half Step. It appeared as if you were going to visit someone at their home from the outside. The window featured writing on it saying, "You earned it." Inside offered a comfortable, alluring ambiance with cushioned booth seating and a rich wood bar. The outside showcased a huge deck and patio. I gladly enjoyed a delicious, refreshing martini, and Jax drank a tasty craft beer. We played ping pong and relaxed outside. It was a beautiful, romantic night. I loved nature and the outdoors, and somehow it soothed my soul. If only I was able to slow down time, so I could stay longer. Instead of being homesick, the thought of going home made my heart ache.

As if he read my mind, Jax grabbed my hand and brought it up to his lips and kissed it. "Please try not to be sad about leaving. If I could keep you here, you know I would not hesitate. I never faced an addiction until now. I am hooked on you, and I am far from satisfied with the little bit of time we were given. Somehow, some way, I will figure out a way for us to spend as much time together as my schedule allows."

I smiled up at him. He lifted my chin and lovingly tucked my hair behind my ear and tenderly kissed me. A tear fell from my eye onto my cheek and he wiped it away with his thumb.

"You are an angel, and I am pretty sure angels do not cry. A smile should grace your lips at all times. When you are happy, the whole world lights up, and nothing makes me happier. Our time together is perfect, and I am not about to let it end just yet.

I hugged him so tight, I thought he would stop breathing. Jax was right. The time I had with him was the happiest I had ever been in my life. It was the reason why it was so heartbreaking to think of saying goodbye. It was nice to know Jax felt the same. I decided to put my faith and trust in him, even though I was laying my heart on the line.

Both Jax and his parents insisted on accompanying me to the airport to send me off with a proper goodbye. Mary and Frank expressed how much they enjoyed my company, and invited me back anytime I wanted to jump on a plane. They promised Jax and I would be the first to see their new home once they purchased it and were settled in.

Mary quickly pulled me aside and said, "Sydney, it was so nice to have you around, and you make Jax so happy. He never found anyone he was interested in long enough to bring them home. I have not known you for very long, but in the short time I have spent with you, I can tell you are a very special young lady. You are definitely one of the last of the good girls. This next year is going to be very trying on both of you, and I ask you to be as patient as possible, and hang in there. My son will be worth the sacrifice, I promise. Frank and I look forward to seeing you again real soon. Have a safe trip home sweetheart." She gave me a big hug and a kiss and then Jax walked over.

I felt so overwhelmed and my throat ached, as I was ready to cry. Jax caressed my face and whispered, "Please try not to cry. This is not goodbye, but rather a see you soon. I will never be ready to let you go. You are my best catch. After the draft, we can work out our schedules to see each other as much as possible."

Jax bent down and gave me the most tender kiss. I responded back, and then the kiss became more passionate. He hugged me and playfully slapped my ass while saying, "Now get going. I want to watch you as you walk away. I hear it is a good view."

I burst out laughing. I loved his sense of humor. Jax seemed to know what to say to make me laugh, and his timing was perfect. I was so close to completely losing it. I believed he would move heaven and earth to see me again. I had such a great time in Texas. It was just so hard to walk away, when every ounce of me wanted to stay. I heard my flight announced over the PA system, so I did a quick wave to everyone and threw a kiss. I had a plane to catch!

Chapter 5 - Romantic Roommates

Sydney and Nina went for a spa day at the Red Door Spa in Atlantic City a couple days after her return home. They were shown to a changing room before the relaxation experience began. After they stripped down to their bra and underwear, they slipped into the softest, most comfortable white robes and slippers provided for guests.

First on the agenda were pedicures. There were so many choices in colors! Sydney picked a coral shade, and Nina chose a soft pink color. Our nail technicians showed us to our massage chairs. What an exhilarating feeling! The robes enhanced the sensation, since they were so cozy and felt like you were being hugged. I was in heaven! Any tension the two of us walked in with had melted away. As our feet were being tended to, we took advantage of our special girl time together.

Nina was absolutely dying for some details. "You better start talking, and you better not leave out one piece of information. I have been left hanging since before you left."

"Oh you poor girl. You are so deprived." She shot me a look, so I giggled and continued. "Okay, okay. I had the most wonderful time in Texas. His parents are so nice and genuine. Mary and Frank introduced me to some of the most delicious Texas cuisine. His mom is an incredible cook, and I think I would weigh three hundred pounds if I lived there full time."

Nina sighed with relief. "I am so relieved his parents are cool. The parents are half the battle. Some parents will not give their approval no matter who is brought home to them. No one is good enough to be with their precious baby. I am very happy they accepted you. How was your time with Jax?"

"Our time together was too brief, however every second was quality time. He showed me around the farm where he grew up. We had a family day at the most incredible natural springs located in Austin. It was a natural swimming pool where a street should have been, and continued for blocks. I never encountered anything like it in my life. Jax and I also hung out at this place which reminded me of an outdoor college party for adults. The entire street featured colorful cottages which were actually bars with decks out back and porches out front. They were all decorated with strung lights so people could be outdoors playing games or lounging in hammocks while sipping drinks and listening to music.

"This sounds so amazing!" Nina exclaimed. "You are so lucky, and I am so happy for you. It seems like you had so much fun in Texas. So how did you leave everything?"

"Jax actually brought up the subject first. He felt we were very compatible with similar interests. Although he has no idea where he will be living after the NBA draft, he promised to make a long distance relationship work. He said it would be worth the extra effort."

Nina grabbed Sydney's hand and squeezed hard. "Holy crap! Jax is under your spell. You did it! I am so happy to hear he truly cares about you. I apologize for doubting him, but I still need you to remain cautious."

"I cannot blame you for second guessing Jax's intentions. You naturally jumped to the conclusion Jax only cared about getting me into his bed, regardless of my feelings, because of the basketball player stereotype. You are only trying to protect me, since you are a good friend. I promise to be careful, but I refuse to hold back my feelings. I will give this relationship everything I have, for the simple reason he is one hundred percent worth it.

Nina and Sydney loved the special treatment they received at the spa. The staff was friendly and very accommodating. They were served finger sandwiches, cucumber salad, and delicious peach smoothies. So refreshing! Personalized makeup palettes were customized for them, and they both received lessons on application. The last service received was a thirty minute massage. What a great day!

After the spa, they went to Smithville Village to leisurely walk around and do some shopping. It was terrific to have quality girl time with Nina. She was such a good friend. And Jax was a wonderful boyfriend. How did she get so lucky?

∞∞∞

Jax was so nervous the night before the draft, he found it almost impossible to sleep. I went to bed knowing I was a prospective draft pick, but what would happen if no one picked me? I was getting in my own head with my uncertainty. It was hard to grasp the reality of what was going to happen the next day. Thinking of Sydney and our good times spent together gave me a break from my own crazy thoughts. Her time in Austin passed too quickly. Just the thought of her kept a smile on my face and comforted me. She was kind, passionate and funny, and I could not get enough of her.

I was in New York for my big day. Part of me wanted to get it over with, so the anxiety would melt away. Patience was not a virtue of mine, and it just added to my uneasiness. On a good note, Nike had a pair of shoes waiting for me in my room, and Bose gifted me with headphones. I was very appreciative of these presents. People say an athlete is fortunate to have the opportunity to be in the NBA. I can appreciate what they are saying, although there is a downside many fail to see. The average person normally has control over their career and where they will be living. It seems like a choice everyone should be given. With the draft, your life is out of your hands. Essentially, you give up your choice of your near future and hand it over to the

NBA. You are on the outside looking in and wondering where you will play and live. You have no power in the decision, and you better go where you are told. It is like playing a game of Pin the Tail on the Donkey. You could very well be drafted and sent to a city you never wanted to visit, but now you are required to live there. Life just became challenging, because it is no longer in your hands. You need to hope and pray an undesirable team did not pick you.

Jax was reading tweets on Twitter from top analysts and watching ESPN analysts who made the situation more tense. It was pure speculation, nevertheless it still was driving me nuts. Jax came across a tweet from Will Smith saying, "Jags stay cool. You are going to make your home in Philly bro. No doubt." It was a great feeling for a celebrity to tweet his excitement about me possibly getting drafted to his hometown. I would be thrilled to go to Philly for two reasons. First it was a young and growing team with plenty of talent and most importantly, I would be closer to Sydney. There were no guarantees, and I wanted to be with her more than anything in this world. I continued praying everything fell into place. My destiny would be fulfilled with Sydney in my future by my side.

Earlier in the day, the prospects and their families ate lunch with Adam Silver, the NBA commissioner. I felt so old at 22 compared to some of the other prospects who were drafted after one or two years of playing in college, and not old enough to drink alcohol yet. I was one of the few actually being drafted after I graduated college. My entire day was scheduled, and I was pleased to have someone shadowing me to make sure I arrived to my scheduled events on time and without hassle.

At roughly 4:30 p.m. a bus transported all of the prospects to the Barclays Center in Brooklyn, New York. The arena opened in 2012 and was a captivating piece of architecture. It resembled copper and was structured with uneven metal panels. The color coordinated perfectly with the neighborhood's brownstone homes. The most fascinating part of the building was at the entrance. There was a big loop with a 3,000 foot LED billboard built into the inner loop. It was very impressive, allowing visitors to catch a glimpse of the inside through the windows above the screen, and people inside were able to look out.

My fellow prospects and I posed for a group photo, and the reality of being part of the NBA draft hit me. I usually grabbed a beer and watched it on television with my father. Suddenly, I was a VIP with people ushering me around everywhere. The special treatment made me feel a little uncomfortable, because I was used to taking care of myself. I was no more important than the next guy and undeserving of special treatment. My agent helped me realize I was not taking advantage of anyone. The individuals waiting on me were getting paid to do a job, so there was no need to feel guilty. Everyone needed to make a living one way or another.

I was escorted to a roped off area and taken to my assigned table in the green room where I would sit and wait for the festivities to begin with my parents, my college coach, and my agent Joe. Joe was very excited to see me again. We shook hands and he gave me a big slap on the back. He said, "Relax and take a deep breath Jax. This is the night you have been waiting for your entire life. Take it all in, and try to savor the moment. This night will go by quickly, so try to enjoy it."

"I will. Thanks for the advice," The phone on the table was like a ticking time bomb. I kept looking at it, willing it to ring. Was it going to ring, or was I going to stare at the damn thing all night? Should I pick it up to make sure it worked, or would it look too desperate? As I sat there impatiently waiting, my foot was moving up and down involuntarily, and my leg was shaking. It seemed as if I was jogging in place. The drinks on the table were shaking and moving around as if there was an earthquake. My dad put his hand on my knee to stop it from moving, and put his arm around my shoulder with a reassuring squeeze. I had sweat on my brow, and my heart was racing. I self consciously touched my hair and brushed it back with my hand repeatedly, as if it was messy. Looking around the room, I could see I was not the only one dealing with a case of the nerves. Other guys had trouble sitting still as well. They were biting on pencils, tapping fingers on the table, touching their ears, biting their nails, rubbing their chin, and cracking knuckles. Smoking was prohibited inside, otherwise the entire place would have been lit up. The arena's wifi was having difficulty keeping up with all the guys on their phones trying to find out what everyone else was tweeting. They were hoping to get some insight as to where the experts believed they were going.

The waiting game was just about over. It was GO time. Who was I kidding though? It could still be a long wait with five hours of draft coverage picks. It was a relief to at least get the festivities underway. The commissioner walked up to the microphone to address the crowd. The draft officially started, and the audience cheered to show their excitement. All the fans were hoping their team would acquire the best draft prospects. The crowd and the millions of viewers watching from home were informed the Philadelphia 76ers were officially on the clock. They had five short minutes to announce their pick. My phone rang and it was a number I did not recognize. I waited so long for it to ring and only received silence in return, so it scared the shit out of me when it did ring. I answered and tried to find my voice. I had to clear my throat. It was my high school coach calling to wish me the best of luck. I thanked him and immediately ended the conversation after pleasantries were exchanged. Seriously?! God dammit. He meant well, though my heart nearly burst out of my chest! I took a few deep breaths to regain my composure and tried to relax.

The phone rang again showing another number I did not recognize. Someone needed to inform callers these phones were only to be used for calls from the drafting teams. I answered

"Hello?!" a little more annoyed and abruptly this time, assuming it was someone else attempting to tie up my phone line with unnecessary polite banter.

The voice on the other end of the line disregarded my displeasure and responded, "Well hello Jaxon, this is Bryan Colangelo, the President of the Philadelphia 76ers. I wanted to personally congratulate and welcome you to our team. I hope you are as excited as the rest of Philadelphia!"

My irritation immediately transformed into elation. "Sir, I uh sincerely apologize for being so ignorant. I was receiving congratulatory calls on this phone, and was trying to keep the line free. Nothing would make me happier, and I sincerely thank you for the opportunity! I would be honored to become a Sixer and play for your team. This is the best scenario I could have wished for myself. Thank you again sir. You made my night with the phone call!"

"Well I am very pleased to hear you were looking to play in Philadelphia. Our organization has the utmost confidence you are the best draft choice for our team, and feel you will be a good fit in our rebuilding strategy. You are a key piece to ensure our future success. We look forward to seeing you again tomorrow Jaxon."

"You will not regret your decision. I am committed to work hard and promise not to let you down."

Yes!! I was one step closer to Sydney, and this was the team I hoped to join, for the simple reason it was a young, growing team with immense talent. They also possessed the chance of winning it all within the next five years. I was feeling very lucky right now to say the least.

My parents jumped up when I hung up the phone, and I could barely contain myself when I told them. We did a celebration dance and hugged and kissed each other. I told them the rest of my conversation with Mr. Colangelo was a blur, but there was applause and celebration in the background when I accepted. They were just as happy to see their son go to the Sixers.

The commissioner addressed the crowd. "With the first pick in the 2016 draft, the Philadelphia 76ers select Jaxon Jones from Elgin, Texas and the University of Texas as their power forward." I made it! Moments later, I walked on stage to shake Mr. Silver's hand. One of the big LED screens showed Philadelphia's reaction to the news. The fans were reveling in the most significant draft party ever held in the city. Draftkings was footing the bill for the big event. Former superstars of the team, Allen Iverson and Julius "Dr. J" Irving were in attendance partying with the fans. It was one of the biggest gatherings in the City of Brotherly Love. Losing so badly the previous season allowed the Philadelphia 76ers the first pick in this year's draft. In this case, losing resulted in success. The fans were out to support and celebrate and were very happy with their new player.

Philadelphia fans had a brutal reputation in the sports world, and if you did not like them, they simply did not give a flying fuck. They were a passionate bunch who loved sports and their teams and were not shy to offer an honest opinion. After my pick, the reporter asked Allen Iverson if he had any words of advice for me. He responded, "Jax, I need to give you fair warning, you will have a rough road ahead of you. Work hard and give the city everything you have to give. If you commit to this team and the City of Philadelphia, the fans will be loyal to you and tell off anyone who thinks differently."

"Wow!" Jax thought. "How many people get advice from one of their childhood idols?" The camera showed the fans. The fans watched the draft pick live on a giant television set up on a stage. They were very thrilled with the results and loved to party to show their appreciation. Jax was now part of a young hopeful Sixers team. He admired how the players supported each other and cheered for each other during games. There was a brotherhood amongst them, and he was eager to be a part of it.

I spent the next few hours talking to the media. Photographers were taking pictures, and I was asked the same questions by a dozen reporters. I was happy to answer each and every one. Basically, I told each reporter how fortunate I felt to be a 76er and was excited to play for the team. I was thankful for the support of my family and my loving upbringing. Luck was not the reason I was here. Hard work and dedication to the constant grind, along with a high school and college coach who believed in me and pushed me to be my best were responsible for what occurred tonight. Now it was my commitment to continue the hard work, keep learning, and trust my new coach to develop me into the best player I had the potential to be. The best word to describe my current feelings was thankful.

Later in the evening, champagne bottle corks were popping and drinks were flowing. It was the best party I was ever invited to, and the only thing missing was Sydney. Hopefully, she was watching the draft and was as happy as I was. I asked her to share tonight with me, however she felt it was too soon in our relationship for her to be here. She said it was my time to shine with my parents and did not want to diminish the moment with her presence. I told her it was completely ludicrous, but there was no changing her mind. She promised to support me from afar and chat with me after the event was finished. My family and I continued the celebration at the Commodore Bar in Brooklyn. It looked like your typical dive bar, but was very clean. The food was surprisingly good, and the bar was open until 4 am. I devoured a tasty catfish sandwich with homemade hot sauce and plenty of drinks to wash it down.

∞∞∞∞

Sydney watched the draft at O'Donnell's Pour House in Sea Isle City, New Jersey with her mom and dad. It seemed like a good idea to view it with a crowd to keep her mind off of her building anxiety. She was attempting to engage in some friendly conversation with some of the locals, but could barely concentrate let alone breathe. She was absolutely on edge worrying for Jax, and the pressure of hoping he would get picked by a team was overwhelming her. He wanted this so badly, so she did not want to see him disappointed. After all, he was driven and accomplished the goals he set for himself.

The draft began, and a hush fell over the bar in anticipation. Sydney felt like her throat closed. Oh God, she was having a panic attack. This was going to be a very long nail biter type of night. The Sixers were officially on the clock. It would be a long shot and a dream come true, but what were the chances? She probably had a better chance of getting struck by lightning, nonetheless she needed to show some faith. The analysts were talking about the Sixers' best options, while management was behind the scenes actually making their choice. Then the camera panned in on the commissioner as he walked up to the microphone. When he announced Jax as the first pick for the Sixers, the whole bar erupted. There was cheering, whistling, clapping, hooting and hollering.

Sydney was laughing and crying at the same time. My mom threw her arms around me, and we began jumping up and down. My dad sprung out of his chair and yelled, "My daughter is dating this young man!" The other patrons looked at him with uncertainty and then at me for confirmation, and everyone grew quiet. They were waiting to see if dad was drunk or full of shit. I concluded the guessing game. "Yes, it is true, although we just started dating." The crowd commenced clapping and cheering again, and some guy at the bar bought a round of shots for each and every one of us. Jax quickly became their own personal friend simply because they were celebrating with someone he was dating.

I was smiling at Jax on television as if he could see me through the screen. Relief flooded through me when I heard he was coming to Philadelphia. I desperately wanted to give our relationship the best chance possible, and my wish was very recently granted. For all the times I did not win 50/50's or contests, this victory was well worth the wait. I was so delighted for him. I never knew anyone personally who made it to a professional sports team. The whole situation was surreal. A half hour later, my phone rang and to my surprise, it was Jax.

"Syd I am a little short on time but I really needed to hear your voice."

"Oh my God!! Jax, I am so happy you took the time to call! My dad took the liberty of informing the entire bar we are dating, so I have been drinking for free for most of the night. Congratulations Baby on your big night, as well as your good fortune of being chosen by the Sixers. Now I can have you close to me where you belong. It could not have worked out any better. I feel like this is a dream, and I never want it to end!"

My dad yelled in the background. "I expect a visit soon Jaxon. Protect my daughter as if your life depends on it. She is my little girl, and you better not break her heart. Or else!...." He was shaking his fist in the air. His beer muscles were kicking in.

I felt my face flush with embarrassment. "Dad! Be quiet. What is wrong with you? Not now!"

"Jax laughed. Tell him not to worry. I will take him out to dinner when I am in town, and he can come see as many games as he wants. Syd, it kills me to do it, but I have to hang up now. I wanted to share my big moment with you. I wish you would have been there with me, but I understand. Please know I could not be any happier and mostly because our dream came true. We are getting a chance to really be together. Oh, my parents asked me to say hello. I will talk to you as soon as I possibly can. I love you."

Sydney nearly dropped the phone. Did Jax just say the L word? She swore her ears must be playing tricks on her. She was about to reply, however the line went dead. "Mom and dad, I cannot believe my ears, but Jax told me he loved me!"

Her mom clapped her hands and giggled with excitement, and her dad attempted to look grouchy. She knew he was merely trying to be protective. The other customers overheard me and erupted into celebration once again. A girl on the other end of the bar bought everyone another round of drinks. If only she had the chance to respond back to him. One thing was for certain. With all of these free drinks, she was getting a bit tipsy. This turned out to be one hell of a great night!

Unfortunately, there was not much time for Jax to catch up on the sleep he lost over the past couple of nights. Anxiety kept him up the night before the draft, and adrenaline kept him up on draft night. At the airport, my parents returned to Texas, and I flew from Brooklyn, New York to the City of Brotherly Love. I was formally introduced to the fans at a press conference. They were very ecstatic and eager to welcome me to my new home. From what I heard, these fans were one passionate group and did not have the best reputation. They were known to be hostile to outsiders and loyal to their team. To be on the safe side, it would be best to work my ass off before the fans came to the conclusion I was the wrong pick for their team. After all, they were not shy about vocalizing their true feelings.

My next stop, after the press conference, was a tour of the new Sixers training facility in Camden, NJ. I was introduced to many more 76er personnel than I could possibly remember. They should have been required to wear name tags. There were almost a dozen co-owners and a couple managing owners. Then there was the coach, assistant coaches, strength trainers, development coaches, and the list went on and on. I would not be surprised if the mascot, Franklin the Dog, had assistants.

The training facility was brand new and quite impressive. It featured a 2,800 square foot player locker room, two NBA regulation size basketball courts with ten baskets, a wellness room, two hot tubs, a recovery pool, and a hydrotherapy room. In addition, there was also a rooftop balcony, meeting rooms, offices for operations, coaching rooms, a press room, recording studio and a film room with twenty five movie chairs. It even had a restaurant with a chef, and a cafeteria so players had everything they needed without having to leave the facility. Players had an area to chill out and socialize, which gave them a chance to bond. Jax appreciated the concept. Basketball was much more than a game to him, and becoming friendly with teammates would be key to playing well together. They needed to have each other's backs at all times, since no one else was going to do it. Previously the team practiced at other facilities, so this was their first private facility. This state of the art center was phenomenal, and the largest in the NBA with 125,000 square feet.

The days following the draft were a whirlwind. My agent Joey set me up with a personal assistant named Jimmy. Up until this point, we only spoke over the phone. This would be our first opportunity meeting in person. He reminded me of Joe Pesci. He was a short, fast talking, funny guy. Jimmy was going to be perfect as an assistant, since he was motivated, conscientious and a hard worker. I told him I needed a house to rent, and he called me within twenty four hours. He told me I needed to check out a house he found, and I needed to act fast. Jimmy was right.

It was a magnificent home located in Moorestown and only a short twenty minutes from the Sixers practice facility in Camden, New Jersey. When I pulled into the driveway, Sydney was waiting for me. I texted her to come look at this house with me, as I had not seen her since Texas. She jumped out of the car and threw her arms around me and gave me a big, long kiss.

Jimmy yelled from the front door. "Yo kids, get a room. At least wait until you rent this house. Then you will have plenty of rooms to christen."

We both laughed and walked up to the house. I put my hand out and said, "What's up Jimmy? It is really great to meet you. This is my girlfriend Sydney."

He gave Jax's hand a hearty shake then appreciatively looked at Sydney. "Well, well look at you sweetheart. You are definitely the better half of this couple." He kissed Syd's hand, twirled her around, and pulled her in for a big hug. She giggled.

I exclaimed, "You know I am used to living in half a dorm which is the size of a closet. This place is the whole dorm building."

"Well Jax," responded Jimmy "I hate to break it to you, but you went from making zero dollars to 4.9 million dollars per year. You clearly can afford a little more space."

"Okay Jimmy, give us the grand tour." This mini mansion included four bedrooms and three baths. The master bedroom featured a living room and a bathroom with a walk in shower so big, I could easily fit my University of Texas basketball teammates in there with me. Other highlights of the home included a hot tub, an indoor and outdoor pool, a theater room, and a built in stone grill. The kitchen was the size of a small Italian restaurant. I might have a reason to learn how to cook some day.

Jimmy mentioned, "Jax, the owners have decided to rent to you for one year with an option to buy, and all furnishings are included. There are five acres which backup to the Rancocas River. This home will give you some land and privacy, and it will not be too far from the practice facility and Philadelphia. I will give you two a moment to discuss this in private. Now try not to use the time to start making out again. Instead, make a decision."

Sydney was so excited. "I love Jimmy. He is too funny and my God, Jax this house is beyond beautiful. You can get lost walking around in here. There are so many rooms. This house is similar to the mansions you see in the architecture magazines. Utterly amazing. You have my vote. I would love to cook for you when I come visit."

Jax replied, "It is a wonderful idea, but I can offer you something even better. I want you to accept the job in Haddonfield, and move in with me. Forget about commuting back and forth or renting an apartment. As you can see, there is plenty of room here for both of us. I know this is sudden, yet my entire life changed with the draft. Everything is so new to me, and it would be much easier experiencing this new adventure with you by my side. All of the newness at once is completely overwhelming: new job, new city, new people, however my new relationship with you is comforting."

Sydney hesitated a moment, and Jax mistook her silence for a NO.

"Syd, I am so sorry. I should not have assumed this is what you wanted. I just thought we are great for each other, and this is the best way to spend the most time together."

"Jax, stop apologizing. There is no issue at all. You simply caught me by surprise. We are moving so fast. I do not want to spoil what we have going on. First you tell me you love me, which shocked the shit out of me. By the way, I love you too. Now you want me to move in with you. It is so sudden. This is completely unexpected."

Jax grabbed Sydney's hands. "Syd, if you cannot see I am crazy about you by now, I need to remind you. I was not looking for a relationship, yet it happened. Now I want to give us the best chance possible to see where our relationship goes. Not to make you even more nervous, but the NBA only has to give me twenty four short hours notice when moving me to another team. I plan on staying here, nevertheless I do not know if the feeling is mutual. We need to make the most of our time together and build on our relationship. I want you to be a part of this wild and crazy ride, and the only way to do this is together. I realize you were hurt in the past, but I can assure you, I am not that guy. Take a chance on me. What do you think?"

She kissed me in response and then started jumping up and down. "Yes, Yes, Yes to everything! I am all in Baby."

I called out to Jimmy. "Jimmy, do you have some papers for us to sign. Syd is going to move in too."

Jimmy said, "Great decision on both parts. Let me get the owners on the phone and finalize this deal. Congratulations!"

Syd kissed me goodbye and added, "I need to run so I can tell my parents in person and start packing. I am so excited Jax. Let me know the move in date as soon as you find out. I will also call my new boss to tell him I decided to accept the position. I was thrilled to see you today, and that alone made my day! It would seem impossible for the day to get any better, but somehow you found a way Jaxon Jones. You decide to rent a gorgeous, gigantic house and ask me to move in with you! This is one of the best days of my life, and you completely swept me off my feet. I love you so much!"

Chapter 6 - No Time for a Young Filly

The next morning kicked off with an interview by Howard Eskin for his Saturday show on WIP radio. The receptionist brought me into the broadcasting room where Howard was waiting for me. We shook hands. "Welcome Jaxon. Have a seat. We are going live in a couple minutes. Just relax, and be yourself. Let the Philly fans get to know you." And the countdown started....3.2.1.

"Good morning and welcome to WIP sports radio with Howard Eskin. Today I have the 76ers number one draft pick power forward, Jaxon Jones also known by his friends as Jags. He is the hope and future of this young team. Jaxon tell me a little about yourself. Where did you grow up?"

The interview opened with a nice and easy question. I replied. "Howard, I was born and raised in Elgin, Texas. It is a small farming town approximately five square miles. The best known person from my town is NFL hall of famer Mean Joe Greene. I went to Elgin High School and played with the Elgin Wildcats."

Howard moved on to the next question. "Your father was a farmer, so how come you decided not to carry on the family tradition?"

This was another easy question. I responded, "It is actually very difficult to survive as a small farmer in Elgin and any other small town for that matter. Combines and tractors cost $300,000 and upward. Weather is another factor which can threaten and limit the crops needed to make a good living. Corporate farms are taking over small farms. They have the big money needed to survive. The younger generations are choosing different careers rather than follow in their parents' footsteps and chance a life of hardship. My parents desired a different future for me, and decided to sell the farm once I finished college. They made the decision for me, and I am thankful for them always having my back."

Howard fired off the next question. "Who influenced you to play basketball?"

The interview continued to go smoothly. I was quick to answer. "Like other fans I have to say Michael Jordan. He is the GOAT (greatest of all time). Basketball was fun to watch with his gravity defying moves and sheer athleticism. He had a lot of fans, and many kids were interested in the game and trying to imitate his moves. The only move I mastered was sticking my tongue out while shooting. My body did not possess the flexibility to perform Michael Jordan's moves."

Howard concurred and moved on with the next question. "When did you begin playing basketball?"

"I started in high school and continued in college with the University of Texas."

Howard played nice up to this point of the interview, but I was well aware of the cockiness he possessed. He matter of factly went on to say, "You were just a mediocre player at best in your first two years at UT so what changed?"

What a jackass, I thought to myself. He went out of his way to embarrass me live on the air. I kept my composure and continued. "I believe a lot of it was psychological. I allowed the disappointment of missing my shot effect my next shots. I sabotaged my own game. I needed to stop being so hard on myself and just play the game."

My statement seemed to shut him up for the moment, but the questions kept coming. "What is your advice to your young fans?"

"In my opinion, have fun and keep working on your skills. Find your weaknesses and turn them into your strengths."

"Your remark covers a broad area, and you are so young to be giving advice. So, where do you see yourself in ten years?" Howard inquired.

I am damn sure Howard knew ten years of playing basketball was wishful thinking, unless you were one of the star players in the NBA. The average basketball player was lucky to make it five years. It was quite obvious he wanted to shake me up with one of his questions and catch me off guard. Not today. I retaliated. "Well Howard, as you are very well aware, I believe I need to finish the first season before I can predict my future for you. Next season is never promised. I am obligated to prove my worth to my team."

"Fair enough, Jax," Howard uttered. "Last question before we run out of time. Is there someone special in your life or should I wait a year for your prediction?"

Shit the bastard got me. He completely caught me by surprise, and I never had the chance to discuss publicizing the relationship with Sydney yet. I was screwed either way. "I honestly cannot find the time to focus on a relationship. Right now basketball is my significant other."

Howard smirked at me and ended the interview. "And there you have it folks, Jaxon Jones has a promising season ahead of him as the new rookie of the Philadelphia 76ers. And after a season of 28 wins and 54 losses, it cannot possibly get any worse, or this town should put them at the curb and call them the 86ers."

Wow what an asshole move!, Jax thought. I wanted nothing more than to punch him right in the mouth, but instead I just smiled at Howard, shook his hand and flipped him off as I walked out the door. For a man who has not liked the Sixers since Allen Iverson, he had some bullshit trash talking aimed at hurting my new team. When he interviewed Embiid, his comments were all about how he had no playing time at all in his first year, and it would really be nice to see him play. He did not believe Embiid was an asset at all for the franchise, especially since he had only played one minute in two years. He rudely declared the Sixers needed him to play seventy RELEVANT games to win a championship and more than thirty minutes a game to win a title.

Additionally, Howard bashed the former Sixers general manager and accused him of purposely tanking the season in order to obtain a top draft pick. If this Jackass did his homework, he would have realized the players were not able to stay healthy enough to win. It was not like anyone cared about his opinion, but Howard seemed to like the current Sixers coach, Brett Brown. This was the only reason I agreed to do the interview. It was ridiculous of me to think a person was capable of changing their cynical ways.

Personally, I was stoked and felt lucky to have Coach Brown as my coach. The players loved him, and he preferred them to hustle when they played. One of his best traits is his open line of communication. The team never needed to wonder what was going on, since he made it a point to let them know. Coach Brown possessed a vast amount of knowledge and skill. His goal was to gain more talent and spend more time with his players. More importantly, he needed to establish a winning culture in Philadelphia. It would celebrate virtue and encourage positive attitudes, successful performances, and high expectations. Not only was Brett Brown an excellent coach, but also a mentor, and he stood for everything I believed in.

When I had my workout with the team before the combine, some of my future teammates affirmed how he demands hard work for their own benefit and not just his own. Coach Brown's goal is to develop players to help them achieve their full potential. The players trusted him and shared a great bond with him on and off the court. Everyone is held accountable for their actions and disciplined when necessary. They liked how he interacted and shot around with them. The players wanted to do their best for their coach and respected him for challenging them. I was only with them for one day, however I was able to see the good rapport amongst the teammates, as well as the strong relationship between the coaches and players.

Despite the Howard Eskin interview not going well, I survived. The real question was, "Would I survive Sydney's wrath if she was listening?"

Of course, Sydney was listening to the interview on the radio. Howard played nice at first, and Jax was answering every question. It did not take long for him to aggravate Jax by focusing on the rough patch in his college career instead of celebrating his acceptance into the NBA with the Philadelphia 76ers. "What a jerk!" Sydney shouted out loud. "You better not take his shit Jax. You better not let him push you around."

She thought Jax answered the question with finesse, and was unsure if she could behave the same in his situation. Howard continued to provoke Jax with his questions. He ended the interview by putting Jax on the spot about his relationship status. Jax hesitated before replying he did not have time for one, and basketball was his only significant other.

"Son of a bitch!" Sydney nearly drove off the road and slammed her palm against the steering wheel in anger. "Seriously!" She turned the radio off and pulled over into a nearby parking lot. She was pissed. When her phone rang a short time after, Sydney declined the call and refused to answer the next ten times Jax called. "I have no time for you either Jax," she mumbled to herself. She went shopping to blow off some steam and drove back to Sea Isle a few hours later. Jax was pacing back and forth outside.

"Sydney, I am so glad you are okay. I tried calling you several times, and you did not answer. I was scared out of my mind something happened to you. I had to drive down to see you."

"You know damn well the reason why there was no answer. Maybe you should have spent time with your basketball instead of me Jax. After all, it is your significant other. I would not want to be a third wheel."

"Oh, so now I understand. It makes complete sense why you did not answer." Jax tried to pull me into a hug, but I pushed him off me and started walking toward the beach. He had to run to keep up with me.

"Listen, I understand you are not thrilled with me right now, but you completely misunderstood and took it out of context."

"Damn right I am not happy with you right now. I sure did misunderstand you Jax. I thought we shared something special, and apparently I do not mean anything to you at all."

"You are throwing a temper tantrum. It is completely untrue and unfair, and you know it. I asked you to move in with me, and I meant it. I did not want to publicize our relationship before checking with you first. Unfortunately, we did not have that conversation yet. I was trying to be respectful by checking with you first, especially with the way your last relationship ended. Believe me, the press will figure it out quickly enough. I would rather enjoy the time we have alone before they do. Our life will stop being private after everyone finds out we are a couple. I am very sorry I hurt you. It certainly was not my intention. I definitely would have talked to you about it first, but I honestly had no idea he was going to ask me the question. Everything has been happening so fast, and I am having trouble keeping up with the pace."

"Okay, well maybe I overreacted just a little. It is not every day I am dating a professional basketball player. I am unaware of what to expect, however I am willing to find out together." I kissed him tenderly. "I am also sorry for getting so mad at you and not talking to you before assuming the worst."

"Apology accepted. By the way, you are extremely hot when you are angry."

I punched his arm playfully and took his hand so he could come inside and meet my parents, before he had second thoughts. "You might as well come inside to meet my parents since you are here."

"Wow, I am not really prepared to be beat up any more today," he chuckled.

Jen and Bobby were thrilled to meet Jax. I really think my dad was in shock at first. He knew I was dating Jax, but his jaw literally dropped to the floor when the guy he had been watching on television walked into his home. He looked as if he needed to touch Jax to make sure he was real and not a figment of his imagination.

My mom was already setting a plate for Jax to join us for dinner. If I gave her too much time, she would be booking our wedding. My dad talked sports with Jax, and he promised to give my father tickets to come watch him play in Philadelphia. It was like Christmas day for my dad. He was being given some VIP treatment and could not wait to tell his buddies the minute Jax left. In the meantime, he put his arm around Jax and said, "Thank you son. I really appreciate the tickets and getting the opportunity to meet you. I need to be completely honest with you for a minute and mention that Sydney is my little girl, and I promise you a world of pain if you break her heart. I heard how some of those NBA players are when it comes to womanizing. I refuse to have Sydney get hurt."

"Dad, you are embarrassing me!" I yelled.

Jax answered, "Sydney it is absolutely fine and understandable. Sir I promise you with all my heart, I care for your daughter very much and do not intend to hurt her in any way. In fact, I asked her to move in with me, so she can accept her new job offer and live closer as we get to know each other better. I would really love your blessing. I have plenty of rooms, and can give Sydney her own bedroom if you like."

Bobby said, "I appreciate you asking Jaxon. You have my blessing, and I am no fool. Believe it or not, I was once your age. I realize you will be sleeping in the same bedroom. My daughter is twenty two years old and a grown woman. Sydney is old enough to make her own decisions, and I completely trust her to make the right decision. As you can see, my wife can barely contain her excitement. You made her a very happy woman too."

Jenny threw her arms around Jax and said, "Congratulations to both of you. I am so happy! Treasure every moment spent together. In your case Jaxon, time is precious, and you will not have a lot of free time. You are going through so many changes at once. It will be nice for you to share them with Sydney. I am sure your first year in the NBA will be very demanding. Welcome to our family. We are all here for you if you need anything. Please do not hesitate."

Jax was truly touched. "Thank you Mr. and Mrs. Fox. Your words really mean alot to me. I will do my best to balance all of my responsibilities. It is impossible to plan ahead, since I have no idea what to expect. With Sydney by my side, I feel like I can face anything life throws at me. Thanks again for your confidence in me."

With the formalities out of the way, everyone relaxed out-side on the deck and enjoyed some wine. My dad took pleas-ure in talking with Jax and telling him some stories from his glory days. He now had one more story to add to the collection as soon as he had the opportunity to tell his buddies who his daughter was dating. Conversation flowed easily, and so did the bottles of wine. My mom asked him about his hometown and growing up. She also asked about his parents. Jax told them a little about his upbringing. It turned out to be good night. My dad showed Jax to the guest room. He knew we would be sleep-ing together in the new house, but not under his roof. If he only knew. Jax and I shared a knowing smile.

On the way to his room, Jax advised me he planned on renting a truck in the morning, and we could move my belongings into the new house. The paperwork was being signed in the after-noon, and he did not want to waste any time. His schedule was about to get hectic quick.

Sydney moved into the house and helped me get organized. We decided she was going to work with Jimmy in areas not related to basketball, to allow me to focus on my game. This would alleviate some extra stress. She would take care of the finances and manage the household. She was also going to read the fan mail on social media and have Jax respond personally to special messages. Sydney would have Jimmy at her disposal to help her with anything she did not have time to handle, once her job began in the fall. She was so excited about her new life with Jax.

∞∞∞

I surprised Sydney with a party on the 4th of July at the new house. I flew my parents in from Texas, and I invited Sydney's parents, family and close friends. I was lucky enough to hire DJ Pauly D to handle the music. Sydney loved to dance, and I knew she admired him. I recruited Mike from Avalon Coffee to work the grill. Sydney was very fond of Mike, and he was quite the grill master. He grilled burgers, dogs, ribs, barbecued chicken, brisket, and steaks. We insisted he party with us after he was finished cooking. He was the type of guy you wanted to hang out with, because he was funny and entertaining. There was plenty of alcohol, although Sydney could have fun without touching a drink.

The guests were all enjoying themselves and having a good time. Our parents really seemed to be getting along and shared many common interests. We both breathed a sigh of relief. The four of them never stopped talking from the time they were introduced.

Sydney was so happy to be the hostess and show everyone our new home. We also had a surprise to present to my parents. Sydney helped me by working with Jimmy to find the perfect home for my parents to retire. Many hours were spent researching not only the best area to live, but also the perfect home. Much attention was given to home layouts, views, easy access to parking, and privacy. Sydney ran over to me and snuck in a quick kiss and a hug, and excitedly asked me when we could reveal the surprise to my parents. The surprise was killing her. I promised her we would do it during dessert.

After Sydney and Jimmy completed their research, they presented their final three houses to me. Despite telling her I trusted her choice, since she spent so many hours on the project, she insisted I make the final decision. Her reasoning was based on the fact of my money being used for the purchase. I chose a spacious two bedroom two bath condominium on South Padre Island. South Padre Island is off the southern tip of Texas and is a tropical paradise. The condo featured gorgeous bay views from the balcony. The island offered amazing views, fishing and swimming, and was within walking distance to the beach. We did get a boat slip with the unit. The house was a treasure, especially since there were amazing water views the moment you walked through the door. The spectacular water view was visible from every room. Furniture and furnishings were included, and covered parking was provided, which was very hard to find. All of this luxury in paradise for $300,000. Jax found no problem paying for the house with his new salary. His parents meant the world to him, so it was his turn to show some love and appreciation.

During dessert I took the microphone from DJ Pauly D and announced, "Mom and Dad, I want to thank you for everything you have done for me throughout my life. You made huge sacrifices so I could play basketball, and you sold the farm because you wanted me to follow my own dreams and not someone else's footsteps. You are two of the most loving and unselfish individuals I have the pleasure of knowing. You continue to put my happiness before your own, and your support is amazing. To thank you, I want to present you with the keys to your new home in South Padre Island. Sydney worked really hard on this project and wanted you to experience life in close proximity to the ocean and bay. Living at the beach brings her peace and happiness, and you deserve the same. The condo includes a boat slip. Once you get settled, I want you to pick out a boat and call my personal assistant Jimmy, and he will take care of the purchase. Sydney and I would love to come and visit once you are moved in and after my first NBA season. Everyone raise your glass and join me in a good luck drink to my parents. Bottoms up."

Mom and dad were crying and ran over to embrace me. Mom was getting my face wet as she kissed my cheek and they both said how much they loved me and thanked me over and over.

"Mom, you are getting me all wet. Come over to the table so I can show you the new house on my tablet."

"Sorry honey, it is not everyday you get a home as a gift. Let me see it. I am so surprised and speechless."

Mom and dad looked at the photos in amazement. I heard a lot of oohs and ahhs. It was a positive sign. They were both gracious and loved the panoramic views.

"Thanks again Jaxon. Sydney, Frank and I want to thank you as well for doing such an incredible job. It is wonderful, and we cannot wait to move in. You are both welcome anytime."

I looked over at Syd who was smiling ear to ear with a look of admiration and love on her face. I realized in that exact moment why she was my happily ever after. She was the woman who would fill my life with love and adoration and keep me as happy as my parents were for many years. I hoped to experience life's journey with her by my side.

Sydney's eyes met mine, and she quietly excused herself and walked over to me. Her timing was perfect as the fireworks just started. They lasted approximately thirty minutes and were so good. The finale seemed to go on forever. Sydney clapped in appreciation and turned to me to give me a big kiss. "Are you having a good time?"

"The best time Babe. Everyone is happy, and Pauly D is making sure the music keeps everyone moving. He really knows what he is doing. He is mixing songs from different genres seamlessly, as if they are supposed to go together. When he feels the energy dropping, he speeds up the song and gets the crowd fist pumping. And he knows when to drop the beat. The dude is phenomenal."

"I totally agree. This party is lit thanks to him. C'mon let me see you fist pump." Sydney was dancing now and kept going until the wee hours of the morning.

$\infty\infty\infty$

Jax brought Sydney to the Sixers training facility to give her a personal tour. He wanted to show her where he would be spending most of his waking hours, and he was also doing a magazine shoot and interview.

Sports Illustrated was there to take pictures to feature Jax on the cover of their magazine and wanted to use the new training facility as the backdrop. The building was beautiful with so much attention to detail. The photographer took action shots of Jax shooting the ball and still shots of him posing.

Sydney sat through the interview. It was unbelievable her boyfriend was going to be on the cover of a major magazine, and she was observing everything, taking it all in. This entire scenario was so unreal to her. Never in her wildest dreams could she imagine living with an NBA basketball player in a house so big her family and friends could move in too.

The reporter asked Jax about his upbringing in Texas and his college years. Then she looked at Sydney and asked Jax if he was in a relationship. "Well as a matter of fact, this is Sydney Fox, and she is the only lady in my life. We met when I least expected to meet someone and really hit it off. I previously decided not to bother looking since I knew my life was going to be so hectic, however fate intervened and brought us together. It has been a whirlwind romance, and I am so thankful for her. We are living together now."

The reporter reacted to this news with a surprised look on

her face, Jax smiled. "C'mon take a look at her. I know it seems sudden, but I am going to have a rough road ahead of me, and I want Sydney to be with me every step of the way. My life is moving in fast forward, and time is not on my side. She is everything I ever wanted in a partner. My focus is basketball and the success of the 76ers during basketball season. Sydney is my life off the court."

The reporter asked Sydney about her career and was impressed when being informed of her acceptance of a position as a special education teacher for autistic children. She also expressed an interest in educating other adults about autism and the best way to communicate with the children.

I almost ended the interview when the reporter had the balls to ask Sydney if I was just a free ride for her cause, but she waved me off. "Not because it is any concern of yours, but if you must know, I truly care about Jax and would never use someone to get ahead in life. I believe in true love. The fact of his money and success is a bonus and not the reason why I am dating him. I had no idea who he was when we met. We had this insane chemistry which blossomed into a romance, and I love what we have together regardless of anyone else's opinion. I will use his money if he offers, to raise awareness for autism and to provide a good education for autistic children. But under no circumstances am I a money hungry fame chaser."

God, I loved her more in this moment than I ever could believe was possible. I was so proud of her. She was driven to help autistic children by becoming an educator and by volunteering her time to teach others about autism. I am glad she accompanied me to the interview, and for choosing to go public with our relationship. My little firecracker put the reporter right in her place, and it was so HOT! Served her right. I could rest easy knowing no one would take advantage of her when I was on the road. The girl could handle herself, and it was making me horny as hell.

The reporter profusely apologized for any misunderstanding with Sydney and took a few pictures of us before wrapping up the interview.

We exited the building giggling hand in hand. I think I drove 80 mph on the car ride home, because I could not wait to rip Sydney's clothes off.

∞∞∞

Sydney did not have much time to get settled before Jax started the summer league. From July 8 to July 18, he was in Utah and Las Vegas. She was nervous and excited for Jax at the same time. Her family watched some of the games at home and at the sports bars. Watching the games was exciting since now they actually knew someone playing for the team. The analysts all agreed Jax was impressive in the summer league.

One article went on to say how the 76ers should breathe a sigh of relief with their number one pick. Jaxon Jones was proving to be a wise choice and seemed to have a promising future. He was not afraid of contact with other players and played competitively. He unselfishly passed the ball to other teammates resulting in baskets and scored buckets of his own during crucial moments of the game. Defensively, he blocked shots aggressively. Jax exhibited a great deal of confidence on both sides of the ball. He took rebounds and used his speed to his advantage when running up the court.

Jax favored the crossover dribble when his defender advanced too close, and he possessed a nice jump shot. He was hitting his twos and his threes easily, but needed to work on his foul shot. This would improve with time and practice and was currently unimpressive. His maturity was revealed when using opportunities to ask coaches for areas of improvement and feedback on his current performance. Overall, he had great, average and forgettable games in the summer league. Jax missed ten shots in one game. He began the summer league very strong but physicality wore him down after playing so many games in a row. He demonstrated increased aggressiveness in the beginning of the summer league but then opponents were getting to him, as he was tiring quicker.

Other critics believed Jaxon would have a tough acclimation, but he was blessed with the skills to overcome the bumpy ride. He needed to adapt to the conditioning, as well as the number of games he was required to play during the season. The number of games was increasing from twenty seven in college to eighty two in an NBA season. His other challenges were extensive travelling and playing with and against veteran NBA players.

Another critic commented, "The sooner Jax realizes the NBA is much different from college, the better. He possesses the skill set and the ability to learn and grow as a player. In the summer league, he experienced a lot of contact going to the rim with very little time left on the shot clock. He is inconsistent, but has potential. In college, he was so fast and rarely encountered problems with the shot clock. His shots went unchallenged."

Sydney was so overjoyed for Jax. This was a marvelous beginning to his professional career. Her phone rang and her dad was on the other end. "Dad, did you hear the analysts on television?"

"I sure did kiddo! You should be proud. I know I am. Jax made a good impression, and he is a rookie. It is expected for him to need improvement. I just wanted to let you know how thrilled I am for both of you. I am certain, without a doubt, you saw his games and surfed the internet for any feedback you could find. Good thing you love sports, since you will be watching a lot more basketball. You are daddy's girl!"

"You know me too well Daddy. I feel reassured now. I was so anxious for him. Jax has tremendous pressure to perform well from his coaches, teammates, and especially the Philly fans. We know how unforgiving our fans can be, since we are part of the same group. I was driving myself crazy hoping he would do well in the summer league."

"Well you can breathe a sigh of relief, so get some rest. In another month, you will be getting prepared for your new career. It will be a fresh start for both of you, and both jobs are equally important."

"Dad, I am not so sure about your statement. I am not being watched by thousands of fans."

"This may be true Sydney, but your teaching will touch the lives of your students."

"I love you daddy. You always know how to make me feel loved and important. Tell mom I was asking for her, and tell her I love her too."

"I will sweetheart. Talk to you soon."

Sydney smiled as she finished the call with her father. He always made her feel wonderful about herself and approved the direction her life was taking. Both of her parents supported all of her decisions, and she loved them dearly.

She decided to take a chance and phone Jax. As the phone rang, she was so excited she did not think any words would come out if she tried to speak. Her heart started to drum faster with the anticipation of hearing his voice. To her disappointment, there was no answer on the other end. She felt her heart sink and was filled with disappointment. She wanted to talk to him so desperately. Sydney walked up to their bedroom and laid down with her book. She drifted off to sleep. When she awoke, Jax was standing over her with a big smile on his face and a bouquet of daisies. Syd tried to jump up to wrap her arms around him but he swiftly pushed her back down.

Jax said, "Stay right there darling. It has been a long time since

I have seen your pretty face, and I intend to join you in your bed. Do me a favor and show me how much you missed me."

"My pleasure." Sydney giggled and Jax pulled the covers over both of them.

∞∞∞∞

They lounged in bed appreciating each other's company. Jax was in deep thought pondering how part of him wished he was not going into the NBA yet, so he could benefit from having a normal relationship with Sydney. He should feel blessed to have made it to the big league and not have any doubts. This was something he wished for and did not take it for granted. It was just a lot to ask of Sydney to hang in there and wait, while he fulfilled his dream. Maybe he was putting too much thought into solving a problem which could be worked out with a little time. He would have to put a lot of faith into their relationship and hope for the best, since time was not waiting around for him.

Jax was playing with Sydney's hair. She smelled so good. Her hair even reminded him of the beach with the scent of coconut. It was so soft and curly. He ran his hand down the side of her face and gently kissed her lips.

He told her, "I am so glad you were home waiting for me. I missed you tremendously. I cannot fathom being away from you once this season and the traveling begin. I did purchase two tickets for every home game, so you can go any time you want to watch me play."

"You are so sweet Jax. Thank you for the beautiful flowers. They are my favorite. I missed you so much too. My heart ached, and I felt like part me was missing. Moving in with you was the best suggestion you could have made. I kept myself busy and have been working with Jimmy to take over paying the bills and taking care of running the household. I also told him how I wanted to handle the fan mail on social media, so it would be more personal. This way, I can tell you personally about your fans and keep myself busy at the same time."

"Thank you babe. I appreciate your help. If you ever find the fan mail too cumbersome, let Jimmy know, and he will delegate the job to someone. I will need to concentrate on basketball 24/7. They only allowed me a week off, and then I start intense training in the gym and prepare for pre season. If we coordinate our schedules, we can maximize the time we have together. I emailed you my calendar."

Syd kissed him. "Jax, try not to worry. We will be just fine."

The pre season workouts were anything but fine. Jax had no clue what was in store for him the eight weeks before the pre season. This definitely was not a college workout. We had a gym for weight training in college, but professional workouts were rigorous and ridiculous in comparison. I was busy from the beginning of the day until the end of the day.

I ate breakfast with Sydney in the morning and was so tired at night, it did not take long to fall fast asleep. The more I tried to stay awake, the faster I fell asleep. My body was exhausted and screaming to relax. The strength and conditioning coach was worse than a basic training camp instructor, and we followed a strict schedule. My body felt like it was training for the Olympics. My coach worked me out with weights, yoga, stretching, running, aerobics and any other punishing exercise he could dream up. Sometimes he had me swim to help my joints, but my muscles were still working. It did allow me to switch to a lower impact exercise to recover some energy.

At the same time, I was strengthening my arms, shoulders, glutes, abs, and hamstrings. I also did weight lifting to make me stronger. If I chose to skip a workout day, I would be punished with a fine. Professional teams did not play around and had high expectations for their athletes. They did not need to worry about me missing a workout, since I was serious about keeping my new job. I needed to perform to my potential or risk being replaced. I waited too long and worked too hard to let it all slip away.

In addition to my intense workouts, I was expected to improve my game. I shot from places on the court where I normally missed. Then I played Around the World and continued until I had at least five hundred makes.

I was required to watch and study film of myself playing in summer camp. My game was broken down and my weaknesses were brought to my attention so they could be worked on until they were strengths. I was advised to keep my head up when dribbling.

I ate, drank and dreamt of basketball. There were basketball skill challenges, ball handling, and footwork exercises. I did figure eights and dribbled the basketball while the trainer launched basketballs at me. There were boxing and plyometric exercises. My body was screaming. It sure seemed as if my trainer got off on brainstorming new tortures for me to endure. He assured me my workouts were to prepare me for the long season ahead and were for my benefit. Increased strength, speed, and stamina were the goals of preseason workouts. If I started the season with a strong body, there would be less chance of injury. If injury did occur, it should be less often and less severe. The eight weeks also kept players focused on the game. My trainer worked with me individually on the court and also when we played five on five pickup games.

I met with a nutritionist who wanted to change the way I ate. I was beginning to feel as if I needed a lot of improvement and was living life all wrong. I needed to learn more about nutrition in order to eat healthier foods. Fast foods were very bad and to be avoided at all costs. In my opinion, I saw nothing wrong with rewarding myself every now and then with a nice, juicy cheeseburger. The nutritionist adamantly disagreed. Somehow, the food I put in my body affected my game play. Since, she did not trust me to make changes on my own, my nutritionist arranged to have meals delivered to my house to ensure her rules were carried out. She said I needed to develop self discipline, and good nutrition needed to become my responsibility. In return, she promised not to make extreme dietary changes.

My days were so tough, I came home mentally and physically drained. There was no time to text during the day. When I was given breaks, I used them to rest, eat, or go to the bathroom before training resumed. Many of Sydney's texts went unanswered. It was not my intention to neglect her. There simply were not enough hours in the day.

I tried my best to eat dinner with Sydney, but sometimes ate with the team at the training facility, since I was already there. It gave me the opportunity to bond with my teammates. My trainer allowed me to take a break on weekends. I spent this time with Sydney. Once the season started, days off would be nonexistent, and there would be weekend games. I was giving our relationship as much time as the team allowed..

One night, Sydney decided to cook dinner and planned a romantic night for the two of us. Unfortunately, I had no idea and ate with my teammates after our mandatory team meeting. When I arrived home, Sydney was sitting at the table with an empty bottle of wine and cold dinner on the table. I have to say, her death glare was not a good sign.

∞∞∞

I decided to surprise Jax with a nice home cooked dinner. Lately, we barely spent any time together due to his long days of training. I went to the grocery store and purchased a couple lobster tails and NY strip steaks. He usually arrived home at approximately 8:00 p.m., so I prepared the meal to be served at 8:30 p.m. to allow some extra time, in case he was running late. I paid attention to all of the small details. Everything needed to be perfect, in order for the meal to be scrumptious. I made french onion soup with caramelized onions, toasted bread, and lots of melted cheese. The steaks were seasoned perfectly and grilled, and the lobster tails were butterflied and broiled. I prepared a fresh caesar salad and baked homemade pound cake for dessert. Pound cake was Jax's favorite dessert. There was a pint of vanilla ice cream in the freezer to top off the cake. I glanced at the clock, and my timing was perfect. It was exactly 8:30 p.m. I uncorked a bottle of cabernet sauvignon and poured two glasses. I took a step back to admire the meal set out on the table before me. I must say, I did a damn good job. I went all out on this meal and was proud of my effort. It was important for Jax to see how much I appreciated and loved him.

I wore a sexy rich burgundy colored satin nightgown. A slit traveled up to my thigh and was trimmed in black lace. It had spaghetti straps with black lace around the decolletage to highlight my girls. Jax could decide which dessert he wanted after dinner.

Now there was nothing left to do but wait for my love to walk through the front door. I could not wait to see the look on his face when he saw this meal waiting for him. I sat at the table and sipped a glass of wine. At 9:00, I drank my second glass. By 10:00 I was fucking pissed. Jax waltzed in at 10:15, and I had polished off the entire bottle of wine. He offered me the biggest, most genuine smile when his eyes met mine. I glared at him and felt like hitting him over the head with the wine bottle. If my eyes could shoot laser beams, Jax would be up in flames.

Sydney did her best not to scream at him. Her voice came out gravelly yet ominous. "Nice of you to let me know you had no plans of eating dinner at home tonight!"

Her anger was unmistakable, so he proceeded with caution. His better judgment told him not to approach her or make any physical contact at this moment. Instead he replied, "Babe, I am truly sorry from the bottom of my heart. I had no idea there would be a team meeting."

"Wait a minute. Did not know or did not care? Am I supposed to sit here at home happily waiting until you decide to show up every night? I spent my whole day planning the perfect dinner for you to surprise you and make you feel special."

"You are absolutely right. I should have called or texted and have no excuse. I cannot apologize enough. It was a rough day today, and the meeting was unexpected. Unfortunately, I ate there in order to go directly to the meeting afterwards."

"So you voluntarily chose to bond with your teammates instead of me?"

"Jesus Christ Syd, do you hear yourself? I understand your disappointment, nonetheless this is my career. I am trying to balance my career and our relationship the best I can. The team wanted to eat together, so I agreed. There is nothing more to it. Stop acting selfish!"

"You Son of a Bitch! Selfish! My whole life revolves around your schedule. I am always here waiting for you when you come home like an anxious puppy. You could probably care less by the way you stroll in any time you please. Well enjoy your cold dinner. I hope you choke on it. I am going to bed ALONE. Go find another room to sleep in tonight. And take a good look at what you are missing. I did this all for you. Maybe you should sleep at the training facility so you are there for tomorrow. You are never home anyway! Goodnight Jax."

She slammed the door as hard as she could for proper effect. I was surprised it did not come off of the hinges. My heart was beating so fast as I turned my back against the door and slumped to the floor crying. I know I overreacted and threw a tantrum, however I could not stop myself. I missed Jax so damn much. It was easier when he lived in Texas. At least I understood distance separated us. Now we lived in the same house, and we were lucky to see each other a couple hours a day. We were merely acquaintances. I felt the need to communicate how he hurt my feelings. I was trying hard to remain patient, yet the waiting killed me. I cherished our time together and expected those couple hours a day. That time was mine, and so was he. Was I being unreasonable? I was reacting as if he cheated on me. I had a good man who treated me like a princess and loved me. He was right about me acting selfish.. What was wrong with me? I was jealous of basketball. Jax made a commitment to me but had a bigger commitment to his professional basketball career. It seemed to be an impossible situation. I had a good cry and fell asleep.

Thankfully, I must have neglected to lock the bedroom door in my fit of rage. Sometime in the middle of the night, I felt Jax's arm wrap around me, and I spooned into him. His hug felt so good and soothed me. I instantly felt loved and hugged him back. My life was perfect when I was in his arms. This is where I belonged, and I would have to learn to be satisfied with any time I could get. Any time with Jax was better than being completely alone.

"I am so sorry and embarrassed for my behavior, I whispered."

"I forgive you and understand completely. I want to make the most of our time together and do not want to spend it arguing. Thank you for dinner. I appreciate the time and effort you put into creating a special meal and night for me. I want another chance, so I reheated everything and want you to come eat with me. I am especially looking forward to dessert. You made my favorite cake. I wanted to wait for you. The meal was meant to be enjoyed together."

Sydney smiled, "I love you Jax. I am famished and would be delighted to eat."

∞∞∞

Sydney woke up extra early to make Jax a healthy breakfast with fruit and eggs before he left for the day. When he woke up in the morning, his muscles were stiff and it took some time to get them warmed up and working again. He always had ice on his body and drank his orange juice down with Advil. The ibuprofen reduced the swelling and pain. His body was going through the most intense workouts he ever experienced in his basketball years.

He walked out to the kitchen and heard Sydney singing and humming. Her mood was much more happier than last night. When she saw him she gave him a big smile and said, "Good morning sunshine! I wanted to make you a special breakfast to start your day off right."

"Thank you Babe. You did not have to ruin your beauty sleep to wait on me."

"Nonsense. I will take any opportunity to spend some time with you. I know you want to forget about my outburst last night, but I needed to say how very sorry I was for my behavior. I promise I will be more understanding in the future." She planted a nice, juicy kiss on his lips."

"Mmmm. You are delicious. I wish I could call out of work, but there is no such thing in my line of work. I promise to do a better job of texting you when I decide to grab a meal with the guys. Spending time with my teammates does not mean I choose them over you. Coach wants the team to bond so we get to know each other and grow closer together as a unit."

"I understand. I was being a spoiled brat and only thinking of myself. We need to let it go and learn from our mistakes. I have a lot to do here between coordinating with Jimmy on household items and getting ready for my new teaching career."

"You do realize I make millions of dollars, and there is no need for you to work. I prefer to have you here anyway."

"Jax, I did not attend college so I could stay home by myself. You are barely home as it is."

"I know, but I will have plenty of time off after the season is over. When we get married, I prefer for you to stay home."

Sydney's expression changed from content to angry. Her entire face tensed, and she slammed the table with her hand. "Dammit Jax, I cannot believe we are having this discussion. We just decided to move on from last night, and you pick another argument. You sound like a male chauvinist ordering me around. I refuse to take orders from you. It is not 1950 for Christ's sake. You have a career, and I have the right to have my own career too. You cannot tell me what to do!"

"We really should not argue, Jax said." He grabbed her hand, but she pulled away.

"I think it is time for you to go to the gym."

"C'mon Syd, we cannot start our day like this. I apologize. You took it out of context. We did not even eat our breakfast yet. Come sit down, please."

"You started it Jax. And marriage? We have to survive dating first. I do not plan to be some stay at home mom who waits for you to come home in an empty mansion, while you travel the country and live your dreams. You need to realize, you are not the only one with dreams."

"Again, I apologize. Of course you should have a career if you want one. I want to take care of you and make you happy. I am simply saying the option exists if you ever decide to choose it. I do not want to see you stress trying to balance work life and family life. We certainly do not need the money. It is not my intention to boss you around. I did not mean for it to come across that way. Can you please sit? We get very little time together."

Sydney could not take his look of dejection and sad puppy dog eyes. It made her mad, because it was impossible for her to stay angry with him. He folded her up in his arms and pulled her in for a big hug and a tender kiss.

"I love you Syd."

"I love you more Jax."

∞∞∞

Sydney was happily eating breakfast with Jax before his training. Jimmy called to say he was a couple minutes away. He wanted to catch us before our day started.

"Is everything okay Jax? It is unlike Jimmy to drop by first thing in the morning."

"I hope so Babe. The last thing I need is bad news."

A few seconds later, Jimmy walked through the front door like a little ball of energy. He spoke as if he consumed ten espressos already.

"Hey kids! I hope you are having a wonderful morning, because it is about to get even better." He dropped a stack of Sports Illustrated magazines on the table.

Jax said, "Oh yeah. I have been so busy, I forgot about my magazine cover and feature story. I hope the reporter was nice, or Sydney will make her regret it."

Sydney laughed. "Hey, I am not normally aggressive. She started it first by trying to make me look like a money hungry bitch."

"Play nice now baby. Give her the benefit of the doubt. She never met you before and had no idea how special this relationship really is. I must say, I was really turned on when you tore her to pieces in front of her crew."

Jimmy said, "Okay, get a room kids."

The three of them studied the cover. It looked great! Jax was in a Sixers uniform with red, white and blue custom Nikes and he was dribbling the ball through his legs. The Philadelphia skyline was the backdrop. It said, "Jaxon Jones - Philly's New Kid on the Block. Can the NBA keep up with Jones?

Sydney said, "This is so cool and creative. It is a play on words about keeping up with the Joneses. You look fantastic on the cover."

Jimmy agreed, "Go to the story kid. What are you waiting for? You are going to be late for your training."

There was a picture of Jax and Sydney smiling back to back in the key with Jax holding and looking at a basketball. The caption read, "Is There Room for Three in the Key?"

Sydney sighed in anticipation, thinking the worst was yet to come with the story inside the magazine. The title of the article was not very promising. Thankfully, she was wrong.

Jax put his arm around Sydney and Jimmy stood behind them as Jax read the story out loud. The article gave a brief history of Jax's upbringing in Texas and life growing up in the country. It detailed his high school and college career and how he was drafted into the NBA. The article had a very positive spin. The story unfolded into Jax and Sydney's romance and undeniable chemistry. There was some background on Sydney and the new teaching job she would be starting soon. It addressed her interest with teaching and starting a charity for autistic children to raise more awareness. Then there were short responses from Coach Brown and veteran players showing their enthusiasm for Jax being drafted to their team. The article wrapped up by letting fans know how busy Jax's life was about to become, and time would tell if the relationship could withstand the pressures of NBA basketball.

"Well, we will show her how it is done! She is lucky she refrained from trash talking me. We can definitely prove her wrong when we are still together next season."

Jax said, "I do not think she is trying to say we will not be together. She is just letting the readers know that being a professional basketball player is a hectic life and being the girlfriend of one is not for everyone. Shake it off. You have nothing to worry about."

Sydney kissed Jax and hugged Jimmy. They were all talking at the same time in excitement for the positive press. Jimmy left and told Jax to get to practice and rattled off about six more items of interest as he was walking out the door.

Sydney laughed, "Oh my God, he is a crazy man, but I love him. He really looks out for you and protects you like a father would protect his son. You made a good choice in choosing him Jax."

"I did a better job in choosing you." Jax kissed her and said, "I really have to get going. I promise I will see you for dinner tonight.

Chapter 7 - Out of Sight But In The Picture

Paul was looking through his mail and the new issue of Sports Illustrated was waiting for him. His favorite Sixer, the highly anticipated rookie Jaxon Jones was on the cover. Paul went to the fridge and grabbed a beer and turned on ESPN. He was going to unwind after working all night and drink a couple beers while reading the article about Jax.

The cover rocked and was very patriotic featuring Sixers red, white and blue colors with the City of Philadelphia as the backdrop. He enthusiastically flipped through the magazine pages to get to the article.

Time suddenly stood still. Paul was blindsided by the image looking back at him. His mood plummeted and became very dark and stormy. He threw his beer bottle, and it crashed against the wall. Shattered glass flew everywhere and beer poured down the wall.

"God damn bitch, Sydney! You always have to ruin everything!"

Paul was accustomed to getting his way with his good looks and boy next door charm. Before Sydney, he coasted through life and never hit a rough patch. Women were just a means to pleasure himself. He really had no interest in becoming further acquainted with any of them.

That is until Paul met Sydney. She refused to have sex with him unlike any of the others. They were all sluts, except for Sydney. She intrigued him enough to stick around and develop a relationship. They dated, yet she still refused to be intimate. He impatiently waited six months until she was good and ready to sleep with him. In the meantime, Paul satisfied himself with one night stands and was very discreet, so Sydney did not find out.

She was worth the wait. His plan was to dump her after he stole her virginity. He was hooked and did the opposite of his initial plans. They continued to date and eventually moved in together. Then, to his dismay, she stopped doing as she was told and became defiant. Reflecting back on their relationship, she was stubborn and not easily intimidated. Sydney refused to be controlled and was very spirited. Paul could not handle being disobeyed, so their relationship fell apart.

He strived to forget about her after getting hit with a restraining order. To add insult to injury, he lost his internship job with the State Police and wasted four goddamn years of college and basic training. When Sydney pressed charges, it was automatically reported to his employer. It was strictly forbidden to have a police record and work in law enforcement. His supervisor called Paul into his office and asked him to take a seat, as he walked over to the window separating his office from the bullpen to close the blinds. It was never a good thing. He informed Paul in the nicest way possible, how he was fucked since he had a record. His career in law enforcement ceased to exist. He would not be allowed to accept any state, local, or Federal jobs. His boss was very sympathetic to his unfortunate predicament, nonetheless his hands were tied. The turn of events could not be reversed or ignored.

Thanks to Sydney, Paul was stuck at dead end jobs making

minimum wage. He was working for a cell phone company inside a Walmart, until they informed him of his hours being cut. Walmart offered him a stocking job on the night shift. His life was a complete mess, and it was all her fault. He wished he never laid eyes on her.

One night they had a huge argument, and he gave her a shove. She fell down some steps. Big fucking deal! She always needed to turn on the theatrics to try and gain pity. He raised his hand to her previously, yet never hit her. He simply wanted to intimidate her enough to shut up and stop bitching and whining at him. After the incident, she told him to stay away and moved out. Paul apologized repeatedly and begged for her forgiveness. For all of his effort and groveling, he was slapped with a restraining order.

To add fuel to the fire, the little bitch recorded their arguments and kept pictures of her bruises when she fell down the steps. It was just a little shove. It was not his fault she was a klutzy whore who bruised easily. Her best friend Nina drove Sydney to the police station and told them all about our arguments. Lies and more lies blah, blah, blah. The police department granted the restraining order and told her she had to press charges for assault. Sydney knew this meant "game over" for my internship as well as my future and tried to tell them she did not want to press charges. It was fucking too late to turn back. The damage was done. I had no say in the matter, which happened to be my fucking life. I should have hit her to teach her a lesson and make it worth all the pain she caused me. If she did not run to the police station in the first place, I would still have a promising career.

I attempted to move on with my life and found a new girlfriend who was a high maintenance, whiny little slut like the rest of them. Here I am scraping by making minimum wage, and Sydney Fox is sleeping with an NBA player, shacking up in his mansion, and spending his money. Her life was too good living in the lap of luxury, and I refused to sit back and let it happen. I decided right there and then, I was going to pay Sydney back for what she did to me.

$$\infty\infty\infty$$

As soon as Jax walked out the door to go to practice, Sydney called Nina. Nina picked up right away.

"Hey Syd, how are you?"

"Sorry to call you so early Nina. I just keep fighting with Jax, and it is driving me crazy!"

Sydney told Nina about Jax constantly being gone long hours, the special dinner she tried to surprise him with, and her most recent argument with Jax telling her she did not need to work.

"Syd, you two pretty much recently met and are starting a relationship under a lot of pressure. Most people have down time to work on their relationship. You are dating a professional athlete who is in the spotlight. He has to live up to his draft expectations with basketball plus endure the pressure of a brand new relationship. Talk about some major stress for Jax. And it is equally stressful for you, since you are left with very little time to spend with your man."

"You are making me feel as if it is my fault, and I should have no right to complain!"

"No, I am simply trying to make you realize, this is not a normal relationship. You hardly get the opportunity to spend time together, so I would not think you want to spend all of your free time fighting."

"It upsets me how we fight. We should not have any issues. This should be the blissful stage of our relationship."

"Listen, time is going to be your challenge so make the most of it. There are not any particular stages in your relationship. You, my friend, are dating a celebrity. Normal rules do not apply. Throw all of the rules out the window. It is obvious you both love each other."

"I really should call you more often Nina. Sorry for biting your head off. You were only being a good friend by putting everything into perspective. Thank you for putting up with me. Enough about my drama. How is Vincenzo?"

"Cenzo treats me great Syd, and I finally found a guy who knows how to treat a woman. I could totally get used to him adoring me. His mom is the old fashioned Italian type who spoils him to death, but she spoils me more, so I cannot complain. We will have to do a double date sometime when your man is not so busy."

"Deal, but let me have some dates with him first."

"Oh and Sydney for the record, I am not always right. I assumed Jax was a typical player in every sense of the word the night you met him. I must admit he has proven me wrong so far. He seems to be a perfect gentleman with Southern charm. You deserve a good man too, especially after asshole Paul.

"Thanks girlfriend. You are always there for me, and I wholeheartedly value our friendship. I honestly have no clue what I would do without you. I promise to call you soon. I desperately need to go back to school shopping soon, except this time around I am the teacher instead of the student."

"I would be delighted to go with you. You know I love to shop, and we can treat ourselves to a girls day out before you start your new job. Hang in there Sydney. Remember, a good man is always worth the fight."

I hung up, jumped back in bed, and dove under the covers.

Nina always gave excellent advice, and she meant every word. She did not sugar coat words just to make me feel better. Although it took her a long time to find a guy worth having a relationship with, Nina was very intuitive about relationships and people. Nina's opinion of Jax was accurate. He was a remarkable man. Sydney already knew what it was like to date a malevolent man and did not want to give Paul a second thought. There was a special place in hell reserved for him, and he belonged in the past.

∞∞∞

Paul was able to pay a large sum of money to have the assault charges expunged from his record. After he appeared to move on with his life, Paul asked his attorney to reach out to Sydney to see if she would be willing to dissolve the restraining order. Paul knew she would agree, because she was weak and wore her heart on her sleeve. The guilt of destroying his life would be eating her alive. Lifting the restraining order would allow her to live with her decision. He really should have stayed with her longer, so he could beat the weakness right out of her body. The woman ruled her life with emotions instead of her brain. He would be doing her a huge favor if he hit her. Maybe then she would use some common sense.

When Paul's attorney contacted Sydney to see if she would consider removing the restraining order, she agreed since her naivety led her to believe people had the ability to change for the better and deserved a second chance. She never meant to ruin his career. Her family and friends disagreed and were strongly against her decision. They were unsuccessful in changing her mind and were unable to make her understand why Paul deserved to lose his job.

Paul was pleased Sydney made the right decision but as far as he was concerned, it was too little too late. She was and always would be a little bitch. He had no remorse in using her guilt to manipulate her decision in his favor.

His future plans included opening up his own detective agency and make a shit ton of money. His cases would help men who were screwed over by the conniving no good whores of women. There were plenty of them out there, and Paul knew first hand what a royal screwing felt like.

But first, he planned on taking a slight detour. He was looking for a night time janitor job for one specific company. Paul applied online and had an interview this week. He would merely tell them he needed this job, so he could take some college courses during the day. Everyone needed to make a buck in order to make ends meet. Paul was confident he was the right man for the job.

Sydney began her new job the Thursday after Labor Day. The holiday was pretty uneventful for her. She longed to go to barbecues and parties to close out the summer with a bang, however Jax was only interested in relaxing and spending time alone. Despite being disappointed, she would not let it show, especially since Jax's schedule was insane, and he desperately needed some down time.

Sydney met with her teaching team the week before the holiday, and they worked on lesson plans. They would need to be tweaked and personalized, depending on each individual student's needs. All assistant teachers were encouraged to contribute to the lesson plans, so they were prepared when they had a class of their own. The school's plan was for Sydney to work one on one with different students during the course of the day, and make sure assignments were completed. She would make sure the students felt confident by helping them work through any problems they were having with any class work. If a student was having trouble comprehending or if they were feeling frustrated, she would find a way to communicate with them until they understood without feeling overwhelmed.

Sydney enjoyed decorating the classroom and getting ready for school to begin. She was so excited to meet the students. Instead of having a back to school night after the school year started, the parents made appointments to visit the week before with their child. This allowed everyone to meet the teachers ahead of time and to give parents a better understanding of the lesson plans without feelings of anxiety. It was helpful to receive input from the parents as to the areas their child needed special attention, and the triggers which set off each child in order to avoid it. There was also a party the Friday before school started with all of the children, so they could meet in a comfortable social environment. The purpose of the party was to make the first day of school less daunting. We brought each child's favorite food, and we played the name game. The kids had a great time.

Since autistic children tend to have anxiety with unstructured free time, the goal was to play games or read stories out loud and participate in activities which were fun. It would not be mandatory to join in, which would hopefully alleviate any pressure. In addition to working one on one with the children, I would also diffuse situations before they became out of hand. I wanted the children to feel like this was their second home, and provide another safe place for them to feel comfortable in. Hopefully the type of environment we were offering would also be conducive to learning.

I was so excited for my new career. It seemed to be the type of job I would love to go to everyday. I felt so fortunate. I had a great relationship, a dream job, and I would be helping children and hopefully making a difference in their lives. Could my life possibly get any better?

∞∞∞

Once the holiday was over, Sydney went to work. I was very busy and had a lot of responsibility with very little free time. Not only was I responsible for a lesson with the entire class, but also my one on one time with each student. It was hard to believe how last week I was bored to death, and my only job was looking at the clock waiting for Jax to get home. Now we barely saw each other, because I was putting in extra hours to get acclimated with my students and their individualized lesson plans.

The individual education plans allowed me to customize the student's learning. My job was to help the children thrive in the classroom, which was no easy task. I did my research so specialized learning could be established in the classroom. Visual clutter was minimized by decorating the classroom in a blue ocean theme, since the color blue was found to be soothing. I also planned to have white noise in the classroom by playing soft background music throughout the day. Each child was going to learn differently and had different triggers for outbursts. Trying to alleviate the trigger would deter the outbursts. I was prepared to make any necessary changes throughout the school year to meet different needs. Alternative seating would be offered as needed, and the classroom would be modified as it became essential.

Visual aids would be crucial to help students understand what was expected of them during the day. I created schedule charts for each child with a color coded picture and a short explanation next to each time of the day. The books for those subjects would be color coded to match the picture. Each child would be given a red stop sign card to use if they needed a break or a yellow card if they needed help during a lesson. These cards would reduce outbursts and stress. Unstructured or free time usually led to increased frustration. There would be cards for free time for reading a book, playing with game pieces, coloring, or nap time. The child would hold up the card showing which activity they wanted to participate in during this time.

When giving instructions to the students, I needed to learn to keep it short and stay away from negatives. It would also be necessary to allow time for the child to process the instructions before expecting an answer. It was essential to make sure I had my student's attention before giving any instructions. The lesson plans would be tweaked throughout the year to provide the best learning experience possible for each child. I would participate in the meetings with the parents and therapists regularly to go over the learning progress and any new developments emotionally in each child's life.

My job was going to require plenty of dedication and flexibility in order to provide the best learning experience for the children. It was a challenge I gladly accepted.

It was a very long first day, and Sydney was exhausted and anxious to get home. As she was walking out to her car, she noticed colored post its all over the driver's side glass. "What has Jax done now? He was always surprising her. He was so thoughtful to take time out of his busy schedule to leave notes on her car. She was so lucky to have him and was unable to wipe the huge smile off of her face. Unfortunately for her, they were not love notes, and they were not nice. There were nasty messages on each one of the notes. Her face drained of color, and her body began to tremble. What a terrible thing to do! It could only be Paul. Son of a bitch. She had moved on with her life and forgot all about him.Why?!

She did not call Jax. Instead, she went straight to the police station to report the incident. The police said it was an unfortunate incident, but there was no way to prove it was Paul. They could not act on assumptions, so there was nothing to be done at this time. I was advised to inform them of any new developments. Maybe he would get sloppy and leave some evidence. Until then, I was to remain patient. I decided not to tell Jax about what happened today. He had enough stress with the start of his rookie year.

∞∞∞

Jax was just as busy with his commitments. Sixers media day was held on Monday, September 25 at the Training Complex in Camden, New Jersey. Twenty seven other NBA teams held their media day on the same day too. All players and coaches were available to reporters between 11am and 3pm. Questions were answered about each team's expectations for the upcoming season. Reporters asked players a wide variety of questions ranging from why they chose to play in Philadelphia, health on the court, twitter comments with other NBA players, etc. There was light hearted recreation across the league. Teams played games, held sing-a-longs, and made it a fun event.

Twenty four short hours later the fun ended when training camp started and continued for four days. NBA camps were shorter than other pro sports camps, because the players work out year long to keep up with the eighty two game grueling schedule which wreaks havoc on the body. These athletes do not show up after months off to just start playing basketball. Some players held informal work outs together. So much work goes on outside of what we see on television. We see a forty eight minute regulation game lasting approximately two and a half hours. What we do not see are the months of working out behind the scenes to get ready for the game. Players' bodies have to be well conditioned. The most common injuries in the beginning of the season are dislocations, strains, sprains, and tendonitis. As the season advances, so do the injuries. Stress fractures of the lower body are common. Even the most conditioned players are vulnerable to injury. Players who spend most of their time on the bench have to work out just as hard to try and prevent injury and be ready to play the game when their name is called to go out on the court.

Exhibition games would follow training camp. Before practices began in camp, players were examined by a team of doctors. These included medical, eye, and orthopedic doctors as well as a physiologist and team trainer. Exercise plans focusing on strength and conditioning would be customized for each player. In addition, players received necessary vaccines, and tests were performed to measure flexibility, body strength, body fat, and oxygen consumption during peak exercise on a stationary bike.

Just because training camp is short did not mean it was easy. Quite the contrary. It was very competitive, extremely intense, and exceptionally fast paced. Players need to abandon any bad habits There is more emphasis on team rather than individual so that players and coaches build relationships. Everyone gets the chance to play and put in some effort. Players without contracts are under extreme duress and fighting for a spot. Anyone who chooses not to exert themselves are immediately cut. Training should not be confused with recreational play time. This is the time for coaches to trim the roster.

The day started early with weights, plyometrics, interval training and cardio. Teamwork began after the workout session. Offensive drills involved passing and dribbling with two on two and three on three. Players learned to dribble less and pass under pressure and try to find an open man quickly. Dominating the ball is adamantly discouraged. Double teaming is also practiced in order to deal with defensive pressure and to get the ball to the open man for the wide open shot. Defensive practice includes protecting the basket, screens, mid range shots and rebounds.

The training camp day ends with a five on five pickup game. This gives the team a chance to work on offense and defense at the same time using the full court. Coaches have the opportunity to try out team strategies to see how they work and integrate each player's specialty moves into the mix. Training camp allows teams to get ready for the upcoming season and establish team goals.

On the other side of the bridge, Paul was relaxing in his recliner taking a short nap, when he heard the phone ring. He quickly jumped out of the chair and answered the phone. The custodial crew manager in charge of the Philadelphia 76er's facility was on the other end of the line. Paul completed his interview three weeks ago, and was advised they were conducting interviews for a few weeks before a decision would be made. The manager happily informed him the job was his if he still wanted it, and he was to start next week. Paul acted excited and accepted the position. He was told he would shadow with a senior employee until they felt he was ready for his own area to clean. His plan was falling into place nicely. The crew manager acted as if he gave Paul the key to the city. In a way this was true, since Paul would be working at the same facility Jax would consider his second home. He was glad he had higher goals in life other than cleaning up someone else's mess. For now, this job would allow him to clean up the mess Sydney made of his life. After Paul hung up, he let out a sinister laugh which was chilling. Other than the laugh, Paul seemed so normal. It was easy to ignore the fact that he was far from mentally stable.

∞∞∞

Paul proved his worth by completing every task he was given and covered shifts any time someone asked him to work. He never missed a day and was very dependable. He was very friendly and sociable and trusted by his coworkers. He was now considered part of the custodial crew family. They worked in pairs and only one pair had access to the locker room. As luck would have it Antwon Davis, Paul's partner, was assigned to the locker room. Antwon was in his late sixties and the old man of the crew. He was all about family and told his stories to everyone. No employee had one bad word to say about him. He was admired by all. Antwon was married to the same woman for fifty years, and her name was Chloe. He had one grown boy, who was a drug addicted loser using heroin, and four grandkids by different baby mama's. Antwon had custody of his grandkids since the baby mama's were either in school or more of a loser than his son Fred. His grandbaby's were all under the age of four and made Antwon a very happy man. He absolutely adored those kids. If Paul had to listen to any more sermons or stories about the grandkids, he was going to snap.

It was important for Paul to maintain self control and keep his focus on the end game. Antwon was the only person in Paul's way of being assigned to the locker room. Paul had to figure out a way to get rid of him temporarily. His plan would not work with Antwon around, for the simple reason he never let Paul out of his sight. In fact, he took so much pride in his job and was unable to trust anyone else to complete the task to his standards. Plus, Antwon was like a father figure to Paul always giving advice and proudly looking on as if he was his special project. Antwon and Paul went out once a week for drinks. It definitely was not by choice. Paul was so sick of hearing Antwon during the day, let alone after work. Despite his growing animosity, he needed to suck it up since there was a job to be done.

One night, Paul decided it was GO time. He went out with Antwon for a few drinks. After an hour or so passed, Paul announced he felt sick and was going to head home. Antwon gave Paul a loving slap on the back, and told him to give him a call if he was still sick tomorrow. He said it would be no problem covering Paul's shift. Instead of going home, Paul quickly walked to his car, and parked it around the corner so Antwon would believe he really went home. He walked back to the bar and took a seat on a pallet located behind the dumpster, with a good view of the door. Paul slipped on a black knit hat and was dressed completely in black like a bank robber. Now he patiently sat back and waited for Antwon to come out of the bar.

Conveniently for Paul, Antwon was alone and preoccupied getting his keys out of his pocket. He was absolutely unaware of Paul's presence. Perfect timing. Paul was quick and light on his feet. Before Antwon realized what was happening, Paul swiftly whacked him behind his knee with a baseball bat. He may have gotten a little carried away swinging for the fences. Antwon cried out yelping like an injured dog, dropped to the ground, and clutched his leg with both hands. He was rocking back and forth writhing in pain. Paul snuck away to his car while Antwon was preoccupied. He pulled the car around and waited in the dark until someone came out and helped Antwon. After all, Paul was not completely heartless, yet he did not possess a conscience or feel one ounce of remorse. When he heard the siren of a nearby ambulance, he drove home and slept like a baby.

Paul woke up the next morning in a rather great mood. He was whistling along to the music on the television and sitting down with a nice hot fresh cup of coffee. Antwon called as he sat down and explained what happened after he went home. Paul was an exceptional actor feigning astonishment and disbelief. Antwon thanked him for his concern and explained how he needed surgery to the PCL, which connects the femur to the tibia. He also added how he spoke to our supervisor Flo to explain Paul was more than capable of taking over the locker room and extra duties. Paul thanked him for his vote of confidence and told him to take it easy. He also promised to visit him when he had a chance, although it may be a while with all the extra hours he was more than happy to work. Antwon told him to worry about visiting, since he had his wife to take care of him. They quickly said their goodbyes and promised to stay in touch.

Hell yeah! It could not have worked out more perfectly. Antwon's wife Chloe said this was a sign from God to stay home and retire. Paul should have felt a little bad for the guy but thanks to his handiwork, he would now have more time to spend with his grandbabies and wife. Antwon did not realize it yet, but Paul gave him a gift last night. Now it was time for Paul to focus all of his energy on Sydney.

Chapter 8 Two Steppin Good Ol' Boy

The Sixers new uniforms were debuted at the first exhibition game at home at the Wells Fargo Center in Philadelphia. They were sharp and were white trimmed in blue and red. There was a circle of thirteen stars with a 76 emblem and the letters were signature style. Jax may have looked stylish, however he was extremely exhausted, and the season had not even started. He did some training in the weight room in college, although the training did not compare to what he was doing now. It felt like he was training for the Olympics.

Sydney appeared to be sympathetic and understanding on the many occasions when he came home and fell asleep on her while watching television together. The more he tried to stay awake, the faster he fell asleep. As he looked up and saw her smiling back at him in the stands, he longed for her compassion and patience to continue. His schedule consisted of strength conditioning, team practice, pre game workouts and watching film. When he finally stopped moving and gave in to relaxation, he could not help but fall fast asleep.

Jax experienced more playing time than he expected in the first exhibition game and tried to make the most of the time. He was frustrated with his performance, since he had a lot of turnovers and was having trouble with his timing. The expectation was for him to get into scoring position quickly and then slow down enough to accommodate the intended play. If that was not disappointing enough, he had six seconds less to work with off the shot clock. In college he had thirty seconds, but the NBA only gave twenty four seconds. Surprisingly enough, six seconds was a huge difference.

Jax felt the disadvantage of being a rookie player. Returning players knew the basic plays the coach ran. The rookie had to learn all the plays as well as figuring out which plays the coach called the most in a game. He had to build a camaraderie with his teammates and try his best not to piss off the veteran players. They were losing valuable playing time when the coach put the rookie in the game. Jax was feeling some doubt and confided in Sydney after the game.

"Babe, I cannot understand why you are putting so much pressure on yourself. Put it into perspective. After all, you are playing in the NBA as a professional athlete. You should feel honored. Ninety eight percent of the population do not get the opportunity. Instead of worrying, we should celebrate!"

"Thanks for being so fucking understanding! You need to get a clue. In case you cannot see, I really do not feel like celebrating. I am tired and you obviously only care about yourself so goodnight." Jax slammed the bedroom door.

"Jax!" Sydney stared at the closed door in disbelief. Her jaw literally dropped to the floor. She was just trying to bring out the positive points. A few seconds later, the door opened and a pillow flew across the room and landed at her feet. She felt bad for making him feel this way. He was completely right. She should have shown more sympathy for how he was feeling instead of pushing his feelings aside. Sydney grabbed the pillow and decided to sleep in one of the spare bedrooms to give Jax a chance to cool off. The last thing she wanted was to upset him further.

∞∞∞

Jax brought Sydney a cup of coffee the next morning before he left for his conditioning session. The team was leaving for a New York road trip for a few games, and the last thing he wanted to do was leave while they were fighting.

Jax sat down on the bed and kissed Sydney's forehead. "Baby, wake up. I brought you coffee."

Sydney woke up and hugged him. "Thank you. I am so sorry for last night. I was an ass. "

Jax kissed her. "There is no need to explain."

"Yes I do need to explain Jax. I feel so embarrassed for my behavior. You were confiding in me and looking for support, and I brushed it off like it was nothing. Sometimes I forget how much pressure you are under to please your coaches and teammates and deal with your crazy schedule. If that is not enough pressure, you are juggling a relationship. I appreciate you and want you to know how proud I am of you. I am not trying to ignore your struggles. In fact, it is quite the opposite. I have so much faith and confidence in you. Just remember, you are never by yourself. I am always here for you."

Jax hugged her. "Sydney, please do not be so hard on yourself. I know you care and was very happy you were there to see me play."

"Good, because I will be at every home game this season. You better get going. You have a big day ahead of you."

"Not before I take you back to our room. I am bringing you back to bed before I leave. We leave for New York after morning practice. I cannot leave you for a few days without a proper goodbye."

∞∞∞

Jax experienced a decent amount of playing time in the exhibition games so naturally, he thought it would continue in the regular season. If he was playing so much, it probably meant he was performing well. In reality, the coaches just wanted to observe his skills to see if he was ready to play in a regular season game, in the chance they decided to put him in. The first team was already decided, and he was not on it. He was on the third team, which translated to very little playing time and more bench time than he anticipated.

His relationship with Sydney improved after their last argument. They both made an effort to improve communication. Sydney also realized she was not in a typical relationship and needed to become more flexible and understanding with Jax's demanding schedule. The practices and trainings were not optional. If he did not show up, he would be fined. Sydney became his shoulder to lean on. Even if she was unable to personally relate to what I was going through, she was more compassionate with regard to my struggles. I was a strong guy, yet sometimes needed to vent. It would be a mistake to vent to the wrong person and have it posted all over social media.

Sydney was a great listener and kept me grounded. Not all of my problems needed solutions. It was enough to know she was there for me. She offered valuable insight instead of telling me what to do with my life. Most people would say, "He is making over four million dollars to sit on the bench. Stop bitching." Sydney told me to be patient and to persevere and train as hard as everyone else, so I could be ready when my time arrived. I watched film on our opponents and became familiarized with their style of play. This would allow me to guard them to the best of my ability if I did get in the game. I never missed a training or a practice. Not because I would be fined if I did not show, but because I cared. I paid attention to the game when I was on the bench and supported my teammates on the court.

Jax believed traveling was great in the beginning of the season. He was treated like royalty. There was no check in, so it was okay to arrive fifteen minutes before takeoff instead of two hours. Instead of wasting time finding a parking spot at a crowded terminal, I simply rolled up to a private hangar and walked onto the team's private jet. There were catered meals, hotels, and traveling to cities all over the country. Sounds like a dream come true right? The jetsetting life of the wealthy NBA player you say? NO! It was quite the opposite, Jax thought. The end of December was a nightmare. He had no idea what to expect on a long road trip. This was a new experience. After a while, the travel was exhausting. There were only twenty seven games in college compared to eighty two games in the NBA. Fifty five extra games was a considerable amount. Three college seasons crammed into one NBA season. Jax was tired, sore and irritable. This was the most extensive road trip of the season, and it was a harsh reality.

The few days before I departed for my road trip were the best. On December 20th, we played home against New Orleans in Philadelphia. During warmups, I scanned the crowd for a familiar face, and there she was looking right back at me. Sydney was sitting in the crowd above the players bench with a big smile on her face. As sure as the sun rises every morning, Sydney kept her promise and appeared at every home game. I did not expect her to make it to every home game, but it made me so happy to see her there supporting me. We spent the next two days together after the game and celebrated Christmas early, since I would be away for the holiday. I had bought a very special gift for Sydney and was pretty excited to exchange gifts. Jimmy helped me with the present, and Sydney was going to be completely surprised.

We shared a romantic dinner and then cuddled by the fireplace. The doorbell rang. Sydney looked at me and said, "Are you expecting anyone Jax?"

"No. I did not invite anyone over. Do you mind answering the door Babe?"

"No no problem Jaxon. Let me see who it is." Sydney answered the door and the only thing there was a big wrapped gift with a bow on it. "Jax no one is here, but someone left a present on the porch."

Jax answered, "Wow, I wonder what it could possibly be. Bring it in here and open it."

Sydney was so excited. Of course I knew what it was since I had Jimmy deliver the gift outside. "What do you think it is?"

"I have no idea, but I am about to find out." As she opened the wrapping, it sounded as if a scratching noise was coming from inside the box. She opened the lid, and the two cutest puppies jumped out wagging their tails. Sydney squealed with excitement and hugged Jax. "Thank you so much! You are so thoughtful. I love them!"

"You are very welcome Baby! I know you were sad about losing your Jack Russell. I saw these two pups and could not resist. I was told they are a Pomeranian Chihuahua mix called Pomchis. They should not grow over ten pounds when they are full grown."

"Thank you so much. They are absolutely adorable. I will take great care of them." Sydney instantly fell in love. They were brother and sister. The boy was black and white, and the girl was tan and black. "This is the best gift ever!" The puppies agreed and were jumping on Sydney and giving her kisses. "Now it is time for your gift." Sydney was so excited. "Okay Jax, you need to open the gift first and then look at the text I just sent. Make sure you do it in order."

"You got it!" Jax opened his gift and it was a framed, autographed Allen Iverson jersey. It was black with white lettering and the number three outlined in red. The background matte was red. It had two 76ers emblems on the top, then the jersey, and a couple pictures on the bottom. There was also a silver plate that said Allen Iverson MVP 2001 Hall of Fame 2016. "Thank you so much! I love it! This means a lot.

"Now look at the text," Sydney smiled.

It was actually a video. I was looking at Allen Iverson. "Jax, Merry Christmas. You have a great girlfriend. Hold on tight to her. Sydney contacted me and told me I was your childhood idol. Other than making me feel damn old, I thank you from the bottom of my heart. I look forward to seeing you play this season. I will see you on the court man."

Wow, I was speechless and floored. "Sydney, thank you so much. I cannot believe you were able to get me such a great gift. It really means a lot. Thank you!" I leaned in for a long kiss. The puppies were jumping all over us and wanted all the attention. We both started laughing. "So what are we going to name these two?"

"How about Jordan and Jewelz?" Sydney answered.

"Very catchy. Jordan after MJ and Jewelz after A.I.'s rapper moniker." Jax agreed and they played and snuggled with the pups the rest of the night.

The team flew out to Phoenix December 22nd for a 9 p.m. game on the 23rd. I spent Christmas in Phoenix and hung out with my teammates on Christmas Eve and Christmas day.

My teammates and I decided to go to the Bar Smith club on Christmas Eve. We mingled at a table in the downstairs bar. A couple girls walked over to our table because they recognized us, and asked to take some pictures together. One of the girls mentioned her name was Lacy, and I took a picture with her early in the night to be a good sport. She took it as an invitation to keep flirting with me. I told her I was not interested in anything else, so she would not get the wrong idea. She listened less with each drink she took. I became a challenge she could not pass up.

I removed myself from the situation and went upstairs. There was a rooftop patio bar with a DJ and a light show. People were dancing everywhere. I had no desire to dance, so I just sat at a table and watched everyone else. Before I realized what the hell was happening, Lacy straddled me and put her rack in my face while trying to give me a lap dance. She was a sloppy drunk. I politely threw her off of my lap, and she became pissed. One of my teammates ended up hooking up with her girlfriend. Little did I know, Lacy was unaccustomed to rejection. She was determined to get revenge, and posted a video her girlfriend took of her giving me a lap dance on social media. The video looked guilty as hell, and of course it went viral.

Paul was having more fun than he should, finding ways to sabotage Sydney's new relationship. It was her turn to experience some of the pain he experienced. He still remembered Sydney's password for Facebook, but could he possibly be this lucky? There was only one way to find out. Paul typed in the password, hit enter, and voila he was in! Stupid bitch never changed her passwords. She posted recently which confirmed her recent Facebook use. Next he created a 76er's fan page and liked it. Sydney was now following the group's page. Paul made the page look official by copying some of the posts from the official Sixers page. Now the group's feeds would show up on her wall, so he could post anything he wanted her to see.

Paul recorded the portion of the Howard Eskin interview asking about a significant other. He created a video with the title "Hey all you Single Ladies, come meet the Sixers most eligible bachelor!" It began with Beyonce's Single Ladies song and showed the relationship part of the interview with exaggerated, shocked emojis. Too bad Sydney was not good enough to be Jax's girlfriend. Poor Syd. Paul loved it. The post generated a lot of comments to help Sydney doubt her relationship with Jax.

Sometimes Paul did not need to look far for news. Jax gave Paul some ammunition with the Christmas lap dance in Phoenix. He edited the video and enhanced the slut's tits and ass and the dumb look stuck on Jax's face. He added appropriate strip tease music and posted it as quickly as he could so Sydney could see the show. The title of this video was, "Sydney Who??? Jax gets a lap dance while his pitiful girlfriend sits at home missing him." It was really too easy to instigate trouble.

When Sydney began her new job, she seemed a little too happy for Paul's liking. One day, he covered the car with post it notes. "Remember me?", "You were lucky to have me!", "You are lucky I just pushed you down the stairs.", "Next time, I will finish the job", "You will never replace me", "Whore", "You ruined my life", "Money hungry bitch", "I should tell him about the real Sydney", "Afraid yet? You should be.", "You better look over your shoulder for the rest of your life", "Karma is a bitch", "You do not deserve to be happy", etc.

Paul was in his car a safe distance away, so he would be able to watch her reaction. It was priceless. She walked toward her car with a big smile on her face. Most likely, she thought Jax left cutesy little love notes for her. Sydney had an extra little bounce in her step as she tried to hurry over and see what the notes said. Paul started counting. Wait for it, and there it is, the reaction he wanted. The color immediately drained from her face, and her smile transformed into a look of fear. She took the notes off of her car as quickly as she possibly could one by one, and looked more anxious after each post it note. Sydney was jittery and looked all around for the perpetrator. She was looking over her shoulder and scanning her surroundings to try and find me. He definitely planned on giving her the opportunity, but not just yet. For now he would revel in the fact of scaring her shitless. It gave him great satisfaction.

Sydney never told Jax about Paul showing up in her life again unannounced in the form of post it notes. The thought of that day gave her chills down her spine. When she saw her car decorated in post it notes, she excitedly headed towards it. Awe!! Jax is so thoughtful to take time out of his busy day to think of me. She walked faster, because she could not wait to get to her car and read the notes Jax wrote. God she loved him!

Sydney was so confused as she read the first note which said "Bitch'. Each note was worse than the next. Oh no, could this be Paul? Then she knew for certain, because the next note said "Remember Me?" Fear filled her body, and she started to tremble. She felt the color leave her face. Why? Just when her life was wonderful, and she was so happy, Paul had to try and sabotage it all. God damn him!!

Once she was safely locked in her car, Sydney called Nina and told her what happened. "That son of a bitch!! How dare he. Call the police immediately Sydney! He is a sick fuck!!" Nina said.

"I cannot tell Jax about this. He has his own problems to deal with, and I refuse to burden him with mine."

"You cannot let this go Syd. At least call the police. Eventually, you need to tell Jax. He is a big boy and can handle the news."

"No!! You better not dare open your mouth. I will call the police right now, and let you know what happens.'

Sydney called Officer Raines who was in charge of the case. He told Sydney to report everything and anything suspicious to him. Right now, there was not enough evidence to accuse Paul of anything. Even though he insinuated his identity, he did not do anything incriminating. Officer Raines explained Paul obviously put a lot of thought into this plan. He told her to bring the post its to him, but could bet his paycheck Paul was careful enough not to leave fingerprints. Sydney promised she would call with any new developments.

She texted Nina to let her know. The response back was, "TOTAL BULLSHIT. He better hope I do not catch him doing anything."

∞∞∞

The team flew out the next morning to Sacramento and had a 10:30 p.m. game the same night. We literally had just enough time to throw our bags in our room and head to the arena for practice. When I finally had a chance to check my phone, there were at least one hundred messages from Sydney. She was not happy, and waiting for a reply made her angrier.

"Oh, I see you had something else in mind for Christmas!!"

"Really?!"

"Nothing to say?"

"WOW!!"

"Did you forget that your life is plastered all over social media where I would see it?"

"How do you think this makes me feel?"

"You are such a fucking asshole!!"

I attempted to call her a few times before the game, but she kept sending it directly to voicemail. I finally left a message." C'mon Syd. You know me better than this. I can have anyone I want, and I choose you. The woman was pissed, because I rejected her. I refused her sexual advances, and she decided to pay me back by posting an incriminating video. Her girlfriend must have taken it when she decided to give me a lap dance, while I was sitting at a table minding my own business. Give me some credit Babe. I love you Syd. The only person I need is you."

I had an average game, at best, against the Kings. The stress of my personal life did not benefit my game at all. I agreed to an interview immediately following the game to the network who televised the game. They were very professional and allowed me to tell my side of the story. After all the questions were answered, I was drained mentally and physically. To make my day even more miserable, a reporter boxed me in on the way to my car demanding an answer to the viral video.

"Jax, what is your response to the video of you clearly cheating on Sydney while she is unknowingly home waiting for you?"

"First of all, my personal life is none of your business. Second, do you have any game related questions?"

"Your game was terrible tonight. Is that due to the guilt of the video?"

"I just held an interview explaining my side of the story, so this is none of your damn concern. If you were really good at your job, you would know her advances were uninvited and unwelcome. A good reporter does not jump to conclusions. Do some research and you will see a young woman, not used to rejection, seeking revenge. You have no right to judge the way I do my job when you cannot even do yours. God damn hypocrite! Now if you will excuse me, I am done wasting my time."

Jax walked away more aggravated than before. God, he prayed Sydney would see through the bullshit.

∞∞∞

Sydney watched the game against the Kings alone, despite ignoring Jax's texts and calls. She was still livid with his behavior. How foolish of her to spend Christmas missing him, while he was on a road trip getting private lap dances. The network announced the exclusive interview with Jax after the game with regard to the viral video. Sydney impatiently waited for the interview. She listened to his voicemail to her and had mixed emotions. She wanted to believe him but should she? The game was over, and the interview was about to begin.

"Good game tonight Jax. Any comment on the little Christmas present you received in Phoenix?"

"We both know I did not play my best game. I agreed to this interview for one reason only. I only owe the most important person in my life an explanation. It is important that my girlfriend Sydney understand the video is not what it seems. It seemed very innocent to me. I was nice enough to take a picture with a fan. She used a nice gesture as an invitation to pursue me. I declined politely and told her I had a girlfriend. I decided to move by going upstairs to a different section of the bar. By removing myself from the situation, I assumed my point was taken. Little did I know, me having a girlfriend was a challenge to her. I was sitting at a table minding my own business and listening to the music. Before I knew what was happening, the same woman finds me and straddles me while giving me an unwanted lap dance. I told her she was wasting her time, and I was not interested. I grabbed her arm and helped her up and off of me. Her friend took a video. She retaliated by posting the video to social media."

"Jax, surely you could have handled it differently? Maybe you gave her the wrong idea?"

"Listen, I was raised to have manners and to treat a woman with respect. It would have been rude to throw her across the room or push her on the floor. It was apparent she was very intoxicated, so reasoning with her was out of the question. Somehow I am the bad guy for acting respectful."

"How does your girlfriend feel about the incident?"

"Well currently she is not accepting my calls, however I am hopeful she will remember how loyal and faithful I am and have been in the past. I would never purposely hurt the woman I love. This is a case of a fan looking for her five minutes of fame, and no one will even remember who she is next week."

"There you have it ladies, Jags only has eyes for his lovely lady, Sydney Fox."

Sydney believed Jax and felt badly for overreacting.

Jax was whooped from his schedule and the added drama. The never ending road trip was wearing his patience thin, and even little things were aggravating him. Back to back games were rough enough, and then he had to deal with flying to different cities and time zones. The only advantage of the constant traveling were the roomy seats on the plane, the luxury buses and five star hotels. The travel schedule was insane. Sometimes we traveled while the rest of the country slept. It was important to keep hydrated for the games which was hard to do with altitude differences and plane travel.

Another benefit of traveling was the time I spent with my team. It gave us the opportunity to bond, and this could only help us on the court. One of the veterans took me under his wing and served as my mentor. He tried to guide me through this tougher than anticipated rookie year. Essentially, he helped me survive the NBA. I am glad I was given the good fortune to lean on him for much needed guidance. The advice he was sharing was valuable and would make an impact on my future in the NBA. JJ told me to keep my head up with regard to playing time and to focus on the game and how to improve. He explained how I had a lot to offer the team, and my skills would be needed in the near future. I needed to remain patient until the time arrived. He not only taught me more about the game, but also how to be a better man. Lately, it was obvious I needed his words of wisdom desperately.

On the 28th, the team flew to Utah for a 9 p.m. game. I played my worst game against the Jazz. They wore you down on every possession and expertly ran the clock down to their advantage. The whole team played disciplined and did not rush or panic under pressure. As a group, they took their time in order to make the best shot. We paid the price if any of us missed our shot or rebound, since the cycle would start all over again. Playing the Jazz felt like a mental beat down.

I could barely get out of bed the next morning. The constant practicing, workouts and game play were wreaking havoc on my body. It was hard to move with all of the aches and pains. I felt like a ninety year old man. Normal people grind too hard at the gym and take a day off to recover. Unfortunately, this was not an option for me. I had to suck it up, because I had another game tonight against Denver. It was time for some ice and ibuprofen and definitely some coffee.

In the meantime, I turned on ESPN, and they were discussing my game play last night. DAMMIT! Last night, one of the opposing players was trash talking me and getting away with cheap shots all night long. No fouls were being called. The refs appeared to be either fucking blind or sleeping. The last straw was when I took a shot to the jaw, and the refs conveniently did not see anything again. I started yelling at the player who dealt the blow. His response was to call me a little bitch.

If the refs were going to let him get away with it, I sure as hell was not. My temper got the best of me later on in the game. I gave him a shove and tripped him up. Before he got up off the floor, I gave him an extra little kick and said, "Now who is the little bitch?" The refs sure as hell saw that one without a problem. Retaliating made me feel better, however it was short lived. I was ejected from the game after a flagrant foul 2 was called. The player who should have been punished was given two free throws and automatic possession. After the game, I suffered the backlash of the media. I turned up the television volume to hear what was being said about the incident.

Sports Center was on and the commentator provided details about the game. "The Philadelphia 76ers lost 80-123 last night against the Utah Jazz. The rookie, Jaxon Jones did not come through at all for his team. He was shut down and only scored twelve points in the game, had eight turnovers, and was ejected from the game with a flagrant foul 2. His behavior was completely unacceptable and disappointing. Jones had a problem with another player's cheap shots and reacted by kicking him in the foot later on in the game when he was down on the ground. Both benches emptied, and tempers flared on the floor. Jax needed to be pulled off the court by his teammates. In my opinion, Jags crossed the line. The rookie needs to learn basketball is physical as well as emotional.

Everyone trash talks on the court. A player should be able to give it, take it, and then leave it on the court when the game ends. If you cannot handle trash talk and physical play, maybe the sport is not for you. The rookie has a lot to learn if he wants to remain in the NBA and become a respected player. Right now, he is attracting the wrong media attention."

∞∞∞

After the game, Coach told me I better get my shit together. He was building a new and better team and did not want another prima donna on his hands. Coach said he expected better behavior from me as a rookie and was disappointed in me. Those words stung more than the discipline. If I was unable to get it together, I would be playing for another team, no matter how well I played. I apologized, and Coach told me I better prove it. Words meant nothing if I could not back them up.

I felt like I was falling apart. The mental stress was giving me anxiety. Was this really what I dreamt of when I wanted to be in the NBA? I was completely unprepared for everything I was experiencing in my rookie year. Where was the dream life? This was complete torture. I spent most of my waking hours preparing for a little bit of play time. Although the team had the privilege of a private jet, I still had to fly to different cities and live out of hotel rooms and suitcases. Half the time, I forgot which hotel room I was in. I just wanted to open the door and have Sydney greet me with her smile, which could light up an entire room. I had a feeling I may never see her smile again between the lap dance and my bad behavior on the court. I really had no excuse. The rest of my teammates seemed well adjusted and were able to handle the traveling without behaving like a jackass.

JJ walked up to me after most of the guys left the locker room. "What the hell is going on with you man?"

"I am fighting with Sydney and this road trip..."

"Let me stop you right there. Save the bullshit for someone else. You absolutely need to put basketball as your first and only priority. Your relationship is extremely important, except not during basketball season. It becomes my business when your relationship problems affect the team. Your teammates deserve one hundred percent commitment from you. Dwelling on your personal problems will not benefit you or the team. You need to put the relationship aside when you are playing, and stop jeopardizing your career. Believe me Jax, I have a wife and family that I leave behind. You are not alone, and I am here for you anytime. Your behavior last night was embarrassing to the team. It is undeniable you were taunted by another player who called you a little bitch, but you acted like a little bitch when you threw the little temper tantrum by kicking him when he was down. The best course of action for you to take right now is to move forward and get over the past. Dwelling on the situation will not fix it. Your behavior was unfortunate, and you need to make damn sure you do not allow it to happen again. Remember, your actions not only affect yourself but the entire team.

"JJ he kept cheap shotting me and getting away with it repeatedly. The refs were not going to handle it, and it needed to stop."

"Jax, did you listen to one word I said? There is no justifying your reaction to not getting a call. Unfortunately, this is how basketball works in the NBA. You will get bullied by grown men. Suck it up. Instead of acting out, shut them up by scoring." JJ had no choice but to deal out some tough love. He knew Jax was reacting to the situation. He was a rookie and still learning. The kid was sleeping in his childhood bedroom a couple of months ago. It was time to grow up and be a man. "I am sure this long road trip added to your stress. It is not easy dealing with travel, hotels, time zone changes, and minimal sleep. I feel your pain bro. You will get through this."

"I apologize for my behavior. Thank you for your insight and advice. I appreciate you not giving up on me man."

∞∞∞

When I was back in my room I tried to decompress. Last summer the idea of playing in the NBA seemed like it was going to be a blast. In reality, it was the opposite of fun. He never thought he would have to work out so vigorously for a forty eight minute game. Jax was under the impression he would be expected to show up an hour before the game. Damn was I wrong. On game day players did a shoot around for an hour and looked at film of the team they were playing. After lunch there was a few hour break. Ninety minutes before the game, players went back to the arena to see trainers, dress for the game, and warmup. After the game, we lifted weights and hung out for a while before going home. It was literally non stop work. Fans only saw a small piece of a basketball player's day on television, and probably had no clue as to the number of hours it took to prepare for a season and each of the games.

Since I finally had some free time, I decided to use it to repair my relationship with Sydney. I picked up my phone for a video chat as my heart pounded out of my chest with each ring.

Sydney's phone started beeping. By the sound of the ring, she could tell it was a video call. She was lounging on the couch drinking wine with Nina. They were spending time at the house watching movies, talking, and drinking more wine. It was going to be a sleepover party.

Nina nudged me. "Pause the movie. I think you made him suffer enough."

"Hello," I whispered to the face staring back at me.

"Please try not to be angry with me. I am so sorry. Please do not hang up on me."

"Jax, sweetheart, everything is okay. I watched your game and heard your interview. I was so angry when I first saw the video on social media with that whore, but I guess I cannot blame her for wanting you. Once I was able to think clearly, I knew you were innocent and would not do anything to hurt me intentionally. You never gave me reason to question your intentions in the past. When we are together, you only have eyes for me."

"I feel so relieved and appreciate you believing in me." He smiled at me shyly, like he was waiting for me to say something else.

"Oh yea, and I watched the game you were ejected from, and saw what happened."

"My coach was furious and told me in no uncertain terms my retaliatory behavior would not be tolerated, and he was not running a daycare."

"Listen Jax, it is your coach's job to instill discipline and channel anger into productive play. You surely could not have expected him to let you off the hook and give you a pat on your back for a job well done. Do not be fooled. He understands you are growing up, and were still living with your parents before being drafted into the NBA. Christ Jax. You have done more traveling then you did in one year of college ball, and you are doing it during the holiday season."

"I know. I need to put the unfortunate incident behind me and move on. The league will fine me $50,000. It is a big punishment for a well deserved payback. He made me so angry Syd, repeatedly giving cheap shots and in my face whenever given the chance. I know it does not justify my behavior. I reacted without thinking. I am playing with veteran players, and I am still trying to learn the system. I realize it will eventually get easier."

"You should not be so hard on yourself. The biggest step is owning your mistakes and moving forward. Some of your opponents use their size to bully other players. Their only mission on the court is to make your life miserable. Other guys will bully you with their trash talk. You simply cannot stop it, so channel your anger into buckets. Stick to what you know best."

"Wow baby! How did you get so smart? I will work on it. I promise. I love you so much Syd."

"I love you more Jax."

"We leave tomorrow to come home. The team has practice, but then I want you to meet me at Bistro Romano in the Society Hill section of Philly at 8 p.m. You deserve a romantic night out and will be properly wined and dined."

"Oh my God Jax. I am so excited, and can barely wait! I have been dying to eat there! I will definitely be there waiting for you tomorrow."

They reluctantly said their goodbyes, and Sydney was giggling like a little girl and jumping up and down. She briefed Nina on their plans for an intimate date and made a quick post on social media. She was having a romantic dinner with her man at Bistro Romano tomorrow night xoxo.

Nina replied, "Good for you woman. You put up with enough nonsense for one week. Make him pay, and order one of everything off of the menu!" She burst out laughing. The wine was going straight to her head.

"Nina, cut it out! You are so bad, yet you are absolutely right. It is too soon to let him know I completely forgave him. I need to drag it out at least for one night anyway. And I am thoroughly going to savor this meal."

They fell on the couch laughing and pressed play to finish

watching their movie.

∞∞∞

The following day, the guys invited Jax to go to the club with them after practice. Jax explained he was taking Sydney out to Bistro Romano at 8:00 for a much needed romantic dinner. They commenced busting his chops when he announced where he was taking her to eat. "Man oh man, you must really be on the shit list if you are taking her there. You are well past sorry or a dozen roses. Are you still in trouble for that lap dance? You must be the only guy in hot water who has to pay a fortune for being completely innocent. Good luck brother. I wish you the best. Our condolences. You had a good run while it lasted." It was all good natured kidding around. They were all close like brothers, and knew all too well the obstacles Jax was encountering.

"You better not forget your wallet. You will need some Benjamins for the restaurant. I hope you bought her a gift too. Should we take up a collection for you Jax?"

Jax looked shocked. "What?! You mean dinner is not enough! I need to bring a gift too? This entire situation is out of control. At least I get to eat."

His teammates were hooting and hollering, and the locker room erupted in laughter. "You have a lot to learn my man. Good luck." They all gave him a slap on the back on their way out to the court.

Chapter 9 - Undying Love

Jax sent Sydney a message asking her if they could change the time to 6 p.m. instead of 8 p.m. Geez, he must really think he is in trouble. She could not wait for their date.

Sydney arrived at the restaurant all decked out in a drop dead gorgeous black dress which hugged her curves in all the right places. The plunging neckline showcased her full breasts and the sparkly lariat necklace ended right at her cleavage. This was not by chance. It was exactly where she wanted his eyes to rest. Jax would need to control himself through dinner and torturously wait to get her home. Just the thought of making him suffer a little bit left a big smile on her face, and it was still there when the hostess greeted her. She was led through the main dining room and received appreciative glances from the men and smiles from the women. Sydney smiled at all of them in return. The hostess turned and walked down some steps leading to the wine cellar. A private table for two with two large white candles in heavy silver candle holders was waiting. The white table cloth was covered with red rose petals. The wall had wine cubbies with bottles of wine laying in them and the top shelf had a very large wine bottle standing up. She never had the opportunity to eat here in the past, but heard the restaurant was known for their limoncello and gnocchis.

The waiter pulled her chair out and seated her. He handed her a white linen napkin to place on her lap and then handed her a rose. She was informed her party would be joining her shortly.

Her date requested her to wear a blindfold. Of course, Sydney happily obliged.

Jax surely went over and above what was expected. He was acting so mysterious and romantic! This was going to be an excellent night. In fact, it would be a night to remember. How was it possible for her to remain angry with him? His attention to detail demonstrated how much he really loved her. She would blindfold him later in bed to return the favor. Syd was completely lost in her thoughts of what she wanted to do to Jax in private, and did not realize she was no longer alone until his leg brushed up against hers.

She blushed and felt her face get hot when she realized Jax must have been watching her seductively lick her lips and bite her bottom lip. Except, Sydney was absolutely unaware that the man sitting across from her was not Jax!

It was actually so much easier than Paul could have imagined. He knew Sydney was going out to dinner at Bistro Romano from her Facebook post. Now he just had to figure out the time. As luck would have it, he overheard the guys talking before practice, as he was getting ready to leave the locker room. They were going to a club after practice but Jax told them he was taking Sydney out to Bistro Romano at 8 p.m. for a much needed romantic dinner. He thought he was going to have to figure out Jax's phone password in order to text Sydney a change in plans. Turns out, the idiot did not have a password. Paul took Jax's phone while he was practicing and texted Sydney to see if she was able to meet him a couple hours earlier. The message sent said he was getting done practice earlier than originally anticipated and wanted to know if it was possible to meet at 6. Sydney texted back almost immediately saying she would be there.

He carefully erased the two messages. Paul called the restaurant pretending to be Jax's assistant so he could change the reservations. The earlier time worked out better for the restaurant too. He could not have planned it any better himself. He probably should be at the casino right now with all of his good fortune, instead of sitting across from Sydney at Bistro Romano.

This night was going to be perfect. For so long, he planned and schemed ways to make Sydney pay for ruining his life. Unfortunately he was unable to plan for the effect her physical beauty would have on him. She looked exquisite and ravishing, and his plans quickly changed in her presence. He would grant her one more chance to make things right with him. They had their entire future ahead of them. She would need to be convinced to see things Paul's way, either by sweet talking or force. The decision would be hers to make, although there was only one outcome. Her life with Jax was finished.

Sydney was clueless that her dinner date was not the man she was expecting. When she thought Jax was in the room with her she happily said, "Jax this restaurant and private room is beautiful, and I could not have chosen a better place myself. I have to really hand it to you for planning such a wonderful evening. The blindfold was a nice, mysterious surprise."

Paul stood up and grabbed her hand, and pulled her in for a kiss. She was still wearing the blindfold. He sat her down so she would not faint when he removed it.

"Okay Jax, I had enough of this damn blindfold. Let me see you! I have not seen you in days!" But something was wrong. When Jax touched her, the hairs on her arm stood on edge. She had goosebumps, and not in a good way. His cologne was different, and something about the kiss was familiar but not enjoyable.

Syd ripped off the blindfold and her breath caught in chest. She froze and was unable to talk or scream. She expected and wanted Jax. Instead, Paul was sitting across from her like Lucifer himself.

∞∞∞

"Hello Sydney. I guess you were expecting someone else, but it is okay. It is time you realize you belong with me."

She was absolutely overcome with fear. Her heart was beating so fast, and her body broke out into a cold sweat. A feeling of lightheadedness came over her, and her hands were trembling. She started to stumble over her words. "Oh my, Oh my God, Pa Paul, wwwhat the hell are you doing here? How did you know I was supposed to be here?"

"All in good time darling." He caressed her hair and tucked it behind her ear. Paul placed his hand on her back and reached over for a kiss. As his lips touched hers, she bit him. He grabbed her by her neck as he tasted a trickle of warm blood on his lips. "Now that was not very nice was it Sydney? If you cannot handle a kiss, how will you handle me ravishing that pretty little body of yours."

"Over my dead body." She frantically looked around, but they were all alone.

"Please do not get any fancy ideas. I made sure we would be all alone in what used to be an underground tunnel. The restaurant turned it into something romantic, but if you make the wrong choice, it will be your final resting place. The waiter will not be returning. I gave him strict orders to respect our privacy, since we desperately needed time alone together. I also told him I would call when we were ready to eat. So sit back and relax, or you will wish you never came here tonight."

She already wished she stayed home and that this was all some sort of bad dream. How did Paul know about their plans, and where the hell was Jax? This simply could not be happening to her. She had to try and scare Paul off. It was worth a try.

"Paul, I have no idea what you are doing here right now, but I strongly suggest you leave immediately. Jax will be arriving here any minute. If you leave voluntarily right now, I promise not to press any charges for keeping me here against my will. We can pretend tonight never happened."

"Oh, cupcake you are so wrong and such a bad liar. Jax is practicing. I sent you the text changing the time. How, you ask? After you destroyed my life by getting me fired from state police or any other municipality, I have been stuck with shitty job after shitty job. I paid a lot of money to get my record expunged and was going to open up my very own private investigator business. But then I saw you on the cover of Sports Illustrated magazine with Jax. It would be unfair if you are able to live a life of fame and luxury. I needed to make you suffer, so I found my way back to you. I work for the 76ers organization as a cleaning crew member at the practice facility and the stadium locker rooms. I am the one who changed the plans. I was going to kill you, but after seeing you, that is no longer possible. I decided to give you, to give us, one more chance. You need to forget about Jax. No woman of mine is going to be with another man. You are mine, and I refuse to share."

Sydney was literally having a panic attack. What the hell was this psychopath thinking? She had to escape. Her eyes were darting around frantically trying to figure out an escape route. When her eyes landed on Paul, he gave her a smug look and then looked down at the table. There was a gun pointing at her. She was alone and screwed.

"Jax is paying for this dinner so pick up your fork and eat. I will not allow you to be an ungrateful bitch. Put a smile on your face too. You look ugly when you frown."

I was given no other choice. I forced a smile and picked up my fork. I would have given anything at that moment to stab him through his black heart with it. I was unable to do anything except for what Paul told me to do with his fucking gun pointing at me.

"The waiter is on his way with the rest of our food so no funny business or he will die."

The last thing Sydney wanted was for anyone to get hurt, so she would have to wait and bide her time. She had to lay on the charm and try to make Paul feel comfortable enough to let his guard down. Ugh, it should be Jax enjoying this romantic dinner with her instead of her worst nightmare. As they began their meal she tried to smile and pretend she was enjoying herself.

"So how do you like the gnocchi Sydney? They used to be your favorite. See I still remember. In fact, I remember everything about you." He smiled creepily.

"They are very good. Thank you." She had to swallow hard to keep the food down.

"See Baby, I knew you would see things my way. I have everything planned for us. I am starting a new life and a new career. The only thing missing is you. You will be my wife, and then my life will be perfect."

"Paul, we should take things slow. We have a lot to work out." He saw a tear drop from her cheek and realized she had been playing him. Up to her old tricks again!

His face went from gentle and caring to dark and mean spirited. "WE do not have to work out anything. You have absolutely no say in this. After what you did, I call the shots from now on. I will let you handle decorating, house cleaning, cooking, and pleasuring me every night."

"Listen Paul, I will never love you and cannot pretend this is okay."

He reached across the table and pulled her by her hair. "Oh you will do what I God Damn say you will do, you Fucking Bitch. I tried being nice, but now you made me very angry. Get up! You are finished with your dinner. NOW!"

"Paul, I am so sorry. Ouch, you are hurting me."

"Unfortunately for you, violence is the only way to get through to you Syd. I did my very best to try and be nice and then you piss me off just like old times. Now you must be punished. Your behavior is intolerable. We are leaving now." He grabbed her and led her thru the tunnel. There was a door at the end of the tunnel, and his car was parked right outside. He shoved her into the back seat and got into the front. He told her if she moved, he would shoot her.

This was crazy. How was this happening to her? Why? Syd's life was going so well and was full of happiness. She found a gentle, kind man who understood her better than anyone. Now everything was in jeopardy. She had to do something.

Paul started the car and pulled away. Syd tried to headlock him from behind. He was coughing and gagging as he was swerving down the side street. If she could just hold on a little longer....

Paul grabbed the gun with the other hand and pistol whipped Sydney on the side of the head with it. She was unconscious and finally quiet. That would give him enough time to get her back to his place. She was like a precious angel when she was quiet.

∞∞∞

Jax was in the locker room happily whistling after practice, and excited for his hot date with Sydney. He picked a romantic setting with a private dining area for two in the wine cellar. It was thrilling thinking about the two of them finally being able to gaze at each other in the candle light while eating mouth watering food and drinking luscious full bodied wine. Jax would appreciate the meaningful conversation and laughter over dinner, and then he would take her home and devour her for dessert. He could barely contain his excitement. Jax picked up his phone and texted Sydney to say he was on his way to the restaurant. There was no response, so he reckoned she was driving.

He spotted her car in the parking lot outside the restaurant and felt instantly aroused, like he did the first time he laid eyes on her. She was his best friend as well as his biggest fan. Jax could accomplish anything with Sydney by his side. He had to stop himself from racing into the restaurant to get to her quicker. When he provided the hostess his name, she hesitated with a perplexed look on her face. "Sir, surely you must be mistaken. Your assistant called and changed the reservation, and your dinner was two hours ago."

Jax stood there looking at the hostess in utter shock. What in the hell was going on? "Wait, what? I made the reservation and never called to change it." The hostess called the waiter over.

The waiter relayed what little information he had to Jax. "I escorted a blond haired gentleman, who claimed to be Jaxon Jones, down to the wine cellar where we have a private table. He requested me to escort the young lady downstairs when she arrived, and he would sit at the bar until I informed him of her arrival. I was given strict instructions to advise the young lady her date would be with her shortly. In the meantime, her date requested her to wear a blindfold and wait. The gentleman went downstairs to meet her once he was notified she was blindfolded and waiting. He was extremely happy with this news, and told me to remain upstairs until he called me with his food order. I am truly sorry sir. We receive many different requests, and there was no reason for me to believe he was an imposter or that anything was wrong."

Jax was trying to figure out who would have wanted Sydney blindfolded to protect his identity. All of a sudden the realization hit. Son of a bitch! Jax stood there frozen in his spot. His jaw clenched and his muscles tightened. Adrenaline filled his body. Sydney only told him about Paul briefly, but he knew without a doubt he was the person whom the waiter described. "Where are they now?"

"Sir, I am sorry to say I have no idea. I went down to see if they wanted any dessert, and they were gone. I never saw them come back upstairs. I have no idea what transpired. I truly wish I could give you more information."

"Call 911 immediately, and tell them you think the young lady was kidnapped by her ex boyfriend who is very dangerous. His name is Paul Reilley. Hurry! Her life may depend on it. And you should not blame yourself. There was no way for you to know what was happening."

Jax called Sydney's parents and filled them in quickly and asked for Paul's address. He was pretty sure it was where he would find Sydney. They asked him to wait for the police. They were afraid it would be too dangerous and not safe to go alone. He told them he already had the restaurant call 911. Help would be on the way. Paul was the one who needed to worry about danger. He had no idea of the rage he just unleashed in Jax.

Furious could not even give justice to the feelings Jax was experiencing at that moment. He got into his car and drove as fast as he could without hitting any cars. This bastard better not have laid a hand on Sydney. Jax loved her with every ounce of his heart and would lay down his life without reservation if it meant saving her.

∞∞∞

Sydney woke up in a strange room, and everything was a little blurry. As the room came into focus, she was looking around to try and figure out where she was, and then it all came back to her like a nightmare. Her head was pounding as if she had a monster hangover. She realized she could not move. Her hands and feet were tied to the bed posts. She struggled to get loose, but it seemed to make the rope tighter and cut into her flesh. Suddenly, she saw him.

Paul was sitting in the corner smiling at her and admiring his handy work. "Hello sweetheart. Well you are a bit feistier than I remember. Please try not to waste all of your energy. You are going to need it. I am going to fuck some sense into you and make you mine. You deserve it after all you put me through. We will be together forever one way or another. Your life of luxury with Jax is over. I own you now."

The situation seemed hopeless. No one knew her whereabouts. Why was this happening to her? Paul walked toward the bed and roughly grabbed her breast. Sydney flinched. He bent down and started to kiss her. She bit his lip again. Paul slapped her hard across the face.

"Oh, so you want it rough? All you had to do was ask. You can have it rough. Bite me again and I will knock your teeth down your throat."

"You will not get away with this."

"Watch me. Now shall we try this again?" He had a knife

strapped to his leg. Paul took it out and held it in front of Sydney's face. It glistened and she could see her reflection in the blade. It was awfully close to her face. She thought he was going to cut her when he made a cut in her dress and ripped it off of her. He grabbed her breast again and roughly caressed it with his thumb. Then he leaned down and kissed her on the lips. She refused to kiss him back.

"You will learn to love me one way or another Sydney. After all, you do not have any other choice."

He tore off her panties next. Paul stood back to admire his prize and then told Sydney how he was going to fuck her over and over until she submitted to him. He took off his pants and underwear and grabbed his cock until it was nice and hard. He was getting ready to mount her when Jax kicked down the door.

"You fucking bastard! Get your hands off of her." Jax flew through the air and tackled Paul onto the floor. They rolled around throwing punches. Jax threw a right hook and knocked Paul out. He was looking at the gun on the chair in the corner of the room and walked over and picked it up. He took off the safety and cocked the gun and Sydney begged him not to do it. She said the police would take care of Paul, and she could not bare to see him spend his life behind bars. Jax was putting the gun back when Paul came up behind him and wrestled it out of Jax's hand. They both struggled for control and fell to the floor. They were rolling around and fighting, and Sydney was screaming. She had no idea what was going on since she could not see anything from where she was tied up. The gun went off. Silence temporarily filled the room. No one moved. They were both at the foot of the bed on the floor. Sydney began screaming for Jax.

Jax finally stood up and untied her hands and feet and scooped her up into his arms just as the police came through the door.

Paul was dead. The police took statements and decided Jax

acted in self defense. No charges would be brought against him. Jax held Sydney close in his arms and carried her to the car.

"You are safe now Baby. It is all over once and for all."

∞∞∞

Jax had no idea how to comfort Sydney and needed some assistance. She cried the entire way home and was inconsolable. He called her parents, so help was on the way. It was hard to believe Paul was the janitor who cleaned the team's locker room. Jax had never seen a picture of Paul before, otherwise seeing him would have raised a red flag. He could not imagine Paul was disturbed enough to get a job with the Sixers and carry out such an extravagant plan to get Sydney back. He could have killed her.

Jax walked over to Sydney on the couch. She was curled up in a ball wrapped up in a plush blanket. He had the fireplace on to keep her warm. She still had not stopped shivering. He went to caress the side of Syd's face, and she flinched and pushed him away. Her reaction wounded him. "Baby it is only me, Jax. There is no need to be afraid anymore."

"It is so easy for you to sit there and tell me not to be afraid! The psychopath found me after he saw me in Sports Illustrated magazine with you. It reminded him of how I was single handedly responsible for destroying his life. There was no way he could allow me to live a happy life. He was convinced I belonged with him, and was going to spend the rest of my life with him no matter how I felt. For God's sake, he almost raped me, and I am not supposed to be afraid!! To top it off, I never told you how he covered my car in post it notes the first day of school and scared the shit out of me. I never told you, because you were busy enough with your own career."

"Those words never came out of my mouth. I would never

think my life was more important than yours. Not in a million years. Nothing on this earth is more important than you God Dammit! I am truly sorry Syd. I never meant for any of this to happen. Somehow you are blaming me." The doorbell rang. Sydney's parents had arrived.

Jax quickly opened the door to let them in, and they ran straight to the couch. She began crying hysterically and begged them to take her home to Sea Isle, where she would always be safe. Sydney confided that she did not feel safe with me, and she would always live in danger dating someone famous.

Jax was left speechless, and felt his heart sink to the pit of his stomach. Tears formed in the corner of his eyes. Sydney's mom spoke to Jax as her dad walked Sydney out to the car.

"Jax, honey, give her some space. It will be the hardest thing you have to do, especially when your instincts tell you to do the exact opposite. I also understand you went through hell and back to save her and ensure her safety. This has been so traumatic for Sydney. I am sure she will realize how much she needs you once she has some time away from the spotlight."

Jax replied, "I am so sorry. I never meant for any of this to happen. She gave me a brief background of her relationship with Paul. I had no clue he was so disturbed or even dangerous."

"There is no need to blame yourself. You had nothing to do with any of this. Paul would have come after her eventually, once an opportunity presented itself. Unfortunately, your fame placed her in the spotlight. You saved her life tonight, and we are forever thankful you showed up when you did. I cannot allow myself to think of what would have happened if you did not come to her rescue. I feel no remorse for Paul's death. He got what he deserved, and she will never have to worry about him again."

Jax stared out the window as his life drove away from him. He was unable to stop the tears falling down his face. His world was crumbling right before his eyes.

$$\infty\infty\infty$$

Sydney's parents spoke to her supervisor at the school to explain the events that transpired, and she was immediately placed on temporary leave. Sydney would be able to return whenever she felt ready to return to work. Everyone loved her, and she was a good fit for their school. The kids she worked with loved her too.

Sydney took the time to relax, read books, and took long walks on the beach. It was winter, so it was like a ghost town in Sea Isle. Jax continued to call, although his calls and texts went unanswered. She needed her space. Syd's mom let her know that Jax wanted her to continue working with the autism foundation, regardless of their personal situation. Sydney was thankful for his generosity, and took him up on the offer in order to keep her mind occupied. She could not bear to think about what almost happened with Paul.

Nina was a frequent visitor, and talking to her was better than seeing a therapist. They were in her room wrapped up in a blanket and drinking hot chocolate.

Nina grabbed her best friends hand. "Syd, I am so sorry for the nightmare you endured. I hated that asshole Paul, and find it hard to believe the lengths he went through to get to you. I was watching the news last night, and an old maintenance worker who trained Paul stepped forward. He told the story of how Paul went out of his way to befriend him. They went out for drinks once a week, and he was attacked one of the nights they shared a few drinks together. Someone hit him behind the knee with a baseball bat. Paul was the first to come to his rescue, but now he realizes Paul planned on hurting him to get the locker room job. It used to be his gig, so Paul had to get rid of him."

"Ugh, how could he do that to an old man just to get to me?"

"He was convinced you ruined his life and patiently waited to get his revenge. That is, until he saw you again and was unprepared for the way you made him feel. He realized he wanted you more than he wanted to hurt you, until you rejected him. It was the ultimate betrayal, and you needed to be punished."

"It is unfathomable I ever let him into my life. How did I miss his mental instability?"

"You need to stop blaming yourself, and Jax. Jax is not and never will be Paul. He is a good man, and he loves you very much. He was willing to risk his life in order to save yours without any hesitation. Why do you refuse to take his calls Syd?"

"Jax is the reason Paul found me."

"Syd, be realistic. Paul could have found you anytime he wanted. He knew where you lived in Sea Isle before you even laid eyes on Jax. It would have taken very little effort to track you down. Paul saw an opportunity he wanted to take. How does it become Jax's fault?"

"Paul is someone I know and look what happened. Jax's celebrity is going to attract good and bad attention. There will be females obsessed with him and fans who want to be him. I cannot put myself in danger again. He will be busy during basketball season and on the road all the time, while I am stuck in a mansion all by myself."

"Well, you could travel with him, if you change your career."

"He will be preoccupied anyway. What kind of life is it to live in a hotel room, or home alone waiting for him to return?"

Nina answered, "You need to take time to reflect and think

about what you really want. It is completely normal to live your life while he is gone. No one expects you to sit idle and wait. Fill your time by doing activities you enjoy. Make some of your own dreams come true. You can find the answer to your dilemma by examining your feelings. How do you feel when you are with Jax?"

Sydney sighed. "He is absolutely a dream come true. Meeting him was a gift from God, but being the girlfriend or even the future wife of a basketball star is a demanding job. I honestly cannot say I am ready to take on such a big responsibility."

Nina put her hand on Sydney's. "You have valid concerns, however the career of a basketball player does not last long unless he is a superstar. Sometimes sacrifices are worth it. If he makes you happy, you have your answer. I am sure you can dig deep to figure out how to make this relationship work to your advantage. Travel to some of his away games, and make the most of the time you have together. Learn to spend time at home with him. Keep in mind traveling so often exhausts him, so when he is home, he may prefer to spend quiet time with you. It is not difficult to see Jax is one of a kind, but you need to figure it out on your own."

"Did I ever tell you how glad I am being blessed with you as my friend? Your advice is so important to me, not only because you are intuitive, but also since you have my best interests at heart. I need someone to keep it real, and not just tell me what they think I need to hear. I just need a little more time alone. I promise I will consider everything you told me and do some soul searching."

Following her discussion with Nina, Sydney decided she wanted to take the Bancroft students to a 76er's game, but needed to speak to someone in the organization first. She spoke to a representative at the Sixers facility and explained her desire to take the students to a game. She discussed the kids' sensory issues, how the crowd would be too overwhelming for them, and the need for more comfortable seats. To make her wish a reality, she suggested the possibility of providing the children with headphones to handle the noise, and little busy toys they could grab and play with during the game. Sydney also mentioned her research of other NBA teams' accommodations for children with sensory issues. One team set aside a separate room, without a view, as a sensory room so kids could go there and decompress if the game became too overwhelming. The public relations department worked with her, and the Sixers Management thought it was a great idea to help out the community and to give the kids a new opportunity. Up until this time, they stayed home and avoided public events, because of the crowd. Sydney recommended special bracelets for the kids so security would know they signified permission to wear headphones. Management would arrange for the kids to be let in at an employee entrance to avoid the crowds. From there they would be escorted to padded front row seats. The room would be ready by the end of February.

Sydney contacted her supervisor with the great news and arranged the outing for the Golden State Warriors game. Everyone was excited about her special project, and Good Morning Philadelphia wanted her on their show to talk about her charity and her recent work. The segment would be aired on the local news channels.

Syd felt a sense of accomplishment. It was a welcome distraction from the terrifying experience she had endured. She did something good for the children and the community.

Jax was thoroughly devastated, but had no time to spare to repair his personal life. His first priority was to finish out the basketball season. Sydney fulfilled his life and brought him so much happiness. They had a great relationship until Paul decided to destroy everything. If living without Sydney did not destroy him, Jax was left to live with the guilt of killing another man. Sure it was self defense, but Jax was not a violent man. There was no need to fight to prove he was a man. The only aggression regularly displayed was exclusive to the basketball court.

After Paul's death, Jax received a lot of unwanted attention in the headlines. The media praised him and was calling him a hero. If a hero felt like this, he wanted no part of the title. Looking down the barrel of a gun was the most terrifying thing that ever happened to me in my entire life. Death staring back at me and trying to wipe out my very existence was an ominous fear I had never experienced. My fight or flight instinct kicked in full force. As we were rolling around on the ground, I was wondering if the scales were tipping in my direction to live. I decided to bargain with the man upstairs. "Please God, tell me today is not my last day on this earth. Good things have happened in my life, but I have so much more to experience. I will do anything to be with Sydney. Let me live."

My heart was beating so fast it felt like it was trying to slam out of my chest. My hearing and sight were superhero strength. I had everything to live for, and I was not ready to die. In that moment of struggle, time seemed to stand still. My life did not flash before my eyes, but I did wonder about the future without me in it. Although my mind wandered, my body went into action with no distraction from the outside world. My emotions switched from fear to fucking pissed off anger. How dare this asshole try and end my life when he was just a worthless piece of shit not worthy of one more breath. The fight became the survival of the fittest, and I was more pissed off than him. My finger hit the trigger and pulled with every ounce of life left in my body. The deafening sound of the gun going off hit my eardrums. My ears were ringing, and I was temporarily deaf. There was blood all over me. Oh my God, was I shot? Nooooo! I really thought I won the fight! I tried so hard. Sorry Sydney. Babe, I tried.

Then I felt Paul's body slump and fall off of me. That is where all the blood came from. I was alive!

I really needed Sydney afterwards, but she was gone and I was all alone. I called my parents before they heard it on the news. They were ready to hop on the first plane back to me, but I assured them I was okay. It was a white lie, but it was necessary. There was no need for them to worry about me. The adrenaline eventually wore off, and I was filled with anxiety in the hours following the traumatic experience.

I waited a few days before texting Sydney. I tried to respect the fact she asked for space. When I did text her, my texts went unanswered. I sent flowers and gifts with the same response. I called Nina to get her advice, since I was unsuccessful. She said she would try and talk to Syd since she liked me and thought I was good for her. Nina told me to hang in there, and she would do her best.

A month passed, and I had a couple of days off. I wasted no time. I needed the rest, but needed Sydney more. I drove directly to Sea Isle and showed up unannounced at Sydney's door. Her parents answered and gladly let me in. I went up to her room, and she was reading in bed. My heart was skipping beats. God I missed her. She looked up at me and dropped her book on the floor.

Sydney appeared startled. "Jax what are you doing here?"

"Well let me see Syd. Where do I start? You refuse to answer my calls or texts, so you leave me with no choice. I am taking you home with me today, and I am not asking but rather telling you. I miss you, and I am tired of living alone."

"I am not so sure I want to come back Jax. I think the celebrity life is too much for me."

"What a bunch of bullshit, and you know it. Paul did not come after you because you were with a celebrity."

"Maybe not, but it is how he found me."

"I totally disagree with you. Paul would have found you whenever he chose to find you. He knows where you live in Sea Isle. He was just biding his time for the perfect moment."

"Maybe you are right. It all has been so traumatic for me. I was almost raped. You have no idea the agony I am going through!"

"Oh please! God dammit Sydney! Are you fucking kidding me? You act as if everything happened to you. Boo fucking hoo. I was there too, remember!? If you are looking to play the blame game, I was forced to stare down the barrel of a cold metal gun and fight for my life in a struggle to save yours. Would it have happened to me otherwise? I think not. Fame had nothing to do with it! Paul would have come after you no matter who you were dating. I have been dealing with the anxiety and guilt of killing a man. And the worst part was not the fact I could have died that night. The worst part was you deserting me as if I did something wrong. Somehow I became the bad guy. I may as well be dead!"

The flood gates opened and Sydney started to cry. Jax cursed under his breath. The last thing he wanted to do was hurt her or make her cry. He simply wanted her to see his point of view. Jax sat on the bed and gathered her into his arms and kissed her hair as he held her head against his chest.

Her sobs continued as Jax hugged her and told her it was okay. He tilted her face up toward his and kissed away the remainder of her tears.

Jax said, "Listen Sydney, it is no one's fault except Paul's that any of this happened. I am so sorry I made you cry. I was so frustrated to be blamed for something completely out of my control. We were there together and should have stayed together. We belong with each other and can handle anything life throws at us. I cannot bear having you out of my life. Giving you time and space is the hardest thing I ever had to do. If you refuse to come back to me then Paul should have just finished me off in his apartment. I love you!"

"I love you too Jax and was so miserable without you! I am so sorry for being selfish and not giving a second thought about how any of this affected you. I am so disappointed in my behavior."

"You do not need to apologize. I just wanted you to realize you were not alone. We both went through a traumatic experience and need each other for support. If I am on a road trip, then feel free to have Nina or your parents over to the house or come down here."

"Good idea, and I promise never to leave you again Jax. I never did get a chance to thank you for saving my life."

"I would gladly do it again Sydney."

"Thank you. Can you help me pack?"

"Darling, I thought you would never ask."

The two of them began to kiss and enjoyed making out like two teenagers. There was plenty of time to pack later.

∞∞∞

Sydney was overjoyed to be back at the house with Jax. There was no need to ask anyone to stay with her. She had plenty to keep her busy when Jax was on the road. Her supervisor welcomed her back to Bancroft with no questions asked. The kids loved Sydney and were delighted to see her again. Her work continued with the 76er's organization to create the special room and accommodations for the kids. Sydney felt exhilarated and wanted everything to be perfect. She arranged a big fundraising event to bring awareness to the community.

She planned a fun night for both the kids and adults with dancing and games. The kids would be free to walk around, and the music would be controlled so it would not be too overwhelming. Sydney was able to get a few local businesses to donate a portion of the night's proceeds to the Autism Foundation. The local movie theater was also offering a day a week to show movies to kids with sensory issues. The lights would be kept on, and the speakers would be at a reasonable volume. Talking during the movie would be acceptable, and kids could get up and walk around as necessary. The local newspapers and news stations praised Sydney's hard work and progress. She explained her goal was to help the children and to allow them to enjoy nights out like other children. The only press she desired was to bring more attention to the children and to recognize their special needs, allowing them to live a normal life.

The kids were thrilled. Sydney talked about the dance party and the upcoming basketball game outing every day to help them become comfortable with the idea of going out. She also incorporated basketball in her lessons and showed the kids pictures and informed them how the game was played. She bought them soft mini basketballs to play with. The kids helped make decorations for the dance. They also made artwork and crafts.

Sydney was so proud of them. Everyone wanted to dress up for the dance, which was being held in the school cafeteria. There was a huge turnout. A projector was set up to make the ceiling look like a starry sky. Lava lamps were on the tables as well as kaleidoscopes. A lounge area was in one corner with throw pillows, bean bags and flip sofas. Other tables had pizza, snacks and drinks for guests. The idea was to let everyone do what made them happy. There was no set schedule. A dance floor with a DJ was open for dancing. It was a very fun and enjoyable atmosphere.

∞∞∞

Jax decided to surprise Sydney by showing up to the dance following practice. He wore a blue pin striped suit with a light blue striped shirt and fancy brown oxford shoes. When he walked into the cafeteria, he was amazed at the transformation. The ambiance was very comfortable and inviting. Sydney and the kids should be happy with their accomplishments . The night was a success judging by the smiles in the room. Everyone was having a great time. His eyes quickly scanned the room and found Sydney. Her smile was so big and could light up the entire room. She wore a stunning blue dress with a sweetheart neckline and a full skirt. Her dark hair was pulled back, but her curls refused to be contained. Tendrils of hair touched her face.

Sydney was so stunning and took his breath away with her beauty. When their eyes met, it was as if the rest of the room disappeared. Her smile melted his heart and made him weak in the knees. He smiled back at her, and they slowly walked toward each other. She grabbed his hand and tugged him onto the dance floor. *All of Me* started to play by John Legend. I pulled Syd in close and we danced. The closeness of her body made my heart race. She looked up at me and smiled. She knew the effect she was having on me. I whispered, "Wait until I get you home."

"Promises, promises."

"I hope you are not busy later, since I plan on devouring every inch of your body."

She looked up at me with a devilish smile and her cheeks were flushed. "Nope, no plans. I look forward to it."

I pulled her in tighter so she could feel my hardness against her leg.

"Oh, you are a bad boy indeed. I will need to put it to good use."

My lips touched hers and I playfully tugged on her bottom lip with my teeth and then kissed her.

The kids were cheering and ran over to us for a big group hug. The song changed to one with a faster beat. We separated and danced with the kids in a big circle. Every person was up on their feet dancing and singing. It was the last song of an amazing night.

∞∞∞

Sydney was applying makeup to get ready to leave for work. Thanks to Jax she was running late. It was well worth it. He needed to leave for an away game in San Antonio against the Spurs. He made her so happy. Syd would not be able to wipe the smile off her face today, even if she tried. It was hard to believe she almost convinced herself that Jax and his lifestyle were the wrong fit for her.

She had been back at his house with their two young pups for a month now. Correction, their house. Jax helped her become the independent, confident woman who was smiling back at her in the mirror. Sydney was emotionally dependent on him but would not want it any other way. When he was home, she wanted to spend as much time with him as possible. And when he was away, Sydney kept herself busy with the autism foundation, teaching, working on lesson plans, reading, and running the household. Sydney's goal was to make Jax's life as easy as possible during the basketball season. He had enough on his mind training, practicing, and playing the game. She empathized with him knowing how hard it must be to live up to his fans' expectations in his rookie year. If a professional basketball career was not challenging enough, Jax decided to take on a new relationship too. She was so glad he valued her and their relationship enough to keep her around.

While Jax was out of town, Sydney arranged for a contractor to come to the house. She had a surprise in store for Jax when he returned from Texas.

Two days later Jax walked through the front door of the house, and Sydney was in the foyer enthusiastically waiting for him. She quickly blindfolded him and grabbed his hand.

"Wow Babe. I barely put one foot through the door and you are trying to get me out of my clothes. Slow down girl. I will be home for a short stretch of time."

"Funny guy. Always jumping to conclusions. Give me your hand, and follow my lead Jax. I have a surprise for you, so no peeking. C'mon."

"What are you up to Syd?"

"That is for me to know and you to find out. Zip your lip. No more questions. Get to steppin." She led him to the indoor swimming pool. Jax immediately smelled the chlorine.

"Syd, I am not dressed for swimming, and swimming blindfolded is not a smart idea."

"Hush. Jaxon. Let me remove your blindfold now."

Jax was absolutely amazed at the vision before him. Sydney transformed the pool room into a tropical oasis. There were palm trees and little gardens set up with twinkling white lights and winding paver paths in between the gardens. A hammock was tied to two trees with sand underneath. Big rocks were set up in a semi circle where the pool curved and yellow and orange pillows were set up against the rocks. A fire pit was in the comfy lounge area. On one end of the pool there were tiki torches and a teak table and chairs. Two grilled steaks with french fries and colorful cocktails with little umbrellas were on the table. Reggae music was piping through the speakers. The other side of the pool had a reclining queen size lounge bed enclosed in sheer curtains. His eyes could not believe what he was seeing. "Oh my God! This is spectacular!! When did you find the time to pull this off?"

"Oh.... you know.... in my spare time. I managed. I figured if there was no time to go to paradise, we should bring it to us. Are you mad? I know I should have asked since it is your house, but then it would ruin the surprise."

"Mad? Quite the opposite. I love it! Are you kidding me? Second of all, this is your house as well. I am so incredibly happy. Speechless actually. This room is so fabulous like you. Thank you so much."

Sydney was jumping up and down, and jumped into his arms and gave him a big kiss. "We should eat. I am starved."

"Good idea. But only if we can spend the rest of the night in here."

"Deal."

∞∞∞

Sydney loved how the relationship was getting better and stronger as time went on. They had good communication, trust, honesty and a mutual respect for each other. There was an abundance of happiness too. Any time spent together was quality time, and they savored every second.

There was just a small nagging feeling refusing to go away. Was it just her or was Jax acting really shady lately? Maybe it was her imagination. She confided to Nina about it, but Nina said she was over analyzing as usual.

"Sorry Nina. Everything has been going so well since I moved back into the house, and I just do not want to lose his interest. You are a great friend. I really have no idea what I would do without you."

"I love you too Syd. Now go get ready. You have your last meeting with the parents before the big night tomorrow."

"Of course, you are right. I want the night to be flawless tomorrow. My goal is for the kids to have a great time. I worked so hard to make it perfect, and Jax has been really busy lately. I just needed someone to talk to and help me put things in perspective."

"Call me anytime." Nina said.

Sydney was getting ready in the bathroom when Jax came home.

"Babe is that you?" Sydney said.

"Oh you are home Syd? I thought you had a meeting tonight."

"I do. I am leaving in a couple minutes. I thought you had practice."

"Yea I wanted to stop home real quick to wish you luck tonight. We had a break and then another session" Jax said.

Syd thought his statement was odd since he just seemed surprised to find her home, but she let it go. She wrapped her arms around Jax and gave him a long, lingering kiss. She felt the familiar longing.

Jax said, "Get out of here before we are both late. This can only end one way and you know it."

Sydney let him go and said, "Okay, okay, point taken. See you later on."

Meanwhile, Nina was at home and had just hung up with Sydney. She had to take a deep breath as she leaned against the wall. She hated lying to her best friend but it was for her own good. Syd would understand Nina had no other choice. She did not possess the self control to say no.

∞∞∞

Jax had to make sure Syd was gone before he made the call he needed to make. He could not afford to get caught. Nina answered on the third ring.

"Hey what's up good looking?" Nina giggled.

"Right back at you. By the way, Syd will be occupied tonight. Do you have time to meet?"

Nina said, "My schedule is wide open. Where do you want to meet?"

"I was thinking something low key. I cannot take a chance of being recognized, and we do not want Syd to find out. It would destroy her."

"I know her better than you do. Stop worrying. She confides in me all the time. I would be the first to know if she suspects anything. My lips are sealed. I will meet you at the parking garage at 7th and Sansom in Center City. Just dress down and wear a baseball cap and sunglasses. We need to make it quick."

Jax said, "Are you sure this is a good idea?"

"Listen, it is the best thing for Sydney especially with your hectic schedule. Stop second guessing yourself. Your nerves will pass after it is done. After all, this is not something you do everyday."

"Okay, you are right. If I am going through with this, at least it is with someone Sydney is friends with instead of a stranger."

"Nina laughed and said, now you are thinking. See you soon Jax. In this case, what Syd does not know will not hurt her."

Chapter 10 - Game Changer

I t was Saturday, March 5th and the big night had arrived. The Sixers were playing the Golden State Warriors and Sydney's autistic students were going to the game to test out the new quiet room and watch the game. She did not have an opportunity to see Jax all day, and her texts went unanswered. Maybe he was simply too busy to answer. The annoying little voice inside her head said he was avoiding her, but she had no time to deal with it today. There was too much to be accomplished. She spent the day on the phone with the Sixers liaison and the Autism Foundation tying up loose ends.

The doorbell rang after her last call. There was a package at the front door. She opened the box, and there was a pair of jeans with white sneakers and a Jax Jones jersey. Under the clothes was a fancy, wrapped gift box. She tore off the wrapping, and it was a silver necklace with a diamond cut silver basketball. Jax was full of surprises. He was so thoughtful. Or was the gift bought out of guilt? Ugh, paranoia and jealousy were getting the best of her again. She really had to stop the nonsense. There was no need to create problems. She texted him real quick to thank him for thinking of her on such a special day. She loved the outfit and the necklace and planned to wear them proudly.

Everything was coming together nicely and on schedule. A bus would take them to a special entrance where the players entered to avoid the crowds. The kids would be given headphones to put on before they entered the building. There was a new VIP seating area at center court usually reserved for the press. Tonight, and for future games, it would be given to children with sensory issues. There was a promotional box converted into a quiet room. Tonight Sydney, the children, and the Autism Foundation would be honored.

The kids were wearing the headphones and clapping when the players walked out for warm ups. Jax smiled proudly at Syd and walked over to the kids to give them Jax Jones jerseys and mini soft basketballs. The announcer told the audience about the new quiet room and VIP section for special needs children. The crowd gave Sydney a standing ovation to recognize her efforts.

The timing was perfect for Sydney to attend this game. She was hype to see Steph Curry play and was even more excited Jax would have more playing time, since one of the players in the starting lineup was injured. Jax needed to take this opportunity to shine.

∞∞∞

Jax was nervous. Sydney was so happy to be at the game for her kids and to see him play. He knew he was going to have to tell her, but the thought of doing so made him sick. How would she react to the news? This certainly was not the time to think about it. He had an important game to play.

He missed some easy buckets. These were easy layups he made all the time. Sydney wore a concerned look on her face. Jax tried to give her a reassuring smile and nod as he went by to let her know everything was okay. At halftime, the 76er Dunk Squad did maneuvers and jumps off the mini trampolines and performed awesome trick shots. The crowd was very entertained and having a great time.

After the first squad completed their turn, the lights turned down and back up as the announcer said, "And here is Jax Jones who wanted to try a trick of his own." Jax had been practicing all week. He ran and jumped up and passed the ball to the next guy as he did a flip. That guy flew in and did a dunk.

Sydney was astonished. What was Jax doing? Did he lose his mind? He was not himself all week, and now he was doing acrobatics and missing baskets during the game. Did he forget he was playing in the NBA? Maybe he spent too much time practicing a trick for halftime instead of working on his game. She was concerned although she had to admit, he was incredible.

He walked over to Sydney and grabbed her hand. He led her out to the court. She pulled back. What the hell was he doing? She sternly whispered in his ear. "I am going to kill you. Why the hell are you dragging me out on the floor in front of all these people?" Jax laughed in response. "Go ahead and giggle like a six year old. Cut it out and let me go." It fell on deaf ears as he kept pulling an unwilling Sydney.

The crowd was paying attention and started to laugh. They began to clap and cheer to encourage Sydney to follow Jax onto the court. Apparently they wanted Jax to let them in on his little secret. There was a chair sitting in the key. Jax gently sat her down, and the guys handed him a microphone and he walked over to me. What was he doing? The rest of the Sixers came out of the locker room. Halftime was not even over. She was going to let him know exactly what she thought later. How dare he embarrass her in front of thousands of people. She hoped to God halftime was not being televised. Sydney felt like she could not breathe. She was having a panic attack. His words interrupted her thoughts.

"When I first laid eyes on you in the club, you took my breath away. You are extremely beautiful with your dark, curly

hair and big brown eyes. I was watching you dance, and your smile and laugh captivated me. Your laugh was contagious and made me want to laugh with you. I knew in that moment I wanted to spend time with you, so I could be the person putting the smile on your face. You are stunning and have such charisma. You live in the moment and possess so much love for life. I treasure the time I spend with you and never want it to end. You had no idea who I was when we met and were attracted to me as a small town farmer named Jackson Jones from Elgin, Texas. You love me for me, and not because I am a professional basketball player.

The best decision I ever made was asking you to move in with me. Our relationship has been far from easy with me traveling all over the country and putting basketball before you. You learned to trust me and found a passion to help autistic children in your spare time. You worked with the Sixers' organization to help create a way for autistic children to attend basketball games like any other child. You are so thoughtful, nurturing and the most unselfish woman I know. Our children will be lucky to have you as a mother someday.

I love you Sydney. You are one of a kind and such an amazing woman. I cannot tell you how many NBA seasons you will have to share me with the sport and my fans. Life with me will always be full of challenges, though I can meet them if you are willing to face them with me. We need to cherish each and every moment we have together. I promise to be *the man you always dreamed of marrying growing up. I know I cannot offer you a normal relationship, however I promise to love you, take care of you, provide for you, and protect you. After my career is over, I promise to spend all of my time with you. There are so many ways to be happy in life, but all the money and fame in the world could not compare to spending my life with you. Sydney Fox, I love you not only for who you are, but also for the man I am with you. Will you marry me?"*

Sydney had to ask herself if this was really happening, or was it just a dream. It felt like a fairy tale. And his speech blew Jerry Maguire's out of the water. She looked around and saw Nina on the sidelines. Next to her were her parents and Jax's parents. So this is why Jax was being so shady. She felt silly thinking something was going on with Jax. She thought he was up to no good when he was planning the biggest surprise of her life. His words touched her heart and soul. Tears of happiness were running down her cheeks. The crowd was going wild applauding and cheering, "Say yes!" She jumped up out of the chair and threw her arms around Jax. In between kisses and crying, she was yelling "Yes!" into the microphone. If it was even possible, the entire arena erupted into louder cheering and applause. They were glad to be a part of Jax's secret. The jumbotron showed Jax pulling out the most beautiful ring Sydney had ever seen and gently slid it on her finger.

They were kissing again as Ed Sheeran's *Perfect* played. Sydney's kids came out to the floor and each one was holding a rose. They each gave her a hug and handed her a rose. Sydney was so touched. This was such a special night. After the song was over Coach Brown grabbed the microphone.

"Congratulations Sydney and Jax. You make a great couple and I wish you many years of happiness. On behalf of the Sixers organization, I wanted to thank you for working with our liaison to set up the section and room for special needs children. They seem to be really enjoying themselves. Now if you have no objections, I need to steal your fiance away from you so we can win a game."

Sydney's parents, Jax's parents, and Nina rushed over and gave their congratulations and went back to the seats with her. Sydney turned to Nina. "Thank you so much for being a part of this special day. You managed to keep a huge secret!"

"I prayed I would not ruin the surprise. The easiest way to accomplish my mission was to avoid talking to you. Of course you called me, so I kept the conversation as short as possible. Sorry Syd, I am sure you realized something was off, but at least I did not divulge the big news. I was grateful when Jax asked me to go ring shopping with him. He figured I would know your style and taste. The man had no spending limit. I have to say, I enjoyed shopping without a budget immensely. It took very little time to pick out your ring, since it seemed like it was made for you."

It was perfect and she loved it so much. The ring was a 1.5 carat solitaire diamond with diamonds in the channel circling around like an eternity band. It sparkled so much, and she was unable to stop staring at it. "Jax wanted to get you a bigger diamond, but I stopped him at 1.5 carats.

"I am so glad you did. This is perfect and entirely my style. I would not desire a huge rock on my hand. You did a splendid job!" They hugged it out, laughing and crying at the same time.

The crowd was hype. Second half was about to start.

The announcers were keeping the home viewers up to date. "If you just started watching tonight's game, Jax Jones asked his girlfriend Sydney Fox to marry him during halftime. The Wells Fargo Center is packed to capacity with 20,318 in attendance. They were not disappointed when she accepted. Coach Brown was relieved when she finally said yes, so Jax could get his head back in the game."

The score stayed close, and the fans picked a great game to come and see. It was always exciting to watch the Golden State Warriors. The fourth quarter was about to get underway. The announcers were totally hype.

"We are in the fourth quarter of this entertaining game. The Sixers are impressive and have been matching the Warriors point for point the entire game, and giving them a fight. This is Jax Jones' first big game in the starting rotation. His teammate Richaun Holmes is injured, so this is his chance to step up. Curry passes to Green who is covered. Green passes to Barnes who fires away, and it is short off the front of the rim. The Sixers have been superb dealing with this dangerous Golden State offense. McConnell gets the ball, dribbles down court, and passes to Redick. He gets the ball open in the corner and lets it fly for the three. That makes it back to back threes for Redick. Curry has the ball and passes to Barnes who answers with a three of his own. Sixers have the ball. Jax passes to Covington who gets inside and misses at the rim. Iguodala comes up with the rebound and passes to Curry. Curry bounce passes to Barnes who is stripped down low by the rookie Jaxon Jones! Jones takes it coast to coast and scores with a thunderous jam over top of Green!! Jones just put Green on a poster!

Curry takes the ball and looks to pass to an open teammate . Barnes gets the ball and is immediately trapped in the corner. This leaves Curry wide open. Big Mistake! He fires from way downtown; BANG the Warriors lead now extends to four at the Wells Fargo Center! Curry is the player they need to worry about and defend. Those are the shots he can shoot and make all day long. He is dangerous, especially when he is hot. What a game!

It feels like a playoff game. McConnell is covered but passes it to Jax who passes it to Covington who sets up the alley oop back to Jax. The crowd is going wild, and the entire stadium is on their feet. The score is 100-98, Warriors with the advantage, with less than a minute left to play. It is so loud in here, and the fans are loving it. This place is electric!!

Iguodala has the ball and throws down court to Curry. Curry goes up to shoot and is fouled by Covington on the three point line. Curry goes to the foul line. The first shot goes in. And so does the second. Curry is an excellent free throw shooter. The score is now 102-98 with the Warriors up. Jax takes the ball down the lane looking to shoot, but has to pass to Covington who passes it across his body back to Jax with twenty seconds left. Jax shoots the three and gets fouled by Green, and the ball goes in anyway! What a play by Jones as he has a chance at a four point play late in the game to tie it! The crowd has been on their feet since Jax's alley oop. Jones shoots, and the ball goes in. We have a tie game 102 all. The Sixers are 21 and 37 and the Warriors are 54 and 4 this season.

Warrior's have the ball. Jax cuts off Curry's crossover, and then strips the ball on the second move. He drives the ball down court and finishes with a reverse layup. It is a costly turnover that Curry cannot make in this late game situation. Sixers are leading by two. Curry dribbles down court and is immediately double teamed as the Sixers do not want to let up a game winning three. This is a bad decision as Barnes is left wide open in the corner. One second left. Barnes takes the shot as the final second ticks off and the ball circles the rim and falls out. The Sixers miraculously win the ball game with an excellent effort by the young rookie Jaxon Jones. He used his time well, and tonight was definitely his night to shine. I am sure he made quite the impression on Coach Brown and should see more playing time as a result of his efforts. The Sixers took advantage crashing the boards and played aggressive against a team who has been winning effortlessly all season.

The Warriors play a fundamental game, are unselfish passers, and they maintain composure under pressure. They have perfected the basic skills of the game, which is why they are so successful. The Sixers presented a challenge and fought hard for the last second victory. Jax Jones played a very impressive game. Richaun Holmes hurt his knee a few weeks ago when a fellow teammate fell into his leg in a season ending injury. The rookie is stepping up for his team and did a great job filling the spot. Coach Brown should be very proud. The Sixers did a great job of anticipating first and reacting accordingly tonight. For the first time, they actually looked like Eastern Conference contenders.

This is a young team to watch out for in the future. Embiid has brought excitement to Philadelphia which has been missing since Allen Iverson played. Now you have Jax Jones and whoever is drafted next year. The Sixers may have the resources to build another Dream Team. The City of Philadelphia has a great win to celebrate. Jax Jones gained a new fiancee, and the crowd truly received their money's worth tonight. The rookie received some negative press a couple months ago for bad behavior, however it seems as if it is all behind him.

People tend to be quick to jump to conclusions, yet they do not realize the stress a rookie player has to endure in his first year. It is hard enough for any player who is not a superstar, let alone one who was just drafted. There are high expectations from fans and coaches. On top of that, a player must deal with travel, training and practice. The pressure of remaining on a team is extremely intense. The NBA only requires twenty four hours notice to a player who is being traded. You can be playing in one city and find out you are no longer on the team and no longer living in that city. An NBA player has no time to find a new home or get comfortable. He is expected to get on a plane and travel to his new city immediately to report to his new team. Sometimes significant others and kids are left behind until a decision is made with regard to moving, in order for everyone to be together. You do not want to act hastily until you are sure you will remain in your new city. Transitions are far from easy.

The life expectancy of an average NBA player is less than five years unless you are one of the greats like Jordan, LeBron, Kobe, Malone, and Shaq. The rookie year is so difficult. I have no idea how he even found time for a relationship. Well Jax Jones should be proud of himself. The fame has not gone to his head, and he is always trying to be a better person and a player. I think he has earned his spot on this Sixers team. I think he will be able to call Philadelphia home for a long time. Congratulations Jax and Sydney."

As soon as he shook hands with everyone after the game, Jax headed over to Sydney and gave her a big kiss, lifting her off of her feet. Steph Curry cleared his throat and interrupted. "Hey man, I just wanted to come over and congratulate you both. It was an exciting night and a great game. I was happy to witness your proposal. Jax you played really well. Hang in there. The rookie year is the hardest. At times it can feel overwhelming, and you question whether it was all worth it. Keep working hard, stay positive, and remain true to yourself. The frustration of your rookie year will pay off. You are part of a winning culture with Coach Brown, and he will help you develop into a great player. Your fiance will give you the moral support you need. Congratulations again. I wish you both the best of luck."

Jax said, "Thank you so much. I appreciate your kind words. It means a lot. My rookie year has been much more difficult than I could have expected. I made some mistakes, and am doing my best not to repeat them. Hey, I am glad you came over. Sydney is a huge fan of yours. I think she was more excited to see you play than watching me." Sydney slapped Jax on the arm and laughed.

Steph laughed and said, "Oh boy, I do not want to be the cause of your first fight after the engagement." He took off his #30 jersey and asked someone for a pen. He signed the jersey and slipped it over Sydney's head, and gave her a kiss on the cheek. "It was great meeting you both. I better get to the locker room."

It was easy to see Steph made Sydney's night. She could not stop smiling. Jax said, "Thanks a lot. Figures he has to one up me. Good thing Steph did not propose first, or I would have been out of luck. You could not possibly possess the willpower to turn him down."

"Oh please. You can handle a little competition."

Jax had fun teasing Syd. "We should grab some dinner when I am done and celebrate. Tell everyone my treat." He kissed her again and ran off to the locker room.

Both sets of parents and Nina ran over, and everyone was talking at the same time. Sydney asked Jax's parents if they knew about the proposal.

"Yes. He told us he was ready to ask you to marry him. He said he wanted to choose the perfect time and asked for everyone's blessings. Jaxon flew us in so we could be here for the big night. It just so happened the timing worked out perfectly. He was able to start in the game, get his big chance, and propose to the love of his life. He certainly used his time to play his best. I would say he had the best night in more ways than one! Sydney, we are so delighted you said yes! We could not have hand picked a better match for our son. We wish you both the best of luck. You both have a very promising future."

"Thank you so much. You are all too kind. I am so happy everyone was included in the engagement. Jax did a great job with the proposal, and I was truly surprised. I am sure it will be on the news too! Oh excuse my bad manners, I am so sorry I forgot to introduce you to my best friend. Mary and Frank this is my best friend Nina and her boyfriend Chenzo."

Syd's parents said Jax drove to Sea Isle to ask Rob if he would give his approval for Jax to marry Sydney. Rob had absolutely no objections. It was an easy decision after seeing how his daughter suffered with Paul. Jax was a good man and perfect for his baby girl. Rob was confident Jax would love and take care of Sydney no matter what the circumstance. He did not possess a mean bone in his body.

They were all enjoying each other's company when Jax strolled out of the locker room all dressed up in a stylish black suit with a white shirt and a red tie. He handed Sydney a large gift wrapped box.

"What is this? Another gift? I think you spoiled me enough for one night. You are so full of surprises Jax!" Everyone anxiously awaited as she opened the box and pulled out a beautiful dress. "Oh my God Jax, I love it! It is beautiful!"

"Well since you had no idea what was really going on tonight, I wanted to dress you for our celebration dinner. I was pretty confident you would say yes."

"You really did think of everything. Oh, and you were so sure I was going to say yes," Sydney teased playfully.

"You better say yes after I flew my parents in from Texas. That would have been a big disappointment to fly all the way to Philadelphia just to hear you say no." He laughed and gave her a slap on her ass. "Now go get changed so we can all go out and eat. You better get used to being bossed around. I am getting a kick out of it."

They both laughed. Sydney asked, "But what about the kids?"

Nina said, "I have you covered Syd. You guys go out, and I will make sure everyone gets home okay.

Sydney's parents said, "You kids go and enjoy yourself. There is plenty of time for us to go out another time."

Jax's parents agreed, "Yes, go have fun. We will see you tomorrow. You get very little time alone, so go and take advantage of it to celebrate."

∞∞∞

Jax showed Sydney where to change, and he happily waited outside the room for her. As she walked back into the room, he was blown away and left speechless by her presence alone. She was a knockout with an off the shoulder form fitting fire engine red dress. The sleeves came down three quarters of the way and then flared into a bell sleeve. The length of the dress hit right above the knee. Her dark curly hair complemented the red dress, and she was dangerously seductive. Sydney possessed an inner beauty which intensified her physical beauty, and she had no idea the effect she had on me. My thoughts were interrupted. She was standing in front of me in bare feet and cleared her throat, "Umm, I have no shoes."

He smiled and handed her another bag. Inside were black Michael Kors criss cross open toe heels. Sydney giggled and put them on. Jax commented, "I love buying you gifts just to see your reaction. And since I am doing so well, here is one last gift."

She opened the box and began jumping up and down. He made her deliriously happy. "Oh my God. These are so beautiful Jax." They were elegant dangling crystal teardrop earrings. The necklace was silver with a solid crystal heart with a thin line of pave diamonds running through the center, turning into a pave heart so the two were joined together. "I absolutely love it!" Sydney kissed him on the lips long and hard.

She emotionally seduced me, and it took every ounce of control to break away. "Stop kissing me, and let me help you with your necklace before I rip all of your clothes off." They both laughed in amusement as Jax secured the clasp. "Every time you wear this, remember our special night, and how I loved you enough to give you my heart." He stepped back and grabbed her hands. Her left ring finger was sparkling with the new engagement ring. His fiancee looked gorgeous and was glowing from head to toe. She belonged to him and was completely irresistible.

They arrived at the Pyramid Club in Center City and were seated at a window table overlooking the entire city. The Club was on the 52nd floor of the Mellon Center Building and had a panoramic view where you could see the city for miles. The top of the Mellon Center was a glass pyramid. The lights of the city enhanced the view, making it even more spectacular. We spotted William Penn, the Art Museum, University of Penn campus, Penns Landing, and even the New Jersey waterfront. The dining room was pretty deserted because of the hour. The service was slow, allowing the food and conversation to be savored. A bottle of Shiraz was brought over and poured for them. They started with Chesapeake Oysters served on bread and aioli. Next they had a delicious pear salad. Steak and lobster was served for dinner. For dessert, a scrumptious chocolate mousse pyramid and New York cheesecake was brought out.

The restaurant was very elegant and the food was presented beautifully. Sydney had to hand it to Jax. Women dream of getting engaged and married from the time they are little girls. In her wildest dreams, she could not have imagined a proposal so well thought out and surprising. Jax proposed to her in front of a live crowd and millions of viewers. The entire night was so special, and it was one she would never forget.

∞∞∞

The next morning, Jax expected to see his proposal on the front page of the sports section. Instead, Steph Curry was kissing Sydney on the cheek, and she was wearing his jersey. The caption read, "The Sixers May Have Won the Game, but Steph Curry Steals the Girl." Jax chuckled. "Very clever!"

Jax wanted to pamper Sydney, so he made her breakfast. He brought a tray into the bedroom. She just woke up and was lazily yawning and stretching in bed.

"Well good morning sleepy head. I brought you some breakfast and the morning paper. I figured you worked up quite an appetite after our late night session."

Sydney blushed and laughed. "Yes, thank you. It was a great workout. Yum. What do you have there? I am ravenous."

"It is breakfast for two. I have a cheese and bacon omelet, pancakes, and french toast. And of course some coffee to keep you awake."

"I can get used to being spoiled rotten. I am going to love being married to you. Smells delicious. Let's eat." Sydney unfolded the newspaper and laughed uncontrollably when she saw the sports section. "Jax, this is hilarious! Oh my God! I am framing this picture. How fitting is it Steph Curry was part of our engagement? I could not have planned a better night."

"What do you mean? I compose a great proposal convincing you to marry me. I put in a tremendous amount of work and effort. Steph simply walks over, says congratulations, and steals the spotlight away from me. You turn all googly eyed and smile at him like a star struck teenager." Jax was giggling the whole time, still trying to keep his composure to act serious. "To top it all off, you make the front page of the newspaper with another man. What the hell?!!" They were both doubled over laughing hysterically now.

"Jealousy suits you." Sydney responded. "Just remember, I said yes to you Jax. After all, you gave me a diamond ring."

Jax gave Sydney a kiss before she turned the page and saw a picture of Jax proposing to her. Details were given about the proposal along with a summary of the game. "It is hard to believe my picture is in the newspaper with two NBA stars, and our engagement is celebrity news. This is extraordinary!"

"Get used to it Babe. I am certain you will see yourself all over the internet and sports and gossip magazines."

"Oh my goodness! They will surely say how Jaxon Jones, the rookie, heartthrob Texan, just broke thousands of hearts across the country last night."

"Thousands? Give me a little credit. I think you meant millions!" Jax laughed.

Sydney gave Jax a nudge and a playful punch, and they both fell over laughing again.

Epilogue

Two months later.....

Jax and Sydney did not want a long, drawn out engagement, so no time was wasted. They decided to get married in Paradise Island, Bahamas. The week before the big day was spent vacationing alone at the beautiful Ocean Club. We were in a luxurious private villa with a fold away wall giving open air access to the beach. Our own private infinity pool was absolutely to die for. It was difficult to tell where the pool ended and the ocean began. The sand was white, and the water was the prettiest shade of blue and crystal clear. Palm trees enhanced the tropical feel and ambiance.

The hotel possessed a one of a kind amenity, a Versailles outdoor garden. The garden was luxurious and majestic, like a jewel in paradise. There were multi level gardens with Bermuda grass and stunning purple bougainvillea plants and bright, colorful hibiscus adorning each level. The bougainvillea is a tropical vine with fancy climbing flowers and was very decorative. Hibiscus plants always remind me of Hawaii with beautiful women wearing flowers in their hair. The manicured, formal gardens were a recreation of a French Garden with rock ridges, stone steps and columns, plants, bronze and marble statues, fountains and lily ponds. The colors were absolutely flawless with purples, blues, greens and grays. Everywhere I looked, each view was more spectacular than the next.

Jax surprised me by booking the wedding at the Cloisters. The Cloisters was formerly a French monastery transported to Paradise Island piece by piece. The surprising part to me was how I could be on a tropical paradise island and with one step was transported back to a medieval time, as if I stepped into a time machine. It was a stunning garden with a French gothic architecture resembling a mini colosseum with steps descending to a gazebo at the water's edge. The roofless design of the cloister was from the 14th century and appeared to be Roman. It sat on high ground, and the white marble columns formed a square with arches between each column. The arches were like windows, offering a breathtaking view of the harbor. Each terraced area was captivating with purple flowering clipped bougainvillea hedges. The area was heavenly and tranquil. The vibrant colors still stand out in my mind and put a smile on my face.

The gazebo where we were to be married was a stone and marble open structure with a stone path leading up to and around the gazebo. There were six columns, and the top of the gazebo was elegant wrought iron vines in the shape of a dome open to the sky. There was a pretty white picket fence with an opening at the gazebo overlooking the harbor. The path leading from the Cloisters to the gazebo was adorned with palm trees.

"Jax, this wedding venue is bigger than any of my childhood hopes and dreams. I feel like a fairytale princess about to marry her prince. This garden is prettier than the Garden of Eden. It is pure heaven."

"Then you must be my angel," Jax replied as he twirled Sydney around and kissed her.

∞∞∞

The next morning, I went to my parent's room to get ready for the wedding. I was surprisingly calm. As I opened the door, I was welcomed with Jimmy Buffet music. Mom was in a festive mood, which was perfect for the occasion. We gave ourselves plenty of time to get ready, so there would be no need to rush.

Nina did my makeup and hair as my mom lovingly looked at me and told me how beautiful I looked. She had tears in her eyes.

"Mom, cut it out! You will have me crying if you start this right now."

"Sorry honey. I will try my best. I love you so much and am so proud of you."

I kissed her on the cheek. "Thank you mom. I love you too. If you are proud of me then you have no need to cry. This is a happy occasion for all of us, so you should only be laughing or smiling when I look at you."

"Okay sweetheart. I am going to have the best time today. How about we drink to good times?"

The three of us drank a couple mimosas and ate some fruit, since our appetite was not so big. We relaxed in our robes and enjoyed each other's company until it was time to get dressed.

Nina brought Vincenzo as her wedding date and excitedly told us all about him. They were pretty serious, and I was so happy for her. She finally found an equal partner, and they truly appreciated each other. They recently moved in together in a brand new townhouse, and the transition went very smooth. There were discussions of marriage, although they preferred to wait a couple years in order to take pleasure in dating first. She lucked out and picked a good guy this time around. Vincenzo was a good communicator and very thoughtful. He knew how to make Nina feel special and loved and was definitely a keeper. Jax and I would definitely be spending more time with Nina and Chenzo after the honeymoon.

When it was time to get dressed, Sydney helped her mom and

Nina. After they were done, they helped Sydney slip into her dress. They had one final group hug before they left the room. It was time to go and get married.

∞∞∞

Jax was nervously awaiting for Sydney in the gazebo. The big day finally arrived, and he was so excited to marry such a wonderful woman. The weather was picture perfect at eighty degrees with no humidity and a gentle breeze. There was not a single cloud to be found in the sky. His dad was standing beside him and reassuringly patted him on the shoulder. Jax chose his dad as his best man He was hard pressed to think of a time when his dad was not there for him, so the choice was an easy one.

Nina was the first to walk down the aisle with a lovely strapless turquoise gown matching the crystal clear water. A violin began to play the Pachelbel Canon D wedding song. Sydney was clutching her dad's arm. Her dad looked over at her, smiled and said, "Shall we?"

She smiled back at her father and replied, "I have never been more ready." The bride walked enthusiastically toward her groom.

Jax's breath hitched in his throat. He never laid eyes on a more ravishing and bewitching woman than the one walking toward him down the rose petal aisle. Jax beamed at his future wife with an ear to ear grin as he quickly wiped a single tear from his eye.

Sydney was shaking uncontrollably from nerves and felt like she was hyperventilating. She had no idea why she was nervous since this was the man she wanted to be with forever, without any doubt . As soon as their eyes locked, her nerves immediately diminished. Jax wore the biggest smile on his face and the most loving look in his eyes. It looked like a tear escaped his eye. He really loved her, especially if she moved him to tears. Sydney suddenly felt the urge to run to him as fast as she could so she did not have to wait one second longer.

Jax thought his soon to be wife looked amazingly drop dead gorgeous in a white gown which hugged her bodice then flowed effortlessly to the ground. She wore a sweetheart neckline and cap sleeves with crystals embellishing the top half of the gown. Sydney's headpiece was a crown of crystals with gold detail and a long veil attaching to the back. She looked like a goddess. Her wedding bouquet was made of fluffy peonies in the shape of a basketball. The flowers were white dusted with blue on the edges and the bouquet holder was red. Jax was extremely touched Sydney went through the trouble to incorporate basketball into their wedding. Sydney's father kissed her on the cheek and shook my hand while confidently placing his daughter's hand in mine.

I felt like such a lucky man to finally have her by my side where she belonged. She squeezed my hand, and I calmly squeezed back. I whispered to her, "You look so beautiful."

"You look very handsome and sexy yourself Jax." Sydney blushed and gave me the biggest smile. Her whole face lit up with happiness. There was no doubt in my mind she wanted to get married as much as I did.

I was a little nervous when it was time to recite the vows, since we decided to write our own. Well here goes nothing.

I, Jackson Jones take you Sydney Fox to be my wife.

I love you unconditionally and without hesitation.

Together we will build a life far better than we could alone.

I promise to support your dreams and respect our differences.

I will respect you as a person, partner and equal,

learn with you and grow with you as time and life change.

I will dream with you and celebrate with you.

I believe in you and the couple we will be together.

Tying the knot symbolizes our connection as a couple .

You are the strength I never knew I needed.

I will walk hand in hand with you wherever the journey leads us,

living, learning, and loving together forever.

One lifetime with you could never be enough.

You are my once in a lifetime.

Sydney immediately kissed me, and was overcome with emotion as a lump had formed in her throat. Her words struggled to get out and her voice cracked as she said, "I love you so much. Your words were so beautiful and moved me to tears. Thank you."

The reverend cleared his throat and said. "Not yet. Stop kissing. It is not time to kiss yet. Let us continue."

Everyone laughed, and then Sydney turned to me and took my hand in her own.

*" I, Sydney Fox **take** you Jackson Jones to be my husband.*

You **stole** my heart the moment I met you.

I promise to be your lover, friend, and **teammate**;

Your greatest **fan** and your ally in conflict.

Our job is not to **compete**, but to complement each other.

There will be no **scorekeeping** since there is no winner or loser.

I will communicate fully and fearlessly.

I promise to give marriage my best **shot**,

and show kindness, patience, and forgiveness,

and take **timeouts** when necessary.

I look forward to **traveling**, play time, and new adventures with you.

You already have the **key** to my heart.

Today, I give you my hand,

and pledge my love, devotion faith and honor.

I promise never to violate your trust.

You are my love and my life today and always.

There is nothing we cannot face if we face it together before the **clock** runs out.

Now it was my turn to kiss her. "Those were the most creative and heartfelt wedding vows I have ever heard. Thank you so much."

The reverend was beside himself. "Not yet Sydney and Jax. When I say, you may kiss the bride, then kiss. No kissing in between. You should not need to practice."

Laughter erupted again and even the reverend could not stop a little smile from escaping his lips.

∞∞∞

Following the ceremony, there was a reception back at the hotel. There was so much food and it was all scrumptious. The food was set up in stations and seemed endless. There was fruit, cheeses, appetizers, seafood, carved meats, pastas, salads, desserts and the drinks flowed endlessly. It was a delectable feast.

Sydney's wedding day was so perfect, it seemed as if it was straight out of a fairy tale. If this was a preview of her future with Jax, then she had a lot to look forward to in her future. She felt so relaxed after the wedding, and was very relieved to be able to fully enjoy the reception.

All of their friends and family enjoyed each other's company, and they partied into the wee hours of the night. My friend Mike was also a DJ on the side, so we flew him in for the reception. It was a good thing he was multi talented. He knew which music to play to keep people on their feet. No one was disappointed, and every seat was empty. Everyone was on the dance floor. Nine months from now, there would probably be a few babies born as a result of the fun had tonight. It seemed as if no one wanted the party to end.

Finally, Jax and Sydney said goodbye to their guests. It was a long day, and they were exhausted. Jax insisted on carrying me into the room. He was always such a gentleman. We helped each other change out of our dress clothes and lay down on the bed. It was only supposed to be for a minute, however we were so tired, we both fell fast asleep.

∞∞∞

The next day we had a very late start. Once we realized we passed out on each other, we felt the need to consummate our marriage immediately. Afterwards, we showered and returned to our bed to take it slow and explore every inch of each other's bodies. No matter how many times we made love, it always felt as thrilling as the first time.

Jax looked at Sydney and his hand brushed her cheek tenderly. "I will never get tired of you as long as I live. I can never get enough of you. Are you ready for some room service? I am famished."

We enjoyed brunch and savored every bite. Both of us worked up quite an appetite. When we were finished eating, the two of us lounged by our private pool and had a relaxing day.

Later in the evening, I arranged a romantic candlelight dinner on the beach. I held Sydney's hand as we walked to our table overlooking the water. The hotel set up speakers playing reggae music. The ambiance was perfect. I picked up a hibiscus flower from the table and placed it in Sydney's beautiful long hair. Together, we sipped martinis and ate conch salad, grouper, filet mignon, and chocolate lava cake. The view was spectacular. A full moon lit the sky and shimmered off of the water.

A reggae version of Stevie Wonder's *Isn't She Lovely* began to play. Jax pushed back his chair and stood up. He grabbed Sydney's hand and asked her to dance. They held each other tight and felt the beating of one another's heart. No words were necessary.

Back at the room, I scooped Sydney up in my arms and carried her over the threshold one more time. We opened up the retracting wall and listened to the ocean as we sipped champagne and held hands. Life was great. I survived my rookie year, and our relationship blossomed and grew. We were unsure exactly what the future held, but together we would face the challenges life had in store for us. As I leaned over to kiss my wife, the television was on in the background. The NBA draft was on, and it was someone else's turn to take over the role of the rookie.

"For the first round pick in the 2017 draft, the Philadelphia 76ers select......"

About the Author

KC Avalon lives in Southern New Jersey with her two boys and husband of 28 years. Sea Isle City, New Jersey is a favorite family vacation spot where many happy years of memories were made. Now the family has a summer home in Southern Delaware and spends time at Dewey Beach, the Indian River Bay and Paradise Grill. The latter is a hidden gem with palm trees giving it a tropical feel.

Made in the USA
Middletown, DE
01 September 2019